THE SECOND DAY
OF THE RENAISSANCE

THE SECOND DAY
OF THE RENAISSANCE

TIMOTHY WILLIAMS

Published by
Soho Press, Inc.
853 Broadway
New York, NY 10003

Library of Congress Cataloging-in-Publication Data
Williams, Timothy, author.
The second day of the renaissance / Timothy Williams.
Inspector trotti 6

ISBN 978-1-61695-720-9
eISBN 978-1-61695-721-6

1. Police—Italy—Fiction. 2. Murder—Investigation—Fiction.
I. Title
PR6073.I43295 S43 2017 823'.914—dc23 2016044299

Interior design by Janine Agro, Soho Press, Inc.

Printed in the United States of America

10 9 8 7 6 5 4 3 2 1

ai genitori

Dolceacqua
Bordighera
Cogoleto
Poggibonsi
Porto Garibaldi

ricordi d'un altro secolo

Glossary

ACQUA BRILLANTE: sparkling water

ALPINI: an elite mountain military corps of the Italian Army

AMORE: love

ANONIMA SEQUESTRI: Sardinian criminal organization specializing in kidnappings both in Sardinia and mainland Italy

ARMA: see Carabinieri

AUTOSTRADA: highway

BALLO LISCIO: Italian ballroom dancing

BANCA DELL'AGRICOLTURA: an Italian bank specializing in agricultural credit

BANCO DEL LAVORO: one of Italy's larger banks, nationalized from 1929 to 1998

BONGUSTO: family name of Fred Bongusto, an Italian singer and songwriter

CAPACI: a town on the outskirts of Palermo, Sicily, where the investigative judge Falcone was murdered along with his police escort

CAPITANO: captain

CARABINIERI: Italian militarized police force

CELERE: riot police

C'ERAVAMO TANTO AMATI: a 1974 Italian comedy–drama

CHIESA: church

CHINOTTO: myrtle leaved orange tree bearing a small, bitter orange, used to produce a carbonated soft drink of the same name

CIAO: hello/goodbye

CINQUECENTO: a Fiat; the investigative judge Falcone was murdered while traveling in a Fiat Croma

COMMEDIA ALL'ITALIANA: an Italian film genre from the late 1950s to the early 1990s that set comedic overtones against a backdrop of the period's social issues

COMMISSARIO: commissioner

COSA NOSTRA: the Sicilian Mafia, a large criminal syndicate overseeing several smaller groups that each control a territory

CROMA: a Fiat; the investigative judge Falcone was murdered while traveling in a Fiat Croma

DOPO MARX, APRILE: A saying that encapsulated the jadedness of the Italian leftist youth with Marxism, literally translating to "After Marx, April"

DUNA: a sedan model by Fiat

ERICE: a medieval town in Trapani, Sicily

FARMACIA: drugstore

FERROVIE DELLO STATO: a government–owned holding company that manages the infrastructure and services of the Italian rail network

GANNA: a brand of fine Italian bicycle

GUARDIA DI FINANZA: militarized police force under the direction of the Ministry of Finance and Economy, with responsibility for economic crime

INDIANI METROPOLITANI: a small, active faction of the Italian far-left protest during the Years of Lead (1976-77)

ISPETTORE: inspector

JUVENTUS: the team of a professional Italian soccer club based in Turin

LA GAZZETTA DELLO SPORT: an Italian newspaper dedicated to the coverage of various sports

LA GRASSA: the Fat One, nickname of Bologna, famous for its cuisine

LEGHISTA: member of the Lega Nord political party, which seeks autonomy for northern Italy

LEGHISTI: plural of the above

LICEO CLASSICO: high school with a humanities- and Classics-based curriculum, and the only kind of school that allowed students access to an Italian university education until 1969

LITTORINA: a rail motorcoach

LOTTA CONTINUA: a political group on the far left; also the newspaper published by the Lotta Continua movement

LUPARA: a sawn-off shotgun traditionally associated with Cosa Nostra

MANI PULITE: a national judicial investigation into Italian political corruption in the early 1990s

MATTANZA: tuna fishing; the expression is used to indicate violent bloodletting in mafia wars

METROPOLITANA: underground/aboveground urban rail network in Milan, Rome, etc.

NARCOLIRE: money in Italy coming from the drug trade

NAZIONALI: an inexpensive brand of Italian cigarettes

NUCLEO ANTI-MAFIA: organized crime unit

NUCLEO POLITICO: political segment of the Carabinieri

OLTREPÒ: hilly area in the Apennines on the south bank of the river Po south of the city of Pavia in northern Italy; famous for its wines

OMERTÁ: Mafia code of silence

OMICIDI: homicide department

OSPEDALE MILITARE: military hospital

PALAZZO DI GIUSTIZIA: courthouse

PALIO: a horse race held twice a year in the center of Siena; even a riderless horse can win

PALIOS: prize (pl.)

PARTITO COMUNISTA ITALIANO: Italian Communist Party

PASIONARIA: Spanish for a highly motivated female activist, often in a left-wing organization

PENTITO: participant or accomplice in criminal activity supplying evidence for the prosecution in court; a grass

PETRARCA: the family name of Francesco Petrarca, an Italian scholar and poet in Renaissance Italy (commonly anglicized as Petrarch)

PICCIOTTO: a young man, especially a young mafioso

PITTORESCO: picturesque

PIZZO: bribe

PO: a river that flows eastward across northern Italy

POLGAI : police training academy

POLIZIA: police

POLIZIA DI STATO: national police force

POLIZIA STRADALE: highway patrol

PROCURA: state prosecutor's office

PROCURA DELLA REPUBBLICA: state prosecutor

PROVINCIA PADANA: an Italian newspaper

PUBBLICA SICUREZZA: the old name for the Italian police force; now Polizia di Stato

PUBBLICO MINISTERO: public prosecutor

PUNT E MES: a dark-brown, bitter Italian vermouth

QUESTURA: police headquarters

RAPIDO: express

REPUBBLICA: a Italian daily newspaper

REPUBBLICHINI: Fascist army and supporters of Mussolini's Republic of Salò, 1943–1945, set up on Lake Garda by the Germans following the Italian surrender to the Allies

ROMA STAZIONE TERMINI: the main railway station of Rome

SAN VITTORE: a prison in the city center of Milan

SCIENTIFICA: forensics

SEICENTO: a city car model by Fiat

SESTO: sixth

SESTO SAN GIOVANNI: a suburb of Milan

SIGNORA: madam, lady

SIGNORINA: miss, young lady

SOSTITUTO PROCURATORE: deputy prosecutor

SPREMUTA: freshly squeezed citrus juice

SUD: south

SUPERSTRADA: highway

TENENTE: lieutenant

TOPOLINO: the Italian name for Mickey Mouse, as well as an Italian digest-sized comic series featuring the Disney characters

TOSCANO/TOSCANI: bitter Italian cigars from Tuscany

TOTOCALCIO: a form of gambling on the results of soccer games; football pools

TUTELA DEL PATRIMONIO ARTISTICO: an arm of the Carabinieri dedicated to the protection and preservation of Italy's cultural and artistic heritage

UNA ROTONDA SUL MARE: a song by Fred Bongusto, an Italian singer, literally translating to "On a Terrace Overlooking the Sea"

VENETO: Venetian(s)

VIA: road

VIDDANI: offensive expression in Sicilian dialect for peasants

ZIO: uncle

1: Florence

THE CITY OF Florence was packed with tourists, with Germans and French and Japanese, talking loudly and flaunting their currencies.

Trotti cursed under his breath. It was another week to Easter, and yet every reasonably priced hotel in the city was full. There had been no reason to expect this sudden drop in the temperature; nor had Trotti been expecting the main railway station to close for the night. Foolishly, he had lingered in a restaurant and now he was shivering in the street. He did not even have a coat. Half past two and the train for Empoli would not leave for another couple of hours. There was no escape from the cold, and Trotti was cursing his own stupidity when he noticed the African girl. She had been standing there for some time, but he had assumed she was just another whore. He looked at her from behind; the overhead neon highlighted her hair and for a moment Trotti thought it was Eva. There was a lurch in his belly, but as the girl moved towards the main entrance of the Stazione Santa Maria Novella, Piero Trotti realized she was a lot younger than the prostitute from Uruguay.

A couple of barefoot children were begging in front of a mobile bar. The bar—probably the only place open in Florence at half past three in the morning—was selling hot drinks on the far side of the road. Trotti scraped money from the bottom of his flimsy pocket and bought two cups of steaming chocolate. He gave the change to one of the children.

He went back across the road.

"For you, signorina."

She turned and the plucked eyebrows rose in surprise.

"Hot chocolate to warm you against this chill," Trotti smiled.

Her lips were almost white in the feeble glow of the station lights. "My mother told me not to take presents from strangers."

"Just a retired policeman."

"Men like you she warned me about." Without taking her eyes from his, she put the styrofoam to her lips and drank.

She must have been in her early twenties. The girl was almost as tall as Trotti, and the appearance of height was accentuated by curly hair, combed outwards. A blue ribbon ran through the curls and was tied into a knot above her neck. She held the cup between her hands—hands that trembled.

She did not have any luggage other than a small bag at her feet and the clothes she was wearing—cotton skirt, blue tights, a sweater and a denim jacket.

"You missed your train?"

Her scuffed tennis shoes were no protection against the Siberian cold. "Perhaps."

"You missed it or you didn't?"

The eyes appraised him from behind the rim of the paper cup. Widely-set brown eyes; Trotti realized why she reminded him of Eva. He felt the pinch of nostalgia.

She blew across the surface of her drink before taking another sip. "I have nowhere to sleep."

"You're not Italian, signorina?"

"Just one of my problems," the girl said in a lilting accent, and then she started to cry.

2: Empoli

THEY HAD TO change trains.

At Empoli, side by side, they sat in an empty waiting room and before long, the girl's head slumped onto his shoulder. Trotti felt the rasp of the girl's thick hair against his cheek and he could smell its warmth.

He closed his eyes and recalled the first meeting with Eva in Milan. A long time ago, before the beating they gave her and her hurried, frightened departure for Uruguay.

He dozed off; the local train pulled into the station and the girl woke Trotti with a sharp jab of her elbow. Grabbing his arm and her bag, she pulled him out into the feeble light of morning and bustled him onto the impatient train, an old, rust-colored Littorina.

After the stuffy coziness of the waiting room, the compartment was cold and the train empty. They collapsed onto upholstery that smelled of cigarette smoke and sweat. The locomotive gave a melancholy hoot to the grey sky and the outskirts of Empoli were soon falling behind them.

They were both too weary to talk, but Trotti was no longer tired enough to sleep. He stared through the window at the rolling countryside of Tuscany, grey-green beneath the leaden sky.

It was quite unlike the flat expanses of Lombardy. Tuscany could have been a different country; it was a different world.

"You're not from Florence?" she asked, as if reading his thoughts. One eye was closed, one eye was looking at him.

"Padania." He laughed.

A frown.

"I'm from the North."

After leaving Bari in the mid-seventies, Trotti had traveled South on only three occasions, and never for pleasure. It was not that Piero Trotti disliked central Italy or the South—unlike the leghista Ubertini in Scientifica, who maintained that you needed a pith helmet and a rifle to venture anywhere south of the Po.

Florence, Rome and Palermo were as much a part of the republic as Milan and Bergamo, Crema and Lodi. It was just that Trotti had no call to go there. He had always been happy where he was, in the city where he belonged, with its winter fogs and with its mosquitoes and its airless heat during the summer.

The softness of the Tuscan hills, even on a freezing April morning, was quite alien to him.

The girl sat before him and soon the second eye closed again as she dropped off.

Surreptitiously, Trotti studied the graceful hands and the long fingers where they loosely clasped the cloth bag. He smiled to himself.

Her name was Wilma Barclay and, speaking in idiomatic Italian, she had told him that she was from America. She was twenty-one—the same age as Pioppi when his daughter had decided she no longer wanted to eat.

No young woman with all the challenges of life before her, American or otherwise, deserved to be left to fend for herself on a freezing night outside Florence SMN.

The train emitted its mournful hoot, a hoot made more mournful by the first snowflakes that battered against the window.

The 6:45 local from Empoli pulled into Siena.

3: Pétain

"GENERAL SPADANO'S WAITING for you."

"General?"

With a remote, patrician smile, the uniformed officer leaned forward and opened the door. "Kindly enter," he said in an educated voice.

Although a policeman himself for nearly forty years, Trotti still imagined that most flatfeet were called Quagliarulo or Scognamiglio and spoke in Neapolitan or Sicilian. Surprised, Trotti thanked the man and obediently did as he was told, entering the office softly, almost on tiptoe, almost intimidated.

He had never seen anything like it; or at least, Piero Trotti had never seen a police room that was Renaissance in style, with vaulted arches and walls covered in delicate frescoes.

"So there you are." Spadano stood up from behind a desk covered with various telephones.

The place smelled of cigars and Atkinson eau de cologne.

Trotti nodded, "You're looking fit."

"Not so bad yourself," Spadano replied. "Except for the paunch and the extra ten kilos you're carrying."

Physically, Spadano was small, and looked even smaller behind the large black desk. He was not wearing a uniform but a dark linen suit, a white shirt and a blue tie. The oblique light from the window had caught his grey eyes. His hair was cut very short and brushed backwards; it was snow-white. "Glad you could make it to Siena, Piero."

"Thanks for the ride from the station."

"I hear you're accompanied."

"An American girl I met shivering to death outside Firenze SMN at three in the morning."

"What were you doing outside Santa Maria at three in the morning?"

"You wouldn't want to know."

"Always were a ladies' man. Good to see you haven't changed."

"You have." Trotti gestured towards the engraved name plate on the desk, "I thought you'd retired years ago, Spadano. You're older than me."

"Perhaps I was." The Carabiniere took a packet of cigars from his jacket and set it on the desk. "Still a few more years before I collect my pension. One of the advantages of rank."

"Last I heard of you, you were in Sardinia fighting bandits."

"In Calabria fighting bandits."

"What brought you to Siena?"

Spadano grinned and gestured to the walls of the office, the painted ceiling, the computers. "Tutela del patrimonio artistico."

"You're a peasant like me, Spadano. What would you know about art?"

"I can't afford to retire yet. I've got a young family to bring up."

There came a muffled shout from beyond the closed window, outside in the medieval city. "I can remember your words, Spadano, as if it were yesterday: 'One thing's certain—I'm not going to find a wife in the Sopramonte. Just sheep, wind and rain—and foul-smelling Sardinian peasants and murderers.'"

"Thanks to you, Piero, I met Signora Bianchini in your foggy northern city."

"How does a general of Carabinieri find the time to have a young wife and a family?"

There was the soft hum of a printing machine in a far corner. Spadano looked thoughtfully at his old friend.

"If you really want something in this life, you work for it." Spadano extended his hand in welcome. "Good to see you again, Piero Trotti."

As the two men shook hands, simultaneously they both seemed to change their minds and hugged each other. "As prickly and irascible as ever. Don't tell me you've given up your boiled sweets."

Trotti took a step back and placed a Vichy pastille in his mouth. He nodded towards an overflowing ashtray, "Pity Signora Spadano hasn't weaned you of those foul Toscani."

The general laughed. "Contraband Toscani from Scranton, Pennsylvania." He gestured to a low divan for Trotti to sit down, then, pulling at the crumpled creases of his trousers, Spadano lowered himself into the armchair opposite. "Coffee?"

A muscular body and a thick neck. Hair that showed no sign of thinning. For a man of well over sixty-five, Spadano had aged gracefully.

"I'm trying to give up coffee. The doctor said it was bad for my blood pressure."

"But not the sweets?"

"My dentist told me to give up sweets years ago." Trotti clicked the sweet truculently against his teeth. "My last remaining vice."

"You had so many. Now tell me about the Signora Scola you're supposed to marry."

"Always thought you'd return to Sicily, Spadano."

"So did I." The general nodded as he opened the pack of cigars, "The day the television showed the blown-up Croma at Capaci, my wife stopped eating. Virtually stopped talking to me. Said she'd never accompany me, said if I took a job in Sicily, she'd return to her little town in Lombardy with Chicco. Wasn't going to have her husband and her child murdered by the Mafia. Sicily didn't need another Falcone or Borsellino."

"Chicco?"

A proud nod towards a photograph on the desktop. "So here I am in Tuscany, looking after our cultural heritage."

"Done very well for yourself."

"My son doesn't get to see the land of his grandparents." Spadano looked round at the office, at the Byzantine murals, red and gold, at the modern furniture. At the four telephones, at the desk and at the slim, portable computer. "Just sitting things out, Piero. Sitting things out until I can retire and take my wife and child home—home to Sicily, where I belong. I don't have to tell you I'm not really interested in chasing up grave-robbers and antique dealers. With age, as you've no doubt remarked yourself, a man's ideals can alter."

"Never aware you had any ideals, Spadano."

"You and I, Piero, we thought we were going to change the world. Instead, the world's changed us."

"The insignia and the pips of the Carabinieri tattooed into your flesh?"

"I never gave marriage a second thought. Not once in thirty years. As you say, the insignia of the Carabinieri were tattooed into my flesh—into my soul." Spadano shook his head as he fumbled with a cigar, "I now have a family of my own. My wife and my son's future's all I care about—as I enter the foothills of old age."

"The pre-Alps."

"Your part of the world, isn't it?"

"To tell me about your happy family life and your retirement plans—is that why you contacted me?"

"I thought you'd like to see me, Piero."

"Perhaps you thought I'd enjoy this weather, too?"

Spadano glanced briefly through the window. He turned to face Trotti. "Something I need to tell you."

"I'm in a hurry."

Spadano put the unlit cigar to his mouth, "Somebody wants to kill you, and I thought you should be told." Spadano added blandly, "A professional killer, Piero."

4: C'eravamo Tanto Amati

THE RAIN RAN down the windows of via Milano and against his will, Trotti started to cry, possibly from nostalgia but probably more from a feeling of loss that he now sensed whenever he started thinking about the past, about his past.

Colleagues in the Questura had given him a video recorder on his retirement, and that autumn afternoon, while the rain pattered against the window of the kitchen, he had watched C'eravamo tanto amati for the second time in his life.

It was the last film Trotti and Agnese had ever seen together. She had put on her mink stole and together they had gone to the Castello Cinema. It was one of the last occasions he would ever get to talk to his wife as a friend, yet eighteen years on, Trotti had little recollection of the evening in 1978 except that the ice cream vendor fell asleep in the front row and had to be awakened by an irate audience during the interval. Agnese, surprisingly mirthful, had laughed happily.

C'eravamo tanto amati?

A typical commedia all'italiana, the film had left no lasting impression on Trotti then. Gassmann, Manfredi and Satta Flores played the roles of partisans who, once the war was over, drifted apart, each following his own destiny as time slowly destroyed any hope of the brave, new Italy that the three friends had fought for.

There was a moment in the film when Gassmann, now a

wealthy lawyer in Rome, recalled his years as a partisan. In a flashback to the hills, he saw his younger self lying spread-eagled on the snow of 1945, killed with a German bullet through the forehead.

While he watched the film with Agnese, it never occurred to Piero Trotti to identify with the protagonists, even though he was of the same generation.

Sitting in front of the television, the retired policeman now wondered whether Piero Trotti himself should not have died earlier. A premature death would scarcely have changed the course of history.

"Like a peasant, you've never learned how to enjoy yourself," Agnese had rebuked him as they walked home, their footfalls echoing off the granite facades of the new town. "Only your work matters, Piero. I don't believe you even enjoy having a family. You're dead—a dead father and a dead husband."

Had Piero Trotti's continued existence served any purpose? Had it brought any lasting joy to the world?

His wife had wanted to believe so for years, but in 1978 she had finally given up and left him and Italy for America.

Had Trotti died, Francesca and Piera would have been just as happy with another grandfather.

Had Trotti died, three men, perhaps four, would still be alive today. Alive and breathing God's air.

In tears in front of the video machine, Trotti saw himself as an old man impatient for his own demise, an old man who had outlived his usefulness.

"A professional killer," Spadano repeated.

For all his professed philosophy and genuine self-pity, Piero Trotti realized he was in no way ready for death.

Not yet.

5: Partisans

THE AFTERNOON LIGHT lit up his features. "You remember Gracchi?" The general had the good looks of a mature film star.

"A common enough name, Spadano."

"You met him back in 1978—when the little girl was kidnapped?"

"You mean Anna Ermagni, my goddaughter?"

"So you do remember Gracchi?"

"Son of the city architect, as I recall. Originally from Turin. Bit of an armchair terrorist."

"More armchair than terrorist," Spadano ran the tip of the cigar along his mouth. "One of the founders of Lotta Continua."

"Gracchi's out to gun me down?"

The grey eyes watched Trotti carefully. "Why do you pretend to forget these things?"

"You expect me to remember Gracchi? Eighteen, twenty years ago. He was important, Spadano?"

Spadano spoke from behind a cloud of smoke, "You never call me by my Christian name."

"Never knew you had one. Gracchi's a professional killer?"

"Gracchi was murdered."

"He got on my nerves, too."

"When you knew him, Piero, it was during the Years of

Lead. Like a lot of wealthy kids, he was overeducated and underemployed. That's why he got involved with the extreme left wing. Lotta Continua and that sort of thing."

"Gracchi accused me of being a fascist."

"Anybody in uniform was a Fascist in the seventies."

"My brother was murdered by the Repubblichini. My cousin Sandro received a German bullet in his scalp. We're not Fascists in the Trotti family."

"You and I are old men, Piero—nobody wants to know about our beliefs or what we fought for fifty years ago. The twentieth century? That's ancient history, now. Who could care less?"

"Then why mention Gracchi to me? I'm ancient history—and I'm retired."

"You were unfair on him."

"Unfair on most people. At least, that's what I'm told."

Spadano resumed, "Gracchi was never a terrorist. Not the Red Brigades and no kneecapping of the bosses."

"I had reason to believe he was involved in Anna's kidnapping."

"You were wrong."

A shrug, "Not the first time."

"Which never stopped you from roughing him up."

Trotti said, "A spoilt, clever kid, he thought he could play on the big boys' playground. Then he went running back to daddy as soon as he got a bloody nose."

"Gracchi spent a year in prison for the murder of a policeman."

"Ancient history, Spadano."

The general repressed a sigh, "My first name's Egidio."

"If it's not Gracchi who's trying to kill me, why mention him?"

Spadano appraised Trotti thoughtfully, was about to say something then changed his mind. He placed his cigar on the edge of the ashtray. "Sure you wouldn't like something to drink? Something to sweeten you up?"

"A coffee, if you've got it."

"Against your doctor's orders?"

"My doctor doesn't spend his nights in the waiting room at Empoli."

Spadano leaned sideways and pushed a button on the Venetian desk. He gave a brief order as his eyes watched Trotti. Then he sat back. "You still haven't told me about your young lady friend, Piero."

"I'd rather hear about your professional killer."

Spadano asked, "Your wife's still in America?"

"Most probably."

"And your daughter?"

Piero Trotti relaxed; a smile creased the tired face, "Pioppi gave birth for the second time last year. In Bologna."

"The boy you always wanted?"

"A little girl called Piera."

"Named after her grandfather?"

"I'd like to think so."

"Let's hope being a grandfather will make you a little less surly."

"Don't hold your breath." Trotti added, "Egidio."

6: Killer

TROTTI GLANCED THROUGH the window. The view belonged to the Renaissance: the duomo against the backdrop of a grey sky. Trotti had the feeling of not belonging; of having been catapulted into an alien world, a medieval world. "How do you manage to stay so healthy, Spadano?"

"All the boiled sweets I don't eat, the sugared coffee I don't drink. And a lot of activity."

"Being married to Signora Bianchini made you rather fat, Spadano."

"Calabria made me fat—but thank goodness, that's all behind me." The general's hand tapped the flat belly. "In Calabria I got no exercise because I spent my time drinking beer and breaking wind in helicopters."

"You mean farting?"

"We have a swimming pool here in Siena."

"Perhaps I should have joined the Arma."

"Not sure you'd've enjoyed the Carabinieri. You always had a problem with discipline, Piero."

"News to me."

"Your ingrained conviction that only Piero Trotti can possibly be right. You were a lot better off with the civilians in the Polizia."

"A lot better off retired."

"I believe you."

The sun appeared briefly through the dark clouds over Tuscany. It cast a sudden light on the dome of the cathedral.

"Farting's rather coarse, isn't it, Piero?"

"Wasn't Pugliese the man Gracchi killed?"

"Gracchi killed nobody; he wasn't even in Milan at the time of Commissario Pugliese's murder—but he spent the better part of a year in prison, and perhaps that's what changed him—teaching on a literacy program."

"Changed him?"

"Gracchi'd gotten his degree from the University of Trento in the late sixties—he was part of the first generation that studied sociology there, then managed to turn the university into a revolutionary hotbed. Ten years later in prison he found himself sharing a tiny cell with four common criminals and he started to realize it wasn't armed revolt that was going to change Italy. Armed revolt or anything else."

"He needed a degree in sociology and a year doing time in San Vittore to understand that?"

Spadano grinned bleakly. "Gracchi distanced himself from the revolt of the proletariat—and from the more radical elements of Lotta Continua who wanted to continue the armed struggle."

"You mean he had a criminal record and he needed to find a decent job with a salary at the end of each month?"

"Gracchi didn't have a criminal record at all. There was no case against him—he was released for lack of evidence. Anyway, his father could've got Gracchi a job any time at the city hall in your foggy little town."

"God help us."

"That's when Gracchi went off to India. Went to meditate with some oriental guru who had all the answers to life's mysteries. When Gracchi came back to Italy, he was wearing saffron robes."

Trotti laughed as he sucked the sugar from his coffee spoon.

"More or less given up on politics, and he was now looking for a spiritual solution." Spadano added, "Gracchi chose to set up a rehabilitation center in Sicily. Rehabilitation for drug addicts."

"Mother Theresa in saffron?"

"He needed a purpose to his life. What else could he do?"

"Start a family—like you."

"He was just eighteen when he married and the marriage'd fallen apart. Gracchi had lost touch with his son, who lived with the ex-wife in Turin. By now Marxism and the revolt of the working classes was falling apart all around him. As Gracchi used to say himself, 'Dopo Marx, Aprile.'"

"I don't recall his having a sense of humor."

"Didn't give him much opportunity, Piero. Too busy kicking his head." Spadano smiled serenely. "He went to Trapani. Though Gracchi's mother's Sicilian, he'd never been to Sicily before—he was born 'up there,' as we say in Palermo. Born and bred in Turin. He wanted to get back to his roots and in Sicily, Gracchi found a new direction to his life."

"Sicily, Sicily, Sicily," Trotti dropped the spoon noisily onto the saucer. "Why d'you keep talking to me about Sicily? And about Gracchi?"

Spadano smiled indulgently.

"I know nothing about Sicily, Spadano. I've never been there and I don't know anybody there—apart from you. I don't give a damn for Gracchi, alive or dead and I don't give a damn about Sicily. Are you trying to tell me there's a contract on my head?" Trotti ignored Spadano's protesting hand. "Is that what you're saying, Spadano? A Mafia hit man out there waiting for me?"

Spadano did not reply while the steady grey eyes held Trotti's.

7: Res Publica

TROTTI HAD FOLDED his arms across his chest. He sat quietly; there was the occasional click of the Vichy pastille against his teeth.

Spadano said, "In the seventies, Gracchi'd've been considered a fool—an outsider and a fool. We Sicilians are a backward people. We've never really been interested in change—particularly if it comes from outside. The viddani managed to change all that."

"Viddani?"

"The peasants, Piero—they went too far. Not the Palermitans but the upstarts, the Corleonesi. The viddani and their drugs made things change. We Sicilians are conservative. Violence doesn't frighten us, but change does. We've always lived with violence—it's in our blood, it's in the dust, it's in the wind. It's something we learn as children—it's all part of the tradition, our sense of being different—of being Sicilian and being better. It took us a long time to realize the changes the Corleonesi were making were directed against us, against Sicilians."

"Still see yourself as a Sicilian?"

"You're a Sicilian for life." Spadano did not smile. "And for death."

"That's why you live in Siena?"

"There was a time when no Sicilian would've ever considered turning to the mainland, turning to Rome for help. During the seventies and the years of Anonima Sequestri, Sicilians didn't care where all the easy money was coming from. A few industrialists kidnapped in the North? The only thing to matter was the narcolire should keep pouring into the economy. The shops in Palermo had nothing to envy those in Rome or Milan, even if they were paying their pizzo to the clans. So what? Who could care less?" Another wave of Spadano's hand. "Sicilians like the winning side and the winning side's the Mafia. We've always preferred our Mafia to the Phoenicians or the Normans or the Arabs or the Bourbons. Or to Rome. That's the way things would've gone on indefinitely if the Corleonesi hadn't started processing heroin. Until then, Palermo had simply been a point of transit between the Middle East and America. But by refining heroin, the viddani introduced their idea of added value—a thousand lire of raw opium could be sold for a million lire. The Corleone sold their refined stuff—not just 'up there' in Milan or Rome but in Palermo and Messina and Trapani. Selling drugs to children—our children. With heroin pouring into Palermo, with syringes lying in the gutter, our retarded, insular emotions began to change. For the first time in two and a half thousand years, we started asking questions about ourselves, about the nature of our thing."

"Cosa Nostra?"

"They murdered General Dalla Chiesa." Spadano was no longer looking at Trotti. "In 1982, it was a choice between our thing and the public thing—the Italian republic. We saw what had been obvious to every civilized human being beyond the Straits of Messina."

"Namely?"

"There's nothing noble or chivalrous about the Mafia. It's not concerned with saving our island, our way of life, with protecting Sicily or the Sicilians. The old myths every Sicilian grew up with—they no longer held water. The Corleonesi wanted money and power—and when necessary, they'd kill anybody who came between them and their greed. In a year, they managed to kill as many people as the civil war in Ireland killed in twenty five years."

"Different kind of war."

"Our enemy'd always been the government in Rome—but when Dalla Chiesa was assassinated, we saw the real enemy—the enemy within. We weren't fighting Italy—we were killing each other. A civil war. Someone put a wreath on Dalla Chiesa's tomb: *Here dies the hope of every honest citizen of Palermo.*"

There was silence in the office. Spadano was looking out of the window, looking downwards into the street.

"Dalla Chiesa's death was the birth of hope." A thin smile as the grey eyes returned to Trotti's. "There was a groundswell of sympathy for people like Gracchi. For people who did useful work, despite the Mafia. Against the Mafia. Useful work for the rest of us—for the honest citizens of Sicily."

8: Lead

"GRACCHI WASN'T INVOLVED in your goddaughter's kidnapping—but he could've been. The Years of Lead, the years of growing up—they weren't easy for his generation. They'd all been to university, there was no fear of unemployment but the choices life offered weren't appetizing. They didn't want to work in the car factories—Gracchi'd slummed on the production line in Turin, he'd worked in Germany and in England and had hated it. But the alternative was to join the doctors, the lawyers, the politicians. The classes controlled by the Christian Democrats and kept in power with the covert support of the Americans. And of the Mafia."

"Not simplifying things, Spadano."

"Piero, all the north—with the exception of the Veneto— and all the center of the country were on the left. It was the South that kept Andreotti and Forlani and all the rest of the Christian Democrats in power. In power for forty seven years while they pillaged our country."

"You sound like a Communist."

"Like a man who's been taken to the cleaners."

"You're not forgetting the Socialists, Spadano? Or perhaps they weren't on the left?"

"Forget Craxi? CAF—Craxi, Andreotti and Forlani. The Socialists came later and they were worse than the Christian

Democrats. They tricked us. They gave us hope of something better—and in the end, they betrayed both our ideals and our innocence." Spadano fumbled anew with the pack of cigars but he did not take one. He had already smoked two cigars and the room was thick with the smell of Toscani. "Gracchi came out of those years fairly unscathed."

"Apart from the year in prison. And the saffron robes."

"He kept his idealism."

"Bravo!"

"He wanted to do something useful—to fight in a just cause in a practical way." Spadano paused. "Some old guard from Lotta Continua went to Trapani with him—including Giovanni Verga."

"Craxi's chum?"

"It was Verga who owned the place in Trapani where Gracchi set up BRAMAN, the rehabilitation center for addicts. Verga'd known Craxi for years—but all this was long before Craxi became prime minister. Craxi's—and Verga's ascent came later." Spadano paused again. "Even Lia Guerra joined Gracchi on his commune. Growing olives and making beads and selling organic food."

Trotti repeated, "Lia Guerra?"

"Lia Guerra always hated you, Piero—with just cause."

9: Lia Guerra

"I NEVER HARMED Lia Guerra."

"You believe that, Piero?"

"Most people tend to forget their grudges with time."

"Fortunately for you."

"She wants to kill me?"

"You were responsible for Maltese's death."

"I had a difficult job to do and Lia Guerra didn't make it easier, Spadano. She was in love with a dead man and she lied to me. I owed her nothing."

"And Maltese?"

"When Maltese got himself killed, I just happened to be sitting beside him in some wretched bar. I didn't even know who he was." Trotti took a short breath, "It wasn't me who fucked up Lia Guerra. First Gracchi and then Maltese—she managed to fuck herself up effectively without any help from me."

"You weren't very nice to her."

"A policeman's not paid to be nice, Spadano. You no more than me, so don't sit in judgment. Even if you're right, at this stage of my life, I really don't care to know."

"You regret what you did?"

"I regret nothing."

"You can be a bastard at times."

"All the time."

Spadano shook his head. He had turned away from the

window. "Piero, you've never fooled me. Beneath that surly exterior there beats a human heart."

"I've fooled you."

"You're no cynic."

"Cynicism's a prerequisite for survival."

"A bastard—but a decent bastard, and that's why I've always liked you."

"Don't feel you have to."

"If you were cynical, you wouldn't now be living in some cramped house in the via Milano on the edge of your foggy city."

"Where would I be?"

"Anywhere, Piero."

"Anywhere?"

Spadano said softly, "Lia Gracchi was an attractive young woman. Her journalist'd been killed and there wasn't much future for her in Milan selling prêt-à-porter at the Porta Ticinese. Of course she blamed you. Who else was there to blame? Bright and pretty girl—and she was alone."

"An addict, as I recall."

"Doesn't even touch alcohol now." Spadano remarked, his eyes on his friend. "Time you helped her, Piero."

Trotti did not hide his surprise, "The crazy pasionaria needs my help?"

"Help her and help yourself."

"Lia Guerra's your professional killer?"

"Professional victim. She went back to her ex-lover in Sicily—she joined Gracchi at BRAMAN in Trapani." Spadano allowed himself a grimace, "With just one little problem awaiting her in Sicily. Gracchi was now married to someone else and had a family of his own—a beautiful wife and a beautiful daughter."

10: Peace of the Senses

"GUERRA WANTS TO kill me?"

"In a hurry, are you, Piero?"

"Forgive the morbid curiosity."

"When d'you last see Lia Guerra?" Spadano asked pleasantly.

"The half-baked revolutionary must be at least forty now. Doesn't she have children or something more worthwhile to do with her time than stick a knife into an old man?"

"If Lia Guerra wanted to kill you, Piero Trotti, I'd've given her the knife."

"Who's out to kill me?"

Spadano held up his hand. "Give me time."

"I was hoping to return to my videos and my cramped house in the via Milano before the fourth millennium."

"Didn't know you were busy." Spadano showed surprise, "Your truffles you've got to get back to?"

"At this moment, a young woman's waiting for me in the Piazza del Campo." Trotti gestured to beyond the cathedral. "It's cold outside, and as much as I enjoy your company, Spadano, as much as I enjoy the excellent coffee and all the hospitality and good taste of Tutela del patrimonio artistico, I'd rather be with her than you. You can understand that?"

"If a young woman could possibly want to spend time with you, I'm sure she's totally immune to the weather."

"I told her I wouldn't be long."

"You really should try to stay alive," Spadano tutted. "It might give you more time for your girlfriends."

"I'm well past the age for having girlfriends." Trotti shook his head sadly, "I attained the peace of the senses years ago."

"You talk such rubbish."

Trotti opened his mouth, but before he could reply, he was silenced by the other man's impatient gesture. "Listen to me for once, Piero Trotti, and try not to interrupt. Keep your head down and your back to the wall."

"Why?"

"You should live out another twenty years."

"Supposing I wanted to."

"Supposing you're allowed to."

Fleetingly, Piero Trotti wondered if his hostility towards the general was not simply jealousy.

Jealousy of the man, jealousy of Spadano's marriage, of his child. Jealousy of the fact that Spadano still had a job to go to every day, a job that gave a purpose to his life.

Spadano took a deep breath and returned to the Venetian desk.

Trotti asked softly, "Who wants to kill me?"

11: Rosalia

"GRACCHI WAS GETTING bored. He was fed up with Trapani, fed up with Sicily. By 1987, he and his wife had spent more than six years at BRAMAN, and it was time for a change."

"Gracchi didn't get on with his wife?"

"A marriage more of reason than of two like minds. Chiara Gracchi's not an intellectual like him—or like Lia Guerra—but she gave him security at a time when he most needed it." Spadano threw a dubious glance at Trotti, "Why d'you ask?"

Trotti gestured for Spadano to continue.

"Chiara was his second wife. Gracchi had got married at the age of eighteen when he was doing his Marxist/Leninist stint on the FIAT factory floor at Mirafiori. Long before he ever met Lia Guerra. His first wife was a teenager who shared a lot of his socialist ideals. Juvenile socialist ideals. From a working-class family in Turin, the girl was called Bettina, and Gracchi married her from a sense of proletarian decorum—or perhaps because he needed to show his parents he'd definitively broken with them. After a few years, things went sour. Bettina wanted a house and a Fiat Seicento. She started seeing other men—and that's when Gracchi left her. Left her, left their little boy and left Turin for Germany."

"Gracchi should've married Guerra."

"He met Lia Guerra a long time later—after Trento, during his Lotta Continua years."

"An arrogant cow. Not my Molotov cocktail at all, I'm afraid."

"Or your Vichy mint. But then, you don't like many people."

"Even fewer as I get older," Trotti mumbled.

"In 1979, Gracchi was thrown in jail over the Pugliese murder. That's when Guerra left him. She went off and started living with your journalist friend."

"The unlamented Maltese," Trotti said.

"And Gracchi met his second wife. He was in prison in Milan, and Chiara was his lawyer's secretary. Very sensible, almost conservative—with a degree in law. The complete antithesis of everything Lia Guerra'd ever stood for. Chiara Gracchi had none of Guerra's passion but she was sensible, with her feet firmly on the ground. And beautiful." Spadano added, almost wistfully. "Still is."

"What made Guerra join him in Sicily if Gracchi was already happily married?"

"What else was there to do?"

"Leave him alone."

"It was her way of returning to the past."

Trotti said, "And returning to Gracchi's bed?"

"These things happen." A sly smile, "You never slept with other women during all your happy years of marriage?"

"Gracchi's wife wasn't fazed at sharing her husband? Remaining silent while he was screwing about?"

"Bit censorious, aren't you?" Spadano raised a brow above the grey eyes. "Gracchi and Chiara had a child. A daughter who was born before they moved to Sicily—born in fact while Gracchi was still languishing in prison. Chiara Gracchi never complained about any infidelities. Not that I'm aware of."

"Women can be funny that way."

"Gracchi absolutely worshipped the kid and was a very good father. His daughter's now eighteen—the name's Elena, but everybody knows her as Lakshmi."

"Rosalia'd've been a bit more in keeping with her Sicilian background. Lakshmi?"

"The Hindu goddess of wealth, Piero. Try not to show your ignorance."

"I don't work for our cultural heritage, Spadano, nor do I have your pretensions to culture—and to long words."

"You should try."

"Or your sense of humor." Trotti asked, "Lakshmi? Gracchi really believed all that Oriental stuff?"

"When Gracchi believed something, he believed it fervently." Spadano had blushed beneath the tanned skin, but his speech remained calm and the grey eyes now gazed steadily at Trotti. He was leaning against the desk. He held an unlit cigar between his fingers. "He'd have his conversion and for a while, the intellectual in him ceased to ask questions. Unfortunately, before long Gracchi would start looking for different answers—for some new Holy Grail."

Trotti winced. "Holy who?"

"Those oriental religions gave him some kind of peace, but the questions would change, and Gracchi needed to find a new set of answers. One of those people who's always searching, always looking for something new. After six years at BRAMAN he was bored, bored of dealing with drug addicts, bored of producing designer olive oil, bored of Sicily. He was looking for a new challenge."

"So he got himself killed? That must've been a change."

"Nobody knows why Gracchi was killed." Spadano started laughing happily.

"What's so funny, Spadano?"

The general of Carabinieri coughed behind his hand.

"Strange sense of humor you have."

"If I knew why Gracchi was killed, you probably wouldn't be here talking to me—you'd have been eliminated years ago. Peace of mind or otherwise."

12: Mattanza

"IN 1987, GRACCHI was invited to TRTP in Trapani. The local television station—a very amateur setup, no bigger than a couple of filing cabinets, a typewriter and a second-hand TV camera—wanted him on a program. This was just before a few elections, and Gracchi was invited along for a debate on local politics. It should've been your typical political broadcast—the sort of thing most local stations put out between some American sitcom and an old Totò film. According to Chiara Gracchi, her husband didn't want to go. Gracchi'd become a recluse."

"What about Guerra?"

"What about her?"

"Screwing her didn't keep him happy?"

Spadano said, "On television, Gracchi rediscovered his old self. He regained all the charisma of Trento and those heady years in Lotta Continua. That night in Trapani, Gracchi mesmerized everybody. Brilliant—people were expecting another dull talking-head, another lump of furniture on the sound set, another double-breasted suit. They got this brash Northerner asking the kind of straightforward questions nobody else would ever've dared ask—questions nobody in his right mind'd ask aloud in Trapani province. This was 1987, the high summer of CAF—Craxi, Andreotti and Forlani. The days of endless rivers of verbosity, jargon and obfuscation. It was before the demise of the Christian Democrats, before Bossi and the Lombard League started using straightforward Italian to talk to the Italian people. Before Mani Pulite. That night, Gracchi spoke simple, honest Italian. Asked embarrassing questions about bribes, about politicians on the take, about Mafia protection in Trapani, about the pizzo, about the clans."

"A bit dangerous?"

"Very dangerous." Spadano nodded, "The phones were jammed with viewers wanting to know who this Northerner was. Asking for more of the same. The manager who'd been shitting bricks suddenly realized he could afford to be delighted."

"Gracchi was asked to stay on?"

"Gracchi'd been one of the editors back in the late sixties with Lotta Continua, but he knew this would be different. Trapani wasn't Milan or Turin. In western Sicily, other rules apply. Being an intellectual and an outsider'd never be protection from the lupara."

"You mean the Kalashnikov, Spadano."

"From the mattanza."

"What?"

"Years ago, when there were still fish in the sea, the Trapani fishermen would sail out and slaughter the tuna in their nets. The sea'd turn red with blood. The mattanza—the slaughter. Gracchi knew what he was taking on. He knew he'd talk too much."

"Yet he accepted?"

"Limelight was a drug for him."

"Even if it killed him?"

"Giovanni Verga asked Gracchi to stay on at TRTP."

"Why?"

"Giovanni Verga was his associate at BRAMAN. Any good publicity for BRAMAN was welcome, indeed was necessary. In the mid-eighties, when Craxi became prime minister, Verga'd started getting into bed with his Socialist chums. Unlike the Christian Democrats, the Socialists hadn't married into the Mafia, so it wasn't as if there was a major conflict of interest. It suited Verga—and through him, Bettino Craxi—to be seen fighting the Mafia in Trapani. Giovanni Verga was delighted to let Gracchi get on with it."

"Giovanni Verga was concerned about the Mafia?"

"Couldn't give a shit." Spadano smiled coldly. "Verga was from Trapani, where his father had been postmaster. He knew all about the Mafia. And he knew Gracchi was setting himself up."

"Gracchi became a television journalist just for the sake of Craxi and the Socialists?"

Spadano shook his head slowly, "Gracchi was an honest man. Honest and middle-class—and though you refused to see it, essentially decent. He hated the Mafia—the Trapani Mafia in particular. Gracchi's real weakness was loving the limelight. He joined TRTP because he fell in love with the studio lights—ineluctably attracted towards them like an insect." The general paused. "There were times when Gracchi would stick his tongue out at the viewers. 'No hairs on my tongue,' he'd say to the camera. Gracchi talked plainly, and he wanted the viewers to trust him."

"They did?"

"A Northerner unafraid to speak the truth about things that everybody knew but nobody dared mention? Can you imagine? Telling everybody the emperor had no clothes. It was wonderfully inebriating—and totally reckless. Gracchi even had priests warning him off, advising him to be careful. Gracchi continued to stick out his tongue, figuratively and literally, and he did some good work—for over a year. Corruption in the hospital, the eternal problem of no running water, lethargy in the town hall. Something quite unheard of in that conservative, prissy backwater of provincialism, where the Mafia's just as prissy and conservative. Gracchi brought his innocence and his righteous anger to Trapani. He also brought his experience as a journalist from *Lotta Continua*. Over the months he worked there, Gracchi trained a group of ex-addicts from BRAMAN and turned them into competent newsmen and TV journalists."

Spadano gave a thin smile.

"A year—and lucky to survive for as long as he did, the stupid Northern bastard."

13: Saracens

ON A CLEAR day, you can see Africa and the foreign coast from where, many generations ago—before the Normans, long before the Spaniards—the Saracen invaders came, sailing beneath the hot Scirocco.

1988 and Sicily has changed little over the centuries, despite the intervening foreign invasions.

September the twenty-sixth.

It is the end of the long summer, that windless, airless Sicilian summer of unrelenting heat. With the advent of autumn, the clocks must go back and darkness falls an hour earlier upon Trapani and the surrounding countryside.

6:58 P.M.

A white Fiat drives away from the city of Trapani and heads towards the hills, guided by high beams that slice a wedge through the dusty olive groves. Behind the car, a cloud of dust billows and then gently settles to the ground. It is dusk and the shadows grow in intensity. Erice, nestling in the mountain, is lost to the blue-black haze of gathering night.

The car slows as it comes to a crossroads. It turns left, goes over a bridge and carefully picks up speed.

A Duna, driven by Signor Gracchi, founding member of Lotta Continua, one-time revolutionary, social worker and now crusading television journalist.

From the studios of TRTP in Trapani, it is just fifteen

kilometers to BRAMAN. Gracchi drives fast this Sunday evening, eager to get home, leaning forward in his seat, urging the Fiat forward, his weight upon the steering wheel.

Sitting beside him is a young woman. She is pretty, has auburn hair and her name is Luciana. Luciana is eighteen years old and is from Milan. She used to be an addict; that was before she came to BRAMAN, before she came to Sicily, before she left Milan. Now, under the careful tutelage of Gracchi's team at BRAMAN, Luciana is learning how to become a television journalist. How to earn a decent living, how to become a productive citizen. Learning how to make the most of a new life that opens like an unread book before her.

Luciana smokes a cigarette as she leans against the car door. With her small feet on the dashboard, she looks admiringly at the charismatic leader of BRAMAN. Gracchi fascinates the young woman.

Gracchi has always been a fascinating man. Thoroughly modern, the bittersweet product of Postwar Italy, with all the conflicting contradictions, weaknesses and strengths of our nation. A flawed hero, an Italian hero, a poet, a crusader, at times even a buffoon. Gracchi is human, he has his frailties and has no doubt committed many mistakes during his forty-two years. Yet here in Sicily, people choose not see the flaws. They overlook his past because no one here can question his dedication to the present: the cause that he has fought for. The cause of human dignity, justice and democracy. No one can doubt his commitment. No one can deny his courage in the unequal fight against the Trapanese Mafia.

A fight lost long in advance, only Gracchi does not realize it.

The Duna runs swiftly past the San Michele church standing at the crossroads.

Gracchi steps on the brake. "What's Lakshmi doing there?" In the failing light, Gracchi has dimly discerned the form of a girl sitting on the steps of the church.

"That's not her," Luciana replies, taking the cigarette from her mouth. "A girl from the village—your daughter has long hair." Luciana laughs. "Long black hair."

Lakshmi is her father's greatest joy. Gracchi, too, laughs cheerfully, glad the day is over, glad to be returning to his wife and his daughter. To his friends—to the one safe haven in this hostile island.

The Duna resumes its speed.

Here in the hills, the Mafia seems a world away, thank God. Seems.

The car approaches the entrance to BRAMAN, gets onto the dirt track, a straight line between the fields. The overhead lights have not been switched on although the clocks came forward this morning.

Away from the scattered houses of the village, the countryside is dark and the road is like a dirty ribbon stretching before the headbeams. The Duna reaches the first zigzag of the hillside, turns left and the window implodes. Gracchi is hit by a projectile and on the rising incline, the car loses its momentum. A jolt as the Duna stalls at the edge of the track.

There are two further explosions.

Signor Gracchi, founder member of Lotta Continua and now anti-Mafia journalist, mumbles something. He slumps sideways and Luciana cannot hear him. She is huddled beneath the seat; all she can see is the blood running from the driver's chest.

The car stops.

Luciana scrambles from the car, bent double. In the darkness, like a stalked and terrified animal, the young woman stumbles forward, caught in the headbeams and blindly running the hundred meters to the entrance of BRAMAN.

Signor Gracchi is wounded, and she must get help. Signor Gracchi has been hit. Signor Gracchi has been killed.

By the time the police reach the car, just twenty minutes later, Gracchi has already breathed his last breath, three weeks after his forty-second birthday.

14: Third Level

THE SUN HAD disappeared and the glow had vanished from the cathedral. The low sky was now uniformly dull above the roofs of Siena.

"Very sorry indeed." Trotti tossed the article back onto the desk. "All my condolences to the lovely widow Gracchi, if you should meet her. And of course, to the not-so-lovely Lia Guerra." He stood up. "Must be on my way."

"Hear me out, Piero."

"Some ex-terrorist gets killed in Sicily?" There was irritation in Trotti's voice. "I'm not interested in Gracchi, Spadano. Nothing to do with me."

Spadano asked, "Another coffee?"

Trotti allowed his weight to fall back onto the seat. "Wouldn't be trying to kill me, would you?"

"There are worse ways to go."

"Being bored to death." A smile broke through Trotti's dour features, "Some proper sugar this time."

Spadano ordered coffee over the intercom before continuing. "In Trapani Gracchi's death came as a shock."

"Gracchi knew what he was letting himself in for."

"People were expecting the killer to be identified. Unfortunately, the Carabinieri made a mess of the enquiry."

Trotti raised an amused eyebrow. "Now you surprise me."

"Carabinieri and the Polizia, for that matter. It was all the fault of the investigating judge. Or rather, the judges. Too many magistrates and too many culprits."

"A classic Mafia killing."

"Too anonymous." Spadano shook his head doubtfully. "When the Mafia kill, they want everybody to know—and to know why."

"Gracchi hadn't made enough enemies in Sicily?"

"Gracchi'd spent his life making enemies—just like you, Trotti."

"Me?"

"Not only the Trapani Mafia. There were enemies in the commune. The killers could've just as well been outsiders as they could've been people working on the inside at BRAMAN. An inmate wanting to get revenge."

"One of the addicts?"

"They're no angels." Spadano said, "Several had connections with organized crime. BRAMAN wasn't the sort of place for people with a cast-iron virginity."

"Why kill Gracchi?"

"Gracchi could be very cavalier." Spadano raised the shoulders of the linen suit, "For all his revolutionary views, he wasn't particularly democratic or egalitarian in his dealings with people."

"*Cherchez la femme.*"

Spadano gave a surprised smile.

"What about his wife?" Trotti asked.

"They no longer slept in the same bed, if that's what you mean."

"You know all about the sleeping arrangements. A dark horse, Spadano."

"Later, suspicion fell on Giovanni Verga. Things'd been deteriorating between him and Gracchi. Despite the carefully cultivated appearances."

"I thought Verga found Gracchi useful."

"Differences over the aims of the commune—and the finances. Gracchi was unhappy about the Socialist dimension, about the money coming from the friends of Craxi—political friends. The third level."

Spadano was now leaning against the desk, opposite Trotti. His arms were folded. He held the unlit cigar to his lips, "In Sicily, a lot of Mafia killings have nothing to do with the Mafia."

There was a knock at the door. The patrician officer entered, carrying a tray: a cup of coffee and a silver bowl of sugar. Bending slightly, he served Trotti, pouring three spoonfuls of sugar into the small cup.

"The name Beltoni mean anything to you, Piero?" Spadano asked.

"Should it?" Trotti stirred his coffee and laughed. Trotti was in a hurry to leave, to get back to the girl, to get to Rome. He had spent his life in smoke-filled offices, feeling tired and fortifying himself with strong coffee and more sugar than was good for him.

The officer nodded towards the general and silently withdrew.

"BRAMAN had been penetrated by people in the pay of the Mafia. That much's certain. The investigating judges believed Enzo Beltoni—an employee at BRAMAN—had been expressly recruited by the Trapanese clan to eliminate Gracchi."

Trotti drank the sweet coffee in a single gulp. His eyes ached; he needed to sleep.

"Beltoni managed to escape before the judge could ask him too many awkward questions. Escaped to Beirut and then to America."

"This has got something to do with me, Spadano?"

"Beltoni's been out of the country now for the last seven years."

"So what?"

After a long pause, Spadano asked, "Sure the name Beltoni doesn't mean anything to you?"

Trotti shook his head.

"You knew his brother well enough, Piero." Spadano added brightly, "You killed him."

15: Beltoni

BOATTI AND COMMISSARIO Merenda were standing together beneath the same black umbrella.

Finally the rain had started to fall, thick drops that fell on to the dusty earth and into the slowly moving waters of the river.

An ugly place, the edge of the city where the old houses gradually fell away and where the surfaced road became a cart track, running parallel to the river—a no-man's land inhabited by a thin phalanx of plane trees. One or two farmhouses beyond the high water mark, mostly uninhabited. Beyond them, the allotments, then the textile factory, its smokeless chimneys and the satellite apartment blocks, squalid beneath the rain.

Trotti and Gabbiani got out of the car.

Toccafondi caught sight of them and hurried over, carrying an umbrella. Despite the warm evening air, he was wearing his uniform leather jacket and gloves. He grinned nervously, touching his beret.

"What is it?" Trotti gestured to where police lines had been put up. A small crowd had gathered, but there was no artificial light other than a police car with its main beam. It was hard to make out the dark, stumpy object that had been cordoned off.

The object cast a long shadow over the ground.

"Looks like a professional job. Badly mutilated, very badly mutilated. And then burned with petrol." Grinning bravely,

Toccafondi closed his eyes. "They cut most of his fingers off. Not a very pretty sight. I couldn't help . . ." He swallowed hard, then the smile returned to his young face.

"Who is it?" Trotti frowned and moved forward.

The arms and the legs must have been tied together behind the back.

Gabbiani remarked calmly, "You choke to death as your leg muscles can no longer resist the tension." He snorted, "And then they burned him. Probably cut his tongue out, as well. Organized crime doesn't like informers. I think he's got a lot to thank you for, Piero."

Beltoni.

Trotti stepped away from Gabbiani's umbrella, ducked under the police rail and moved towards the black lump.

Surprisingly, the flames had left much of the face intact. Everything else was carbonized—black like a burnt tire—but the face was untouched, cheek against the ground. The long hair had been singed and the empty mouth lolled open against the dusty earth that was forming rivulets of rainwater.

Trotti crouched down in the headlights. The rain was now falling heavily, running down his face, seeping through his clothes.

Piero Trotti looked at what had once been the body of Beltoni: addict, drug-dealer and police informer. Thirty-five years earlier a mother's baby, and now dead.

No more hunger or thirst, no more desires, greed or pride. The true peace of the senses. Tortured, strangled and burnt to little more than a cinder lying in the dust beside the river Po.

"Too many deaths, too many deaths," Trotti repeated to himself.

Somewhere towards the city, there was a distant whine of a siren.

Trotti stood up.

"Gabbiani, for God's sake, give me one of your Nazionali."

16: Kisses

Spadano had offered him lunch, had even proposed driving out to eat somewhere in the surrounding hills, but Trotti declined. He was in a hurry to join the American girl and catch the first train to Rome.

The general of the Carabinieri insisted upon lending Trotti a warm coat.

"Be careful, Piero," were his parting words. "An awful job to get the blood stains out. Take care of my coat, even if you won't take care of yourself."

Perfunctorily they shook hands.

Trotti turned away and, feeling the weight of Spadano's troubled eyes on his back, walked down the hill from the cathedral, through the twisting streets of Siena.

Trotti had reluctantly accepted the Gracchi folder; it made his heavy bag still heavier.

A biting, wintry wind scurried across the vast openness of the Piazza del Campo, yet all the bars and cafés were doing good business. Tourists sat outside on the terraces, despite the cold and despite the threat of more snow.

Trotti looked for the girl.

Wilma was not waiting for him at the place where they had agreed to meet.

Trotti felt exposed in the windy piazza and was in a hurry to get away from the open square.

(*"My advice's to lie low and be careful, Piero."*)

He entered several restaurants where lunch was being served.

No American girl, just the smell of good food.

It was in via di Città that Trotti found a café to his liking. The place was both warm and empty; no sign of all the tourists. Trotti opened the glass door and walking the length of the bar, went to the window that backed onto Piazza del Campo.

He sat down and before long, the barman took his order of hot spremuta.

Trotti's eyes felt gritty and he wondered if he was going to come down with influenza. He needed to sleep. When the squeezed grapefruit juice came, it was sweet and hot and it rasped against the edge of his throat.

With a frequent glance at the Piazza del Campo—in high summer, crowds thronged the square, jostling to catch sight of the Palio and the horses that the Sienese bet so heavily on—Trotti thumbed through the files that Spadano had given him.

Outside, the clock on the tower chimed midday.

A couple of tourists arrived in the bar. A man and a woman, they were probably English, in their late forties. The man was wearing the same waxed jacket that Pioppi had given Trotti a couple of winters earlier. He wore a matching hat that hid much of his face and he talked loudly to the woman. She sat with her legs together and her hands neatly on her lap when she was not drinking her hot chocolate. She was too attentive to be the man's wife, yet there were no subtle intimacies to suggest that they were lovers. They looked happy, like old friends who had met after spending much of their lives apart.

The woman wore a wedding ring; the man did not.

Trotti sipped his spremuta as he sorted the photocopies— papers from the Palazzo di Giustizia in Trapani, newspaper articles, several photographs and an envelope containing a set of handwritten poems.

(*"Beltoni's back in Italy, Piero. You don't want to go looking for him? Then my advice's to lie low and be careful. Stay with your daughter in Bologna. Stay with your grandchildren. With Francesca and the little Piera. Try to stay alive."*)

The couple laughed and Trotti raised his head. They were talking with animation and seemed fascinated by the bar. Trotti heard the word "pittoresco" pronounced in an unsubtle accent. The couple were talking about the bar.

Picturesque?

Trotti set down the photocopies and looked around, looked at the boxes of Baci chocolates lined against the mirror, at the plastic tablecloths, at the tinted photographs of earlier palios. For Piero Trotti there was nothing even faintly picturesque about the place; the only memory he would retain was the spremuta, twice as expensive as even the dearest bar in his foggy, northern city.

The woman laughed again and the man produced a minute black box. Trotti realized it was a camera only when the man opened up the front lens.

Trotti resented their cheerfulness, and when the man placed the small camera on the glass shelf, beside the chocolate boxes, to take a photograph of himself and his companion, Trotti brusquely rose to his feet, gathered the documents and hurriedly left, going out into the cold of via di Città.

17: Legalese

A FEW PEOPLE huddled on the platform, waiting for the local train to Chianciano, but they stood close to the walls, close to the posters, out of the biting wind, away from the track.

It had started to snow again.

There was blood on Trotti's hands, and in the fall, he had torn his trouser leg.

Limping slightly, Trotti entered the station bar. It was full and the air was thick with rancid smoke. He found a table beside the postcard stand and sat down to wait the twenty minutes until the train was due.

He ordered another hot spremuta, but this time drank it fast. He was coming down with some infection; his throat was uncomfortable and the skin around his lips had begun to flake from the cold.

The palm of his hand hurt; grit from the paving had worked its way under his skin.

NO SIGNIFICANT ELEMENT HAS EMERGED FROM FOLLOWING UP THE THEORY OF AN INTERNAL CONFLICT WITHIN BRAMAN. EVEN IF THE RETICENCE OF SIGNORA CHIARA GRACCHI APPEARS HIGHLY SUSPECT AND HER VERSION OF THE EVENTS LEADING TO HER HUSBAND'S MURDER

ARE SIMPLISTIC AT BEST, THERE IS NO CON-
CRETE EVIDENCE TO SUGGEST THAT EITHER
SHE OR VERGA ACTUALLY WANTED GRACCHI
REMOVED OR INDEED, KILLED. LIKEWISE,
THERE IS NOT THE SLIGHTEST OBJECTIVE EVI-
DENCE THAT GRACCHI'S OLD FRIENDS AND
EX-COMPANIONS IN LOTTA CONTINUA WERE
CONCERNED BY THE FACT THAT HE HAD, ONLY
A MONTH BEFORE HIS DEATH, BEEN SUMMONED
BY THE JUDICIAL AUTHORITIES IN MILAN
TO EXPLAIN A POSSIBLE INVOLVEMENT IN
THE MURDER OF COMMISSARIO PUGLIESE
OF THE PUBBLICA SICUREZZA, FOR WHOSE
SLAUGHTER GRACCHI HAD ALREADY SPENT A
YEAR IN JAIL, AND CONCERNING WHOM NEW
INFORMATION HAD BEEN MADE AVAILABLE TO
THE SAME JUDICIAL AUTHORITIES IN MILAN.

Trotti looked up, escaping the turgid language of the
Sostituto Procuratore who had spent two years investigating
Gracchi's death in Trapani.

(*"Stay with Pioppi and the little girls."*)

EQUALLY UNFRUITFUL WERE THE INVESTIGA-
TIONS INTO A POSSIBLE MAFIA INVOLVEMENT.
NONE OF THE WITNESSES GIVING STATE EVIDENCE
AT ANY TIME MENTIONED A KNOWN CONNEC-
TION BETWEEN GRACCHI'S ASSASSINATION
AND THE TRAPANI BOSS, ROBERTO PALERMERI.
ALTHOUGH THERE WAS UNDOUBTEDLY A MOTIVE
FOR PALERMERI'S WANTING GRACCHI REMOVED,
FOLLOWING A SERIES OF POPULAR TELEVISION
PROGRAMS IN WHICH GRACCHI HAD OPENLY
DENOUNCED PALERMERI AND HIS TIES TO THE
POLITICIAN MARIO AGRATE, THERE IS NO EVI-
DENCE OF A LINK BETWEEN PALERMERI AND
GRACCHI.

Trotti had to read the typed page a couple of times in order to penetrate the legal jargon.

(*"Beltoni's back in Italy, Piero."*)

His finger followed the text.

ENZO BELTONI, UPON RECEIVING INFORMA-
TION FROM THE LESS-THAN-HERMETIC TRAPANI
COURTHOUSE, TO THE EFFECT THAT HE HAD
BECOME A FAVORED SOURCE IN THE ENQUIRY,
CHOSE TO ABSCOND AFTER AN INITIAL INTERRO-
GATION. HE LEFT TRAPANI WITHOUT WARNING
AND WITHOUT PERMISSION. HE IS NOW BELIEVED
TO BE LIVING IN AMERICA.

BELTONI HAD ENTERED BRAMAN AS AN EX-
ADDICT IN 1985, BREAKING WITH HIS HABIT
OF HEROIN. AGED THIRTY-TWO, AND BEING OF
HIGH INTELLECT, HE BECAME A CLOSE COLLABO-
RATOR OF SIGNOR GIOVANNI VERGA. ALTHOUGH
GIOVANNI VERGA KNEW OF BELTONI'S PAST—
BELTONI HAD MURDERED IN AMERICA WHILE
STILL AN ADOLESCENT AND HAD SPENT SEVERAL
YEARS IN A NEW JERSEY REFORMATORY—AND
ALTHOUGH SIGNOR VERGA WAS AWARE OF TIES
THAT BOUND BELTONI TO THE TRAPANESE
MAFIA, NEITHER VERGA NOR INDEED GRACCHI
WERE CONCERNED ABOUT THE MAN OR WOR-
RIED THAT HE MIGHT BE A SPY FOR THE LOCAL
CRIME ORGANIZATION. AS A SIGN OF THEIR
FAITH, BELTONI WAS GIVEN CUSTODIAL RESPON-
SIBILITY AT BRAMAN. GIOVANNI VERGA CLAIMS
BELTONI EXECUTED HIS TASK SATISFACTORILY. IN
AN ORGANIZATION AS HIERARCHIC AS BRAMAN,
GIOVANNI VERGA AND ENZO BELTONI WERE
EXCEPTIONALLY CLOSE, ENJOYING STRONG TIES
OF FRIENDSHIP.

BELTONI ALWAYS MAINTAINED HIS INNOCENCE
IN GRACCHI'S MURDER. HE WAS, HE CLAIMED,

ON DUTY AT BRAMAN AT THE TIME OF THE
MURDER.

The train hauled into the station as Trotti stuffed the photocopies back into the file.

He went out onto the freezing platform, pulling at the collar
of the Carabinieri coat. His hand hurt.

She was accompanied by a man who helped her onto the
train. She laughingly thanked him as he bundled her bag
through the carriage window. Wilma was wearing a bright,
new anorak and a matching woolen bonnet. Leaning out of
the train to receive a farewell kiss on the cheek, Wilma never
noticed Commissario Piero Trotti.

She smiled charmingly at her youthful friend.

18: FFSS

THE LOCAL TRAIN was maddeningly slow.

Piero Trotti had not wanted to enter the crowded compartment, preferring to sit on a fold-down seat between the two carriages. Here, without the upholstery and fittings, the smell of burnt diesel, along with the clatter of the wheels and the biting cold, worked its way through the shifting plates beneath his numbed feet.

The pain of his grazed hand had become warm, almost pleasant. His bruised knee was stiff.

It had started to snow again.

Trotti stared at the passing countryside through the narrow windows of the folding doors. Tuscany no longer appeared soft and gentle as it had in the early light of the morning, and he was increasingly unhappy about going south.

He was tempted to get out at the next stop, tempted to take the first train north, back to Bologna or even back to the Po valley. Back to where he would feel at home. To where he would feel safe.

(*"You really should try to stay alive. It might give you more time for your girlfriends."*)

He turned his glance away from the window and looked at Wilma. She was sitting with her back towards him. Her head was bowed; he saw the curly hair pushing from beneath the edges of the woolen bonnet. She showed no interest in the people round her. She was probably reading.

The train dutifully ran its tedious course across the Apennine plateau, crossing swollen rivers and wet, winding roads. The villages all seemed the same when seen through the damp panes of the train. Empty stations, platforms deserted except for the awaiting station master, reluctantly plucked from a warm office and now shivering beneath the red cap (and plastic cover) of rank.

The *Littorina* finally reached Chianciano.

Trotti deliberately avoided Wilma. He yanked at the collar of Spadano's coat and clambered from the train. Clutching his bag to his chest and limping, he took the underground passage—despite the cold, it smelled strongly of urine—to the far platform where a sleek locomotive was already waiting on the main line.

It must have been an earlier train that had been delayed because when the ticket collector found him, ensconced in a spacious armchair, Trotti had to pay a supplement for a rapido as well as a fine for not having the right ticket.

The fine applied even to retired functionaries of the state, the ticket collector explained apologetically, even to Carabinieri officers. He filled out a yellow coupon and deftly tucked Trotti's thirty thousand lire note into a leather pouch.

Trotti did not resent the extra cost. At least he had avoided the American girl.

He opened the documents on his lap and started to read. He coughed. His sore throat was getting worse and his knee was swollen.

19: Falcone

ON THE NIGHT of July 9, 1943, Sicily was invaded from North Africa by American, Canadian and British forces. Thirty-eight days later, the conquest of the island was complete.

The invasion secured the return of Allied troops to Europe. Coming after twenty years of Fascist repression, the invasion, engineered by the American secret services, also secured the triumphant return of the Mafia to Sicily, putting paid to Mussolini's campaign to destroy the Honored Society.

With Sicily invaded, Italy quit the Axis, changed sides and joined the victorious Allied camp. Two years later, Mussolini was caught, shot dead and suspended by his ankles, along with his mistress, in Milan. The war was over and in a referendum, Italians voted to abolish the monarchy that had allowed the rise of the Duce.

On June 2, 1946, the Italian Republic came into being.

In the hope of thwarting a growing separatist sentiment among Sicilians, the new republic granted the status of autonomous region to Sicily. The Sicilian Region was made responsible for fiscal affairs and accordingly, in 1952, just like the Bourbon monarchs before them, the elected members of the Sicilian Region entrusted tax-raising to private enterprise.

Mario Agrate, heretofore best known to the police for his smuggling activities in Trapani province, had married the daughter of a Palermo tax collector during the last year of the war.

Aided by his cousin Luigi Agrate, Mario Agrate pushed his father-in-law into premature retirement and promptly took over the family business. Rather than the standard cut of three and a half percent on all taxes raised, Mario Agrate now took ten percent.

With a virtual monopoly on tax collection, the cousins grew rich fast. By 1960 they had become landowners, developers and the biggest wine producers in Western Sicily. They also entered politics.

According to a 1977 report of the governmental anti-Mafia agency, the Agrate cousins controlled the ruling Christian Democratic party in Trapani. Mario Agrate owned a yacht, and it was aboard his luxurious boat that the cousins enter-tained high-ranking politicians from mainland Italy.

The Christian Democratic party, predominantly Roman Catholic, moderate and pro-Western in viewpoint, was held together by its opposition to Communism.

For thirty years, the Agrate cousins were good Catholics and committed anti-Communists; for thirty years the cous-ins ensured that Trapani voted massively for the Christian Democratic party.

Everybody was happy: the Agrate cousins prospered, their fiscal activity was never threatened by state intervention, while the Christian Democrats in Rome could count on Trapani for its vote.

There were many rumors about Mario Agrate and the Mafia, yet no link was ever shown to exist, even if, in Sic-ily, no one could be as rich as Mario Agrate without having influential friends. Mario Agrate had many influential friends in government—and the government never changed.

Then, in 1981, a Freemason scandal involving public servants brought down the national government, and for the first time in the thirty-five year history of the Italian Republic, a non-Christian Democratic premier was elected. There was a new balance of power in Rome.

At this time the Corleonese clan was embarking upon its murderous struggle for the control of organized crime in Palermo. The city became more dangerous than Beirut at war and the new government responded by sending the Carabiniere general and national hero Alberto dalla Chiesa to Sicily.

In September 1982, Alberto dalla Chiesa was murdered along with his wife, gunned down in his car as they left the Villa Whitaker. The Italian nation went into a tailspin of shock, angered that the country's most respected soldier could be eliminated like a common criminal, like a cheap picciotto of a warring Mafia gang.

The government's response to dalla Chiesa's murder was astonishingly immediate and understandably, Agrate was dumbfounded when policemen arrived in his offices in Trapani. Like a lot of powerful men in Sicily, Agrate was used to respect from the functionaries of the state.

That he was above the laws of the Republic had heretofore never been questioned.

"Can the Christian Democratic party allow the persecution of its allies in the business community?" Mario Agrate thundered publicly in the columns of the national weekly, L'Italiano.

It was more than a rhetorical question; it was a signal to the Christian Democrats in Rome. A clear signal—and a clear warning.

On the far side of the Atlantic, a retired mafioso living in Argentina had been arrested and extradited first to the USA, then to Italy where he agreed to collaborate with the Palermitan judges. Most of the Mafioso's close family had been eliminated and in his opinion he was no longer bound by omertà, by any law of silence. The pentito talked non-stop for days on end about the Mafia to the investigating judge, Giovanni Falcone. Though poorly educated, the mafioso was a highly intelligent man who knew and thoroughly understood the workings of the Mafia. The depth of his knowledge was impressive.

Although he never openly mentioned the 'third level' of Mafia activity, the pentito mentioned the Agrate cousins and their political immunity—immunity that was, he said, the pay-off for the votes that the cousins had always garnered for the Christian Democratic party.

Dalla Chiesa was murdered in September, 1982. In August 1983, the Socialists came to power, sharing it with the immovable Christian Democrats. Bettino Craxi—a Socialist—became prime minister.

The justice portfolio was passed to a Socialist in Craxi's coalition government and it was not immediately apparent that a new thief had come to the banquet. In the early years of the Craxi administration, the interlopers were still new to the spoils of power. A party with its roots in the north and center of Italy, the Socialists in 1984 preferred popular support in mainland Italy to the support of the Mafia in Sicily.

As for the Agrates, the writing was on the wall: their easy deal with the Christian Democrats could no longer be taken for granted.

For the first time since Mussolini, the investigating judges in Palermo received political support in their battle against the Mafia.

They prepared their massive Mafia maxi-trial in the knowledge that they had the support of the national government in Rome.

To the surprise of everybody, the Agrates were arrested.

In their late sixties, the cousins were the only politicians among the four hundred mafiosi to be put on trial in the vast, underground bunker of Ucciardone prison.

For the first time ever in Sicily, the question of the third level of Mafia activity was raised in public.

The third level, the court was told, was the political level of the Mafia.

The third level was the level at which the Italian Government and organized crime worked together, to their mutual benefit and to the prejudice of the Republic.

The third level was the level at which the democratically elected government of the sixth wealthiest nation in the world colluded with gangsters and criminals.

Luigi Agrate died of cancer before the end of the trial. Mario Agrate, on the other hand, was sent to prison, condemned to five years for Mafia activity.

Had a new dawn broken in Sicily?

On appeal, Mario Agrate was released after having served just eighteen months.

Bettino Craxi's Socialists were beginning to have second thoughts about fighting the Mafia.

20: Topolino

"TRYING TO HIDE from me?"

Trotti looked up in surprise.

The smile was bright, the white teeth sparkling. "I thought you were joking about being a Carabiniere."

"I gave up joking years ago, signorina."

The girl appeared puzzled. "You really are a policeman?"

"That's nothing to joke about."

"A real policeman?"

"Don't I look real?"

"A uniformed policeman?"

"A real policeman, retired now, thank goodness." Trotti smiled anew, "Polizia di Stato, not the Carabinieri. Don't be fooled by the coat. Lent to me by a general of the Carabinieri."

"It suits you."

Perhaps the remark was pure courtesy; perhaps the American girl had said it without thinking, but Trotti was both pleased and flattered. It was years since he had last thought about his personal appearances. It seemed even longer since any woman had sought to flatter him.

"Somebody hit you?" she asked, the smile gone. "Your face is bruised."

"Somebody bumped into me."

"You're hurt?"

"Tired and in need of sleep." Trotti added, "We both did well in Siena. I got a new coat and you got a new jacket."

She put her head to one side, "You're not hurt?"

"Your anorak looks warm."

"A man gave it to me."

"Lucky girl." Trotti emitted a mocking whistle, "What sort of man?"

She pointed to the logo of a grinning automobile at her chest and the matching logo on the woolen bonnet, "The sort of man who owns a car rental business and who needs to employ a girl with English and secretarial skills."

"You've got secretarial skills?"

"I work with children," Wilma replied. "I was waiting in the bar where you left me and he sat down beside me. He even bought me a hot drink before taking me to his house. I got to meet his wife and the two children. It was his wife who insisted on my staying for a meal."

"Nice people."

"I fell asleep." Wilma shrugged, "Not used to spending nights in cold railway stations."

"Who is?"

"Sorry I missed you in the Piazza."

Trotti turned to glance out of the window.

The fast train sped south. In the empty compartment, he had the feeling that they were in a small room, just him and the girl, and that some film was being projected on the far side of the window. The cheerless countryside and the battering rain against the window had nothing to do with either of them.

"Why sorry? You don't even know who I am."

"Didn't you say you were going to Rome? Didn't you say you were a policeman?"

"Then you did believe I was a cop?"

Her smile was slow, the smile of a little girl who knows she has been caught telling fibs and who can rely on her charm to get out of a sticky situation. "I thought you were a detective."

"I used to be a detective—not a very good one."

"I was hoping you'd help me."

"Your mother told you to be careful of men like me."

"You looked after me in Florence. You bought me a drink when I was freezing—when all the other men thought I was just an African prostitute."

"I never gave you an anorak."

The far door slid open and the ticket collector entered the coach. Since looking at Trotti's ticket, he had acquired a red scarf that he had tucked under the lapels of his blue-grey suit. As he came along the central aisle, he nodded to Trotti and smiled at the girl sitting curled up in the armchair beside him. Then with the pneumatic *whoosh* of the sliding doors, he was gone.

"I thought you didn't have any money, signorina. You can afford a first class ticket?"

Wilma had kicked off her shoes. "I never intended to catch this train. Way out of my class. Then, in Chianciano, I saw you scuttling along like an irritable mouse."

"An irritable mouse?"

"A mouse in a military overcoat."

"And the ticket collector?"

She grinned. "What about him?"

"If the collector'd asked you for your ticket?"

"I would've given him a lovely, innocent smile and told him the truth about this little girl from America who'd got on the smart train by mistake."

Trotti touched her sleeve, "I can lend you the money."

"I'm looking for my father," Wilma said, studying Trotti carefully. The grin turned wistful.

"You've lost him?"

She did not blink. "You can help me find my father, can't you, Ispettore Trotti?"

21: Petrarca

"YOU WORK WITH children?"

"I'm an au pair," Wilma nodded. "Staying with an American family in Milan, looking after the two little boys."

"Why hang around the railway station in Florence?"

"I have a few days off." For a moment, Wilma appeared irritated. "I'm on my way to Rome."

Trotti said, after a brief silence, "I used to deal with children."

"You enjoyed it?"

"It made a change."

"How would a policeman work with kids?"

"Abused children—a couple of years before I retired. We set up our own little center and even collaborated with the city hospital."

She sat to one side, opposite Trotti, with a leg folded beneath her and with the other knee propping up her chin. "Before coming to Italy, I was studying child psychology at university."

"I didn't enjoy working with abused children." Trotti leaned back into the deep armchair as the fast train—it was called the *Petrarca*, the ticket collector had told him—hurried through the late afternoon towards Rome.

Rain rather than snow now battered against the window.

"I ended up with more than enough problems of my own. Child abuse? Piero Trotti abuse."

"You love children, ispettore." It was a statement.

"The job had nothing to do with loving children."

"Then why get involved? Not enough robbers in this country of yours to keep every policeman busy?"

"A girl was being molested." Trotti breathed out noisily, "A sweet little thing and we managed to help her. The newspapers heard about it and of course after that, everything turned political. Mainly the leghisti. You'll soon discover, everything's political in Italy. Everybody—the politicians, the doctors and my superiors—they all wanted me to stay on with the center. Suddenly Piero Trotti was everyone's favorite flavor."

Wilma's smile broadened.

"I was even asked to postpone my retirement for a couple of years."

"You didn't?"

Trotti raised his flat hand to eye level. "I'd had enough."

The girl was looking at him attentively. "When I met you last night—this morning—in Florence, I knew you were good. You're a kind man."

He opened his eyes in astonishment. "People tell me I'm irascible and selfish. An irritable mouse."

"A kind man," she repeated, more to herself than to him.

Trotti snorted mirthlessly. "I'm the sort of man who carries a big stick, who believes in right and wrong. The man who puts criminals in prison."

"Criminals who don't buy a first class ticket?"

Trotti gave a weary smile. "I hated it. With children, you can never know the whole truth. Not until it's too late, not until the damage's been done. Children are always the victims—and through no fault of their own. There's neither stick nor carrot. It's all about protecting lives, protecting children when they've been betrayed by the people supposed to protect them." Trotti shook his head, "Too depressing."

"Protection's more important than sending a culprit to jail."

Trotti laughed sourly, "Hitting people over the head and throwing them in prison—that's my specialty, that's what I do well. The big stick. I can deal with perverts, just as I can deal with thieves and pimps and murderers." Trotti looked at her and he caught his breath, "You can't teach an old dog new tricks. I'm not a nurse, not a social worker—just an irritable mouse." He pushed his hand through the thinning hair. "For goodness sakes, I didn't even look after my own daughter."

"You say a lot of things you don't mean. Anyone can see you love children."

"Twenty years ago, Pioppi stopped eating. She almost died. That, so I'm told, was my fault."

"She was trying to tell you something."

"That I wasn't the perfect father."

"Eating disorders are a frequent problem in adolescent girls. Various causes—including causes outside the family—can trigger anorexia."

"Don't use that word." Trotti jerked his hand sharply, "It's not a word I like." He returned his glance to the window, to the endless passage of the wet countryside.

"You have grandchildren, ispettore?"

"Two girls," he said to his reflection. "Francesca and Piera."

"Your wife must be beautiful."

"I'm sure she must."

22: Nissan

"I'M FROM CHICAGO."

The word sounded distant and exotic.

"An orphan." Wilma's eyes met his, "I never spent time in an orphanage or anything horrible. The happiest childhood, in fact—even if I was the only black kid in the neighborhood. I grew up near Northwestern University, in a very white part of town. So white I often wondered what I was doing there."

"What were you doing there?"

"My parents live in Evanston."

"That's where you learned Italian?"

"At high school. And then here in Italy." She added simply, "It's important I should learn the language of my origins."

"Where we come from, where we're going to—I'm not sure that's so very important, signorina. It's what we do along the way that counts. Or perhaps what we don't do."

"You say that because you know who you are, you have your roots."

Her vehemence surprised him and Trotti was momentarily silenced. He turned and looked at her young face in admiration. "If your father's black, it shouldn't be too hard to find him in Rome."

Wilma's white teeth sparkled. "Why on earth does everybody assume my father's black?"

"Possibly because you're black."

"Europeans all seem to think only black men can have children with white women. But black women?" Wilma shook her head in impatience. "Black women like me?"

"Very few black women in this country."

"You're forgetting the African prostitutes hanging outside the station in Florence. The ones you didn't give the hot chocolate to."

Trotti replied stiffly, "All very recent, signorina."

"Wilma."

"The prostitutes from Africa and Eastern Europe—that's new for us Italians."

"My blood mother was a nurse in the US Army. With the medical corps in Padua."

"You know her?"

Wilma held up a finger to accompany a lopsided smile. "I met her just once." The girl moved her legs on the seat. She was now looking at Trotti carefully, as if apprehensive of his reaction. "She wasn't very interested in me when we finally caught up with one another."

"She came looking for you?"

"I had to wait fifteen years before having that pleasure. She'd left the army by then and was living in Los Angeles. My father took me there to see her. I needed to know who she was." A shrug. "She was married and working in a private hospital. Somewhere classy near Beverly Hills." The girl stopped, "You know America?"

Trotti shook his head. "I once spent a weekend in Switzerland."

"Switzerland?"

"I should've stayed at home."

Wilma smiled perfunctorily. "This woman—my mother— has a husband from Jamaica who's a successful doctor. A lot older than her. Not that I ever met him. I was the little secret she had to hide and so she couldn't take me home to meet her wonderful family. She refused Pa's suggestion of going to a hotel. So we just sat there in the airport. Didn't really have much to say to each other, my blood mother and I. The nurse—ebony black, with beautiful skin, so slim and elegant, with her long, straight hair and her lovely clothes and shoes—was in a hurry to get away. Away from the reminder of a past she'd chosen to forget."

"Why did you want to meet her?"

"The three of us went to a Burger King." Wilma bit her lip, "Your own daughter—your own flesh and blood that you haven't seen since the day the baby came squealing out of your belly, your own daughter who's flown halfway across a continent just to see you—and all you can spare's a half-hour at a fast-food stop in a food court in LAX?"

Trotti frowned.

"At the Los Angeles airport. She had her family to think about. Her husband and the two little boys—she showed me a photograph of them, bless their hearts. Two boys that she was putting through private school. The husband had no idea she'd had a child by another man."

"She felt guilty, Wilma."

"Why agree to see me? It wasn't to go to Disneyland that Daddy and I flew out to California." The nostrils flared as Wilma breathed in. "All I wanted was a sign. A sign she cared, a sign that I was more than just a genetic coincidence. You know what she showed me? A photo of her car. A red Nissan. I wasn't asking her to feel guilty. I can understand the situation she must've been in—a black Army nurse who'd an affair with an Italian. She didn't have to worry about me—I'd been lucky, very lucky. I grew up in a wonderful home, in a wonderful family, with very loving parents."

"It's what you do—not who you are—that counts. Why bother with the past?"

Wilma smiled bravely. "My adoptive parents gave me more love than my real mother could dream of. A lot more. And they don't even have a red Nissan."

23: Penn

"DADDY DROVE DOWN to Tennessee. That's where I was born—in Memphis. I'm told my birth was one of the happiest days in Mom's life. At last she had a child, a little girl to call her own. She'd been trying to have children for years."

A moment's pause as the girl looked at Trotti.

Trotti said, "I'd've liked more children—perhaps a son. A little brother for Pioppi."

"Who wants boys?"

"They have their uses. Some grow into policemen who can help young women."

"My parents went back to Chicago and they never saw or heard from my real mother again. Not until the meeting in Los Angeles. My dad's a teacher and less than a couple of months later, Mom was pregnant. At the age of forty-two—would you believe it? Pregnant with twins. She spent the next eight months in the hospital. Thank God our insurance paid." Wilma nodded brightly. "Two gorgeous little girls, two daughters for my parents and two wonderful sisters for me." She added, "The girls are in college in Philadelphia."

Trotti waited.

"I'm different." Wilma's face was not sad, but the set of her jaw, the tightening of the muscles betrayed an inner conflict. Wilma reached out across the seat, opening her hand, the pale palm up. "When I was a little girl, nobody ever mentioned my skin—not even when we were buying clothes together or getting cosmetics. But of course it was always there, unspoken."

"Your parents'd told you about your adoption?"

"Not the sort of thing they could've hidden from the only black girl in a white family." Wilma laughed and at that moment, she was so pretty, so young, so sweet, so innocent that Trotti could not stop himself from sharing the laughter.

"There, at the airport in Los Angeles, I realized this woman who had given birth to me fifteen years earlier, this beautiful nurse, just like a Hollywood actress with her beautiful clothes and lustrous hair, smoking one cigarette after another and scarcely touching her food and never daring to look me in the face—I realized I had absolutely nothing in common with her. Except, perhaps, that we were both black and that neither of us liked hamburgers. When she was gone and Daddy took me back to the hotel, I didn't even cry." Wilma paused. "I was glad she was . . . so insignificant."

Trotti said nothing.

"That day at the airport in Los Angeles, I realized that part of me's American, but another part of me is from Europe. And that's how I decided I needed to find my father."

"One disappointment's not enough?"

"I'm not asking him to love me," Wilma retorted. She ran a hand through the strands of hair that poked from beneath the woolen bonnet, "I just want to see him—that's all I ask. Just see him so that I know where I'm from. Just see him." Wilma shrugged. "See if he cares. See if he knows."

24: Madonna

"PISANELLI'S GETTING MARRIED on the sixth."

"The sixth of April?" Wilma said, a happy smile creasing her young face. "That's so romantic! The first day of the Renaissance."

"Easter Saturday."

"On the sixth of April in 1327, Petrarch first saw Laura and fell madly in love with her."

"Who?"

"Laura was a Frenchwoman—just nineteen years old. Petrarch's family had gone to Avignon in exile."

"They lived happily ever after?"

Wilma retorted, "Of course not—Laura was already married, but that didn't stop Petrarch from immortalizing her name in his sonnets—*Rime in vita e morta di Madonna Laura*. She inspired in him a passion that's proverbial for its constancy and purity. And started the Renaissance."

"My friend's waited twenty years to marry his fiancée, my goddaughter." Trotti snorted, "Not sure Pisanelli's a poet, though. His passion may be constant, but I wouldn't swear to its purity."

The *Petrarca* pulled into Roma Stazione Termini.

The weather had improved and Trotti was unreasonably surprised.

Having lived most of his life in the Po valley, he was unused to a Mediterranean climate. Admittedly, he had once spent two years in Bologna, but there the weather was just as damp and cold as at home. A further three years had been spent in Bari where Trotti could recall no particularly mild climate—no doubt because while in the south, he had spent nearly all his time in dim offices.

(*"You always put your job before your family, Piero."*)

Stazione Termini appeared smaller, cleaner and a lot brighter to Trotti than the grand central station of Milan. There were no pigeons just as there was no glass-covered canopy to keep out rain, fog and cold.

"Traveling in style, commissario?" Pisanelli's broad smile was waiting for him. "First class, eh?"

"The bastards make me pay a fine for the luxury."

"That's what comes of having communists in the government."

"The first time we've had communists in forty-five years," Trotti said.

"First time you've traveled by train in forty-five years. No wonder you couldn't find anybody to drive you here."

"The Ferrovie dello Stato's always been criminal." Trotti stepped down onto the platform. "A retired functionary of the state's got to pay thirty thousand lire over and above the first-class fare for a wretched train that's late."

"Half an hour early, you mean."

"The train's late, Pisa—just me that's early. It was delayed at Chianciano and I got on. Hence the fine."

"Welcome to Rome," Pisanelli said cheerfully, holding out his right hand for Trotti.

"At least I didn't keep you waiting, Pisa."

A shrug. "I have a lot of free time these days."

Trotti put his bag down on the platform and looked appraisingly at the younger man as they shook hands. Pierangelo Pisanelli had been sitting on the edge of a boxed concrete flower bed. A couple of shrubs and a discarded can of Chinotto, a few cigarette tips.

"Looking good, Pisa."

Pisanelli had lost weight since they had last met, and as he pulled himself upright onto the crutch, he appeared shorter than Trotti remembered him. Shorter and more frail.

"No need to worry about me, commissario." Pisanelli must have caught Trotti's glance, for he laughed. "The worst's over. This"—he tapped the unbent leg with his hand—"got me away from your dreadful city."

"You like Rome?"

"I like being with Anna," Pisanelli replied, and the freshness of his smile pierced Trotti's heart. "Forty-three years old and I'm marrying a woman almost half my age. A very lucky man."

Trotti nodded. "I always told you that."

A raised eyebrow. "Your goddaughter's about the only thing I have to thank you for, Commissario Trotti."

"She hasn't forgiven me, has she?"

"I see your hens and your mushrooms and your chestnuts are keeping you fit." Pisanelli put his head back and the long hair ran against the collar of his suede jacket. "Apart from the bruised face, you're not looking at all bad yourself. Bruised face and a paunch. Pity about the Carabinieri overcoat."

"I almost died of exposure in Siena."

"Your fault for going there."

"She hasn't forgiven me, has she?"

"Forgiven you for what?" Pisanelli's steady eyes held his.

"Your getting hurt."

"Do I look hurt?"

Trotti made a movement of irritation. "Anna still holds everything against me."

"It wasn't you who drove the car off the road."

"It was me who got you to run all over Lombardy on my wild goose chases."

"I miss all that," Pisanelli answered wistfully. "That and your bullying and all your obsessions, commissario. Plus the smell of your sickly, synthetic rhubarb sweets."

Trotti smiled, but the pain in his heart lingered as he picked up his bag. Taking the younger man by the arm, he walked across the busy concourse of Stazione Termini.

25: Verdi

"IT'S ALWAYS RUSH hour in Rome—any time, night or day. That's why the place's eternal."

The evening sky had cleared to the west. It was raining, but the drizzle was almost pleasant against Trotti's skin; the air was softer and warmer than in the hills of Tuscany. Here winter was over and Trotti was tempted to remove the overcoat. He had forgotten about his sore throat and his bruises.

They stepped out of the station.

The lights and their reflections along the wet roads beckoned enticingly. Trotti, retired now for nearly a year, had the strange sensation of being on holiday. Piero Trotti, who had never been young or carefree, felt pleasantly young and carefree.

He caught a deep breath, and at that moment he saw Wilma; she was being accompanied by a well-dressed couple to an awaiting car. Perhaps before climbing into the back seat, the young face turned in the evening rain to glance at him.

Trotti could not be sure in the failing light.

Wilma was going to stay with friends of the American family for whom she babysat. Trotti had given her Pisanelli's home number.

He watched the sleek car disappear into the swirling city traffic.

The Eternal City.

His sense of excitement was almost inebriating in its intensity.

"Don't have much luggage, commissario?"

Trotti swung round to look at Pisanelli. "I'm not staying forever."

"You've got a suit for the wedding, I hope." There was concern in Pisanelli's voice.

"Just flippers and a snorkel. And a present for Anna."

The two men walked along the long row of taxis.

"I'd've married at the town hall, but Anna wants this to be a very special occasion."

"You only get married once, Pisa . . ."

Pisanelli shot him a sideways glance.

"At least, in theory."

"For years I thought I'd never get married at all." Pisanelli balanced his weight on the aluminum crutch. He had shaken free of Trotti's guiding hand.

"Tell me about your future wife, Pisa."

"What do you want to know?"

"Nothing to stop you having children, I hope." Trotti gestured towards Pisanelli's crippled leg.

"Lost none of your tact, commissario."

"Anna always wanted a family. Ever since she was a little girl."

"I hope to be family enough for her."

"Anna wants children that grow up. The kind of children that have hair on their head."

"As delightful as ever," Pisanelli retorted, not without bitterness. "The life of enforced inactivity hasn't altered you, commissario."

"People say I've grown worse."

"Calumny." Pisanelli asked, "You're going to tell me what happened to your face?"

"Somebody pushed me over."

"I know the temptation."

They followed the taxi rank to where a yellow cab stood alone. The driver was standing out of the drizzle beneath a domed perspex shelter. He gave a smile to Pisanelli, a nod to Trotti and like a clever magician, produced an umbrella from behind his back. He took Trotti's bag and placed it in the capacious trunk.

Pisanelli said, "Trastevere."

Trotti interjected, "That's where you live now, Pisanelli?"

"Don't you want to be near the Pope?"

"I want to be with my goddaughter."

"I've booked you into a hotel."

The car smelled of new plastic and naphthalene. Pisanelli clambered awkwardly onto the front seat where there was more room for the unbending left leg. "Anna's very busy before her wedding," he said over his shoulder.

"You invited me to stay with you and Anna."

"The bill's paid for four nights—or for as long as you care to stay."

The taxi pulled away from the curb and headed towards via Nazionale.

"I want to see Anna."

"Don't fret."

"Can't I see Anna now?"

"You're very special for her—always have been."

The wiper started its rhythmic beat; beyond its sweep, the city lights multiplied and twinkled in the raindrops of the windshield.

"Still angry with me, isn't she?"

"If Anna were angry, she wouldn't have invited you to her wedding."

"You invited me."

"A big mistake."

"I'll go back, if that's what you want. What Anna wants."

"So susceptible, commissario."

"It's to see my goddaughter that I've come down to Rome."

The driver's window was open and the damp air smelled of car fumes.

"Nearly seventy years old and you still behave like a petulant child. Of course you'll see Anna."

"When?"

"Her family's staying with us at the moment. The apartment's very small."

They waited a long time at the traffic lights off via del Corso. The memorial to Victor Emmanuel was a brightly lit wedding cake against the darkening sky.

Soon the taxi was running over a bridge, over the Tiber, into Trastevere.

Pisanelli said softly, "Give her time, commissario."

26: Athletic Club

DESPITE THE TOXIC fumes of the traffic, the trees were already in bloom along the via Sidney Sonnino.

The taxi dropped them off at a tram stop; the driver, both brusque and friendly, handed the umbrella to Trotti as he pulled the bag from the trunk. With scarcely a glance at the bills Pisanelli gave him, he took the money and the umbrella and then returned to the driver's seat. A screech of tire rubber and the red lights joined the endless flow of cars.

They crossed the busy road, Pisanelli walking slowly beneath the light drizzle and refusing Trotti's proffered help.

"Why do the Romans all sound like people on television?"

"Because the people on television are all Romans," Pisanelli said. "You'll like this hotel."

The sound of the Corso fell behind them as they entered the side streets of Trastevere. The same cobblestones as those of Trotti's city, fished from a river bed and neatly tapped into the ground. The houses appeared cheerful, as if illuminated by the optimism of permanent good weather. Lights were coming on and there was the smell of cooking—oil, tomatoes and garlic.

"I'll get to see Anna before the wedding?"

They took a couple of left turns where the streets got narrower.

The streets reminded Trotti of his own city on the Po; as in his city, there was no sidewalk, but these streets were less cared for, less clean. Oil slicks on the cobbles, accumulated piles of detritus by the side of the road and between the parked cars, rusting Vespas and glinting new motorcycles. There were the incongruous reminders of a rich heritage: the unexpected fountain or an ancient engraving set into a building, a luxurious villa beyond a high wall.

Trastevere was both quaint and dirty.

"I wouldn't like to live here."

"Nobody's asking you to," Pisanelli retorted. He added, "You know my family's from the South."

"Always thought you were from Sondrio, Pisa. From the Alps."

"My parents went north during the thirties, when Mussolini was trying to make the Alps a bit less Germanic and a bit more Italian."

Pisanelli stumbled as they moved along a line of parked cars. The crutch tapped against the cobbles.

There was purple bougainvillea climbing down the brick of a wall. Beyond the wall stood a clinic or a hospital, and Trotti caught a glimpse of a few sprouts of grass and another forlorn fountain. He also caught sight of a nun.

"You're going to like this hotel."

"Who are you trying to convince?"

The Hotel Toscana was hidden behind a couple of cars. There was an entrance and, set back from the road, a wooden doorframe with a ground-glass window.

The door would not move under Pisanelli's hand. Stepping back, he rang the bell. A distant tinkle and after a while, they heard scratching in the lock and the door was opened by an old man with white hair and a smiling face.

He beamed at Pisanelli. "Commissario Trotti?"

Pisanelli gestured. "This is Commissario Trotti. He's booked for four nights."

"A gentleman's just phoned for Commissario Trotti." The old man ushered them into the gloom of the hotel. He was wearing a red and black striped waistcoat; he could have been a superannuated player from Milan AC. "Wouldn't leave his number, so I told him to ring back later."

27: Zapping

"THAT YOU, PIERO?"

A grunt.

"That you?"

"How d'you know I was here?"

"I spoke to your goddaughter. You told me you were going to stay with her."

"She's a busy woman, three days before her wedding."

"Signorina Ermagni's charming—although she didn't seem particularly pleased to hear from me."

"I'm not particularly pleased to hear from you, either. You want your coat back, Spadano?"

"Keep the coat, Piero. It suits you."

"So I'm told," Trotti remarked coldly. "I'm about to go to bed. I haven't slept for thirty-six hours and I can smell your cigars from here."

"I'd like you to see Lia Guerra. You left in such a hurry to get back to your American girl, I didn't get the time to tell you Guerra's in Rome."

"I'm not interested in Lia Guerra, Spadano. Nor in Gracchi."

"For your own good."

"My own good at this moment is to sleep."

"Lia Guerra lives in the via Tempio, opposite the synagogue."

"Spadano, I'm going to spend a few days in Rome with Pisanelli and Anna. On Saturday, I'm going to the wedding on Lake Bracciano and then I'm going back to via Milano, my video machine and my cousin's cooking. Please don't ask me to do favors for you."

"For yourself, Piero."

"I've got better things to do."

"Near the Colosseum. Via del Tempio, 26. Top floor."

"I couldn't give a damn."

"You couldn't give a damn Beltoni'll kill you?"

"Beltoni's not important."

"Trotti's important—and Beltoni'll kill Piero Trotti if Piero Trotti's not very careful."

"Kill me? I'm not that interesting."

"You don't know Sicilians. His brother was murdered and he holds you responsible, Piero."

"I know them well enough to know that I have nothing to fear."

"And if he kills you?"

"If Beltoni kills me, I won't have to fear him, will I?"

"Not afraid of dying, Piero?"

"I'm an old man."

"You're being foolhardy."

"I can live with foolhardiness—not with fear."

"Lia Guerra knew Enzo Beltoni well."

"A good life—wife, daughter and now two granddaughters. I can't complain. Remember the Fascist signs they used to paint on the walls, Spadano? *'Better to live a day as a lion than a hundred years as a lamb.'*"

"Ancient history. Do yourself a favor, Trotti. Speak to Guerra."

"Ciao," Trotti said and he put the receiver down.

Trotti showered and climbed into bed.

He stretched out, feeling his tired muscles, feeling the bruise on his face, feeling the dull pain in his knee. Yet, despite his fatigue and the missed night's rest, he could not get to sleep.

He turned on the television and switched between the mindless pap of the Berlusconi stations.

After ten minutes he turned the television off and turned the bedside lamp back on.

"I'm not interested in Lia Guerra, Spadano. Nor in Gracchi."

Trotti started to read.

28: All You Need Is Love

PRINCE MAGAZINE: ARE you a Communist?

Gracchi: I am absolutely nothing. My parents were Communists—my father worked his way up the ladder at Fiat, then studied in the evenings to become an architect. It took him ten years. When I was growing up in Turin, there was a picture of Stalin on the kitchen wall. For all that, my parents sent me to the priests. Five years of schooling with the Rosminian Institute of Charity, then seven years with the Salesian brothers. It took me a long time to see that with their centralized structure and their hostility towards intellectual independence, the Church and the Communist Party were really the same thing. Neither had faith in the individual.

It's the individual who counts.

Communist? I nearly joined the party, you know.

In Trento, as a student, I believed in the existence of classes, just as I believed in the oppression of the working class. Lotta Continua became my platform. No doubt as a response to that period of tension—the forces of progress had been silenced and then killed off by Pinochet in Chile—Lotta Continua slipped out of control and became too radical. And violent. I found myself at odds with my companions. Soon Lotta Continua was no better than the Partito Comunista Italiano that it so despised. Good friends of mine became apparatchiks, toeing the line while using Lotta Continua for their personal aims. "Power to the people"—I was beginning to have second thoughts. Power to the person, power to be free, power to live one's life to the fullest. I was concerned with the pursuit of happiness, the pursuit of *my* happiness. The Beatles were more important than either Marx—Karl or Groucho.

The apparatchiks learned to hate me. Dope was now part of my revolution. They said I was setting a bad example for the working masses on the factory floor. I told them the masses were already under the influence of cheap red wine.

As a punishment for the drugs, my long hair, my clothes and my women, Lotta Continua sent me to cool my heels in Palermo, then to Padua where I taught at the university. [*Laughter.*] I taught sociology during the day and screwed my sociologists at night—something very special about the girls from the Veneto—beautiful, church-going and slightly crazy. The Rector told me to take my salary and stay away from the university.

Prince: Perhaps he was jealous.

Gracchi: Not long after that, I was wrongly arrested in Lombardy—a little girl had been kidnapped—and I spent a couple of nights in a pokey, provincial prison where I was interrogated by a policeman who ate sweets and pretended to be stupid— at least, I think he was pretending. That he—or anybody else—could believe me capable of kidnapping a child I found quite unbearable. Let me tell you something—and you can quote me. Children are the justification for our struggle, they are our hope and—forgive me if I sound like a Salesian—they are our redemption. Lakshmi—my daughter—for nine years now has been my source of joy, my true *raison d'être*. Her smile gives sense to my life.

During those days in prison, a fellow inmate—a defrocked priest who'd got a couple of nuns pregnant—talked to me about India. He gave me a book on transcendental meditation. In prison, you always try to sleep as much as possible—it's the safest way of killing time. I can remember sitting up all night in my damp cell of that horrid, humid city on the Po, reading the book.

Prince: Destiny whispering in your ear?

Gracchi: A few days later, my mother died. I realized then how much I loved her. A hard woman, but I appreciated her more in death than I ever did in life. One morning I woke up and the two most important things in my life had gone forever. My mother was dead. Lotta Continua was dead. One of my best and dearest friends, another founder member of Lotta Continua, Antonio Cocco, was in prison and his beautiful young wife had been gunned down by the Carabinieri.

I felt terribly alone.

My generation had got lost. There was no longer any place for the kind of constructive movement I had always wanted. There was nothing but emptiness around us. No more dreams, no more hopes, no desires. Nothing mattered anymore.

That's when I decided to go to India.

There's no doctrine, there's no discipline in Indian philosophy. Life's a game; learn to live with yourself. If you can love yourself, then you'll learn how to love other people. In India I came to understand all forms of society, on the left or on the right, are coercive. In wearing saffron, in embracing transcendentalism, I found freedom.

Zen says, "Stop running after a goal. What you're looking for is within you." I'd been running for thirty-two years—obtuse, arrogant and schematic. I'd never learned to look at myself. I had never learned to relax.

I'd already met Chiara during my imprisonment and we liked each other. It was fun—but then one day she smiled at me and she said, "I'm pregnant." I already had a son by a first marriage but I hadn't been a good father. Yet when Chiara said those words, I suddenly understood the meaning of life.

Prince: The meaning of life?

Gracchi: Life goes on. We don't have tenure; we're passing through and it's our job to make the best of it, for ourselves and for others.

29: MGM

THE PHOTOCOPIED SHEETS had slipped from his hands onto the floor, and now muffled shouting came from the street.

It was nearly nine o'clock in the morning before Trotti awoke in the dark room.

Using the remote control to turn on the television, he watched twenty minutes of an old American film before finally pulling himself out of bed.

He threw open the blinds.

Eyes blinking in the sudden light, Trotti looked out onto the new day. A cloudless sky above the terracotta roofs of the Eternal City. Somewhere a bird was singing hopefully, and there was the smell of coffee and petrol fumes in the air.

The muscles in his shoulders were stiff from hauling his suitcase through the streets of Siena. The sore throat had gone; his lips had healed. His knee was stiff but did not hurt. The spremutas and their vitamins had done him a world of good. Trotti was refreshed after a good night's sleep.

A spring morning in Trastevere.

As he looked down on the street three stories below, Trotti was aware of feeling unreasonably cheerful. Leaving home and coming to Rome for a few days had been a wise decision, even if his cousin was not happy about the prolonged absence. Too bad.

As for Wilma, she was young enough to be his granddaughter. He had found her company delightful, but Trotti knew that she could never be interested in an old man like him. A very old man like him.

It was good to see Pisanelli again.

Trotti shaved to the music of the Hollywood fantasy. In the bright mirror, he examined his features. The bruised cheek had turned yellow. Beneath the lathering soap that smelled of almonds, his skin showed further signs of aging—less supple, less elastic.

(*"Who knows, you should live out another twenty years— supposing you're allowed to."*)

Trotti laughed and grazed his chin with the razor.

He showered, got dressed and polished his shoes on the overlap of the counterpane.

Leaving the Carabinieri coat hanging from the back of the door, he was about to leave when the bakelite telephone by the bedside started to ring.

Trotti barked ungraciously, "What do you want now, Spadano?"

Wilma Barclay gave a girlish laugh at the other end of the line.

30: Austerlitz

TROTTI WENT DOWN the narrow stairs to the reception. Nobody was in sight, even though Trotti had been told the hotel was full. The American film continued, cheerful and unheeded, in the gloomy entrance hall. Animated shoes danced around Fred Astaire for an absent audience.

The Hotel Toscana smelled of floor cleaner, and somewhere he could hear a woman shouting.

He dropped his room key on the counter and went out into the city.

He was surprised to find himself whistling a tune from the musical. Trotti had never liked American music, not even at the end of the war when jazz was the popular antidote to twenty years of Fascist culture. Piero Trotti preferred opera, Italian opera. At least you could understand the words.

The Piazza Santa Maria in Trastevere was only a two-hundred-meter walk from the Hotel Toscana, and Pisanelli was already waiting for him, reading the newspaper on the terrace of a bar. He sat slumped in a chair, his left leg and the crutch held out straight before him. His sunglasses were pushed back onto the receding hairline. The suede coat had been draped over a spare chair.

"You never whistle, commissario. Why the good mood?"

"Been waiting long, Pisa?"

"Not more than a couple of hours."

Trotti nodded to the blue portable telephone on the table-cloth. "You could've called the hotel."

"You needed to sleep."

"You should've woken me."

"I don't want you tired and irritable."

"I'll have time enough to sleep in my grave."

It was indeed a beautiful morning, with a warm sun shining on the open square and the central fountain. The freezing cold of the Apennines seemed a world away. Walls blossomed with wisteria.

Trotti placed a hand on Pisanelli's shoulder. "Your future wife doesn't need you this morning?"

"Best if I'm out of the way," Pisanelli replied. "Anna's with her family. With her father and her brother, Piero. And her stepmother."

"How's the young Piero?"

"Doing well at the technical institute. Studying computers."

"Named after me, you know, Pisa."

"We all have our cross to bear. How'd you find the hotel?"

"I slept well."

"I'm not sure I trust your good moods," Pisanelli remarked grimly.

In the piazza, gypsy children were playing football, occasionally breaking off to beg from the passersby. A few clerics and Japanese tourists entered the church or emerged from it.

The tourists showed little generosity towards the shoeless young beggars; they clutched their cameras.

Again Trotti had the impression of playing hooky, of being on a stolen holiday.

The smile left his face. "What d'you do with all your free time in Rome, Pisa? With your pension, you no longer need to work."

"Still recuperating from the accident, commissario."

Trotti laughed.

"You find that funny?"

"You don't get bored recuperating?"

"You don't get bored in your foggy northern city? You

were supposed to leave that place for your house in the hills, commissario."

"Anna Maria put a stop to all that, I'm afraid."

"Anna Maria?" Pisanelli raised an eyebrow in faint amusement. "Another of your American ladies?"

"My cousin from Holland—the woman with the Count Cavour spectacles. She always hated Santa Maria, always hated life in the hills. Almost as much as she hated Holland. Anna Maria doesn't want to spend the last years of her life in the place where she grew up."

"Cousin?"

"You met her, Pisa. She took a liking to you."

"My disarming, youthful smile?"

"Now the grandchildren are married, Anna Maria's returned to Italy—and to via Milano."

"An improvement in the cooking arrangements, I hope."

"You liked my boiled eggs."

A waiter who had been hovering by the open door of the café surged forward and brought the list of drinks to their table. Trotti smiled in surprise and ordered coffee and two croissants. Like a diligent student, the waiter took notes. He had long, thin hands and a weak, ingratiating smile; his cheeks were creased in deep wrinkles. He gave Pisanelli a radiant nod and nimbly returned to the interior of the café. Seen from behind, the waiter's waistcoat was unnaturally narrow.

Trotti threw a glance at the open *Repubblica* that Pisanelli was reading.

The medical section.

"Very interesting," Trotti said flatly and turned away.

"I try to educate myself as best I can," Pisanelli remarked. "I'd hate to remain an ignorant peasant."

"Many advantages to being a peasant, you know." Trotti's eyes wandered to the church on the far side of the piazza, beyond the noisy children. "Slow, stubborn but not necessarily stupid."

Pisanelli returned to the newspaper.

Trotti said almost absentmindedly, "I never did believe in coincidences."

Pisanelli looked up, "Coincidences?"

"Not in my line of business. Not after thirty-eight years as a policeman."

31: Cherchez la Femme

PISANELLI TIPPED HIS head and asked expectantly, "What coincidence, commissario?"

Trotti was still looking at the church, "A couple of days before I was about to leave for Rome, I got a call from Spadano."

"Your Carabinieri friend?"

"Friend in a manner of speaking. High-ranking general now, and based in Tuscany. Claims he's working on art protection—Tutela del Patrimonio Artistico—but I'm not sure I believe him. Not sure I believe any Carabiniere. Spadano says he's marking time until he can retire to his native Sicily." Trotti gave an apologetic shrug. "I suppose somebody's got to live there, Pisa."

"You ever been to Sicily, commissario?"

"God forbid."

"What does your Carabiniere friend want?"

"The general had some important news and he asked me to drop in on my way to Rome."

"How did he know you were coming to the wedding?"

"No idea, Pisa."

"You're part of our artistic heritage he's protecting?"

"I'm old enough."

"You could do with renovations."

Trotti smiled.

"You see, commissario, you do have a sense of humor."

"After spending a couple of days with Pioppi and the little girls . . ."

"How's your daughter?" A wolfish grin from Pisanelli as he moved in the armchair to face Trotti.

"Instead of catching the direct train from Bologna, I stopped off in Florence." Trotti did not conceal his annoyance. "Thought I'd do some sightseeing. Foolishly, I missed my connection."

"Not used to public transport, commissario. Things'll get easier with practice."

"I nearly died of frostbite in Florence."

"With all that sugar in your blood?"

"While waiting for the first train—they closed the station, not even a waiting room to get away from the cold—I bumped into the pretty black girl you couldn't take your eyes off last night at Termini."

"What girl is this?"

"Glad to see your hormones are still functioning, Pisa. One thing less for poor Anna to worry about."

"Wasn't it you, Commissario Trotti, who had a black lady friend? From Uruguay, I believe, who did some very inventive things to your interior decorating."

Trotti took a deep breath, "I traveled with the girl, and together we got into Siena on the early morning train. The Carabinieri were waiting for me at the station. We dropped the girl off in a bar."

"Spadano still smokes those awful cigars?"

"Spadano thinks my life's in danger."

"Rhubarb sweets are no more dangerous than the noisome Toscanellis he smokes. What'd your Spadano want to tell you?"

"A long time ago—at the time when Rosanna Belloni disappeared—there was a Sicilian who was murdered in my city."

Pisanelli nodded. "A small-time dealer called Beltoni who liked to consume what he was supposed to sell?"

"They cut his tongue out and then tied him and burned the corpse. Not a pretty sight."

"Aren't you forgetting I was there, commissario?"

Trotti said, "His brother wants to kill me."

Pisanelli took up the *Repubblica*.

Trotti pushed the paper back onto the tablecloth. "This brother once worked for Gracchi. The same Gracchi that we—that you and I arrested when your little Anna was kidnapped, back in the Years of Lead."

"That's your coincidence? All that was a long time ago, commissario—nearly twenty years."

Trotti's face broke into another smile, "You were in love with Anna even then."

"Anna was six years old."

"Surprised you've managed to stay out of prison."

The waiter brought the drinks. He placed the tray on the table, winked at Pisanelli and pirouetted before gliding off to a different table.

Trotti emptied three envelopes of sugar into his drink. He resumed as he stirred, "Gracchi spent a year in prison. At San Vittore in Milan. Accused of involvement in the killing of Commissario Pugliese but he was released for lack of evidence. Went to India and then to Sicily."

"To set up a center for addicts in Trapani."

"You knew?"

"I read the papers." Pisanelli fiddled edgily with the pages of the medical supplement, "When you let me."

"Gracchi was probably murdered by Beltoni." Trotti set the spoon down and took a tentative sip at the frothy coffee, "Beltoni didn't have an alibi for Gracchi's murder. This was in 1988 and the Procura della Repubblica in Trapani was bent on making a quick arrest. Wanted to show they were combating the Mafia." Trotti winced. Cocoa powder speckled his upper lip. "Beltoni ran away. He escaped from Trapani and went into hiding in America."

"So?"

"He was in the United States when they murdered his twin brother—our friend, the dealer. Trussed the poor bastard up like a goat and burned him."

"So?" Pisanelli repeated.

"They murdered Beltoni's brother in our quiet, provincial city while he was helping me with an enquiry."

"The brother's out to get you? That's the problem?"

Trotti touched Pisanelli's arm, lowering it and the newspaper, "A couple of months ago in Trapani, the judges interviewed Gracchi's widow. They now want to talk with Giovanni Verga—Socialist and close friend of Bettino Craxi."

"So?" Pisanelli repeated.

"Verga's in Nicaragua. He's believed to have become Chiara Gracchi's lover sometime before Gracchi's death."

"*Cherchez la femme*, as you always used to say."

"The Mafia connection may just be a diversion. If Chiara Gracchi's being questioned by the pubblico ministero and if she's shown to have been involved in her husband's death, it'll mean the Mafia theory was a red herring all along. A red herring to get the wife and her lover off the hook."

"To let them get away with murdering the husband?"

"A crime of passion, Pisa, and not a Mafia killing as everybody believed."

"Which'd mean Beltoni's innocent?"

"Innocent and free to come and go. Free to return to Italy."

"Free to avenge his brother's death and kill Commissario Trotti?" Pisanelli put his head back and laughed with genuine amusement. "Piero Trotti's scared of a Sicilian hitman on the loose?"

Trotti finished the coffee in a greedy gulp and scraped at the undissolved sugar at the bottom of the cup, "I don't like coincidences."

Pisanelli was still laughing, "What coincidences?"

The gypsy children had ceased their soccer game. The piazza had become quiet. Even the conversations at the adjacent tables had slackened. The svelte waiter, for a moment relaxing, was watching Pisanelli from the entrance to the café.

Trotti lowered his voice. "The girl you couldn't take your eyes off last night."

"What about her?"

"Wilma grew up an orphan in America."

"So what?"

"She's Gracchi's illegitimate daughter."

32: Nunc Dimittis

"A sweet girl."

Pisanelli laughed cynically. "Sweet like your Uruguayan lady?"

"It was me who went up to her outside the station, Pisanelli. It was me who got involved. I saw Wilma standing alone in the cold, her young face pinched by the wind, and I felt sorry for her. She was shivering and I bought her a hot drink."

"You spend too much time trying to save prostitutes from themselves."

"She's not a prostitute."

Pisanelli shook his head. "Of course not."

"A young American in search of her father. She's been in Italy for six months—working as a babysitter for a family in Milan."

"And you believe her?"

"Why should Wilma be lying?"

"Why should Wilma be telling the truth?"

"She thinks I can help her."

"Impressed by the Carabiniere coat, no doubt."

Trotti grinned with boyish pride. "She said it suited me."

"There's no reason for you to help her, commissario—other than she's got a pretty face."

"I trust her, Pisanelli."

"You trusted the Uruguayan whore—and that never stopped her from running off with the Trotti family silver."

Trotti said tamely, "I know I can trust her."

"Can you afford to?"

Trotti had picked up the mobile telephone and was playing with it absentmindedly.

Pisanelli sighed. "That thing costs a lot of money, commissario. Don't want you calling Uruguay."

"I never gave Gracchi a second thought in twenty years, Pisa. Then within a couple of hours, a general of the Carabinieri and a young American woman are both talking to me about Gracchi. Both asking me to make enquiries about him."

"Choose the company you keep more carefully."

"More than a coincidence."

"You're being used, commissario. It wouldn't be the first time."

"Used by who?"

"You'll soon find out."

Trotti pointed the telephone's aerial at his friend's chest. "You remember Guerra?"

"Gracchi's old girlfriend?"

"You remember her, Pisa?"

"Last time I saw Lia Guerra, she was scuttling down into the subway in Milan. Back in 1982. Wearing a blonde wig and on her way to a clinic in Switzerland. Trying to avoid you, commissario."

"Really?"

"Trying to avoid you—like so many other people."

"She stayed in Switzerland for several years." Trotti said, "Then Lia Guerra went down to Trapani in the mid-eighties. She wanted to be with Gracchi—unfortunately the ex-boyfriend had married another woman."

"Which wouldn't've stopped Gracchi from screwing her."

"Delicately put."

"Gracchi'd screw anything that moved—and a few things that didn't."

"Gracchi found Guerra a job at the commune, and she worked with him at BRAMAN."

"She hoped Gracchi'd leave his wife and go back to her?"

"Spadano says Gracchi'd never've left his daughter."

"So he got murdered," Pisanelli said.

"Gracchi got himself murdered, Pisanelli, and everybody thought it was the Mafia silencing a noisy journalist." Trotti pushed the empty cup away. "Lia Guerra'd been an addict herself and she felt empathy for the people on the commune. Several months before the murder, Giovanni Verga sent her here to Rome to run the public relations for the commune."

Pisanelli took the *Repubblica* and folded the paper on his unbending knee.

"It's Guerra who's been pressuring the pubblico ministero to reopen the file."

Pisanelli tilted his head in mild interest. "Why bother?"

"Guerra loved Gracchi."

"Gracchi's dead."

"She'd always loved him—ever since the years of lead when Guerra and Gracchi were playing terrorists."

"She's got any children?"

Trotti shook his head.

"A silly cow," Pisanelli observed. "She spouted left-wing politics, the revolution and all that crap. Beneath the facade, she was a woman like all the rest."

"All the rest, Pisa?"

"Guerra was a good-looking girl. I could've fancied her myself. She should've had children."

"It's not too late."

"I've never known a woman to put the dictatorship of the proletariat before a home of her own, a family and a white Fiat."

"You were good to her, I recall. Silly cow, Pisa? You stopped me from arresting her."

"You manipulated her."

"Hardly."

"Her politics gave you no right to treat her the way you did, Trotti. You despised her."

"Not at all."

"Despised her because she was taking heroin," Pisanelli said.

"I had a job to do."

"She was protecting Maltese."

Trotti grunted, "And now, eight years after his death, she's protecting Gracchi."

"Silly cow."

"Guerra's never believed the Mafia killed Gracchi, but with Beltoni absconding, the case was very conveniently closed. The Procura had wound Gracchi's murder up to its own satisfaction and life could go on in BRAMAN. And in Trapani. A Mafia killing with Beltoni as the executor—it suited everybody."

Trotti's fingers toyed nervously with the telephone, and his glance went from the piazza to Pisanelli and back again. "Except Lia Guerra."

"What does it all matter, commissario? Gracchi's dead—been dead for years. Nobody's going to bring him back. It's not your problem."

"Spadano's thinks I should find out who killed Gracchi."

"You're joking."

"You know I have no sense of humor."

"You owe Spadano a favor?"

"Spadano was good to me over my wife."

"Twenty years ago."

"Southerners never forget."

Pisanelli imitated Trotti's flat Lombard accent. "*Piero Trotti's a functionary of the republic. He neither gives favors, nor does he ask for them.*"

"You have a good memory, Pisanelli."

"From hearing the same things repeated over and again?" Pisanelli's amusement vanished. "You really want to help Spadano?"

"Spadano wants me to help myself."

"Could you care less?"

A shrug. "My life's in danger."

"Scared of being shot down by a Sicilian killer?"

"I've never been afraid of death."

"You really are scared, aren't you?"

"Wife, daughter, a family of my own." Trotti pressed the telephone aerial against his chin. "I always told myself I could depart in peace when the grandchildren came along."

"Piero Trotti's *Nunc dimittis?*"

Trotti shrugged. "The grandchildren."

Pisanelli asked, "What about the grandchildren, commissario?"

"I left Spadano in his magnificent office and went into the center of Siena, looking for the American girl. Believe it or not, Pisa, I was frightened. Despite the cold, I was sweating. The big, empty piazza—I felt naked and vulnerable. More scared than I've ever been in my life."

"Getting old and senile?"

"More scared than when the American bombers flew over Santa Maria all those years ago."

Pisanelli had set the paper down. He was smiling and his eyes were fixed on the older man's face.

"My grandchildren—I want to see them grow up. I want to see the girls become young women. I want to be there, I want to enjoy their childhood because I never had a childhood of my own. And I never enjoyed Pioppi's early years—too busy being a policeman. I wasn't a good father. Who knows, perhaps that's why she stopped eating."

"You're turning into a human being?"

"Be there for my Francesca and my Piera. For this adventure they call life. I want to be there—just as I want to be there for your children, damn it, Pisa. For the babies of this marriage of yours to Anna."

33: Ciuffi

AT THE OTHER tables on the terrace, the customers chatted or read the morning paper in the warmth of the spring sunshine.

The waiter had disappeared.

"Guerra hated you, commissario, and with good reason. Why help her now? Why help Spadano?"

A young man in sunglasses dismounted from a battered Vespa. He was wearing a dark lumpy suit and a red tie.

"Go back to your foggy little city, commissario. Forget Guerra. Go back to your Dutch cousin and her Count Cavour glasses. Forget Trapani."

"It's not too late to help."

"Feeling guilty, Commissario Trotti?"

"Don't think I know that word."

"After all these years of throwing your weight around, you're having remorse?"

Trotti fidgeted with the mobile telephone.

"Finding the truth isn't going to stop Beltoni putting a bullet through your head."

"Or leaving me tied up in the trunk of a car—just like his twin brother."

"Let the Procura in Trapani get on with it. It's their job. They've got the logistics—and the armor-plated cars."

The gypsy children stood around aimlessly. One tapped

the deflated football with his hand. Several older boys had sat down on the steps of the fountain and were in conversation. They appeared to be trading, placing pieces of paper on the steps.

The man with the Vespa approached them, smiling cheerfully. He had a small head and the long hair was combed backwards to where it touched his collar.

"You'll go to Sicily?"

"I'm going home after your wedding."

"You'll be safer there."

Trotti gestured to the piazza as if it were a foreign country. "Going back to where I belong."

"Not going to bother with Spadano or Lia Guerra, then?" Pisanelli sounded relieved.

"There's also Wilma wanting my help."

"A lot of people all clamoring for favors from a retired flatfoot with a conscience. How very popular you are, commissario. Your Wilma doesn't know Gracchi's been dead for nearly a decade?"

"Clearly not."

"She's leading you on."

Trotti tapped his friend's wrist with the mobile phone. "Why lead me on?"

"She's a woman and she's pretty. Because you're a gullible male. And because you're a retired policeman."

"Can't she get someone young and dynamic to do the job? Why ask an old man?"

Pisanelli shrugged unhappily. "Goodness knows."

"You're supposed to be good on female psychology, Pisanelli."

"Flattery will get you everywhere."

"Remember that nurse at San Matteo who admired you so much, Pisa? She was convinced you understood women."

Pisanelli's smile vanished as he shook his head, "On the contrary, commissario, your friend Ciuffi maintained I was a phallocrat."

"The nurse in obstetrics. You've forgotten her?"

"A phallocrat, Trotti."

"No need to mention Ciuffi."

"A balding phallocrat—but then, Ciuffi only had eyes for you."

"I'd rather you didn't mention Brigadiere Ciuffi."

"Poor thing loved you blindly and wanted to marry you. The wise old man of the Questura and the pretty young police-woman." A laugh. "May-September."

"I don't know what you're talking about."

"You'd've never married Ciuffi."

Trotti whispered hoarsely, "Why bring all this up, Pisanelli?"

"You'd never've gotten a divorce."

"Ciuffi and I were colleagues." The knuckles around the blue telephone had turned grey.

"Ciuffi worshipped the ground you walked on. Like a duti-ful little puppy, she did everything you asked her to."

"Be silent, will you?"

"Most probably she'd've ended up marrying some boring, rich lawyer husband in that godawful, damp city of yours. Instead, the stupid girl got herself killed."

Trotti had turned away; he was looking at the man in the sunglasses. The man stood in conversation with the older boys. His trousers were short, not quite touching the top of the scuffed shoes. The shoulders of the jacket were padded.

Behind the sunglasses, the face seemed familiar.

"A silly young woman in love with an irascible old police-man."

Trotti was silent.

"Not as if Ciuffi was the first police officer to be killed in the line of duty."

Trotti swung round and banged the table with the flat of his hand. "Shut up, damn you! Shut up, Pisanelli!"

The cups rattled.

Heads were raised. People at the neighboring tables turned in their seats, lowered their newspapers.

A hush came over the terrace. The church bells chimed ten o'clock.

The man had pushed the sunglasses up to his forehead and was staring at Trotti and Pisanelli. The broad smile showed white teeth.

"No longer the dark-haired Latin lover of Lombardy, you know," Pisanelli went on amiably, "I'd hate to think you were falling in love again, Trotti. Not at your age. Not with another wretched black woman."

34: Aluminum

THE TWO MEN took a taxi and went over the slow green waters of the Tiber.

"Nice of you to help me," Trotti said evenly.

Pisanelli sat in the front of the taxi, his leg stretched before him.

"You don't have to, of course. I'm surprised your in-laws don't need you."

"Someone's got to keep an eye on you now that there's a price on your head," Pisanelli answered glumly.

"Don't worry about me, Pisa. Just keeping myself amused in this city."

"Visit the sites. Go to the Colosseum, go to the Spanish Steps. Visit the museums. Find yourself a whore, if you must. Try out one of the transvestites."

Trotti waited before asking in a casual voice, "You noticed he was carrying a gun?"

"Either a gun or a pump for his Vespa." Pisanelli turned his head awkwardly. "You really are scared, aren't you, commissario?"

The taxi-driver lifted his head quizzically and his eyes met Trotti's in the mirror.

Trotti averted his glance. He looked out of the window at the city. "The same man as in Siena. The man who knocked me over in via di Città—I was coming out of the bar."

"You said you didn't see his face."

"I was on the ground, but I saw him from behind. The same man."

"Not very likely if he's friends with the gypsy children."

The yellow taxi moved into the narrow streets near the Colosseum.

At the entrance to the via del Tempio, there was a roadblock.

Two vans; several alert and wary Carabinieri stood around wearing bulletproof jackets. They toted semi-automatic guns.

The taxi turned onto the street and stopped with a squeal of brakes.

A couple of officers scrutinized Trotti and Pisanelli as the two men clambered from the taxi.

A sergeant in a beret moved sideways, crablike, towards the taxi, a hand on the butt of his weapon. With the other hand, he gestured for Trotti to halt.

The driver did not wait for payment; the yellow car slid rapidly backwards. The exhaust pipe reverberated angrily as the taxi vanished into the morning traffic by the Tiber.

"Visiting Signorina Guerra," Trotti announced.

As Trotti's hand went towards his pocket, the Carabiniere jerked the gun up menacingly.

The sergeant's face was immobile. The right eye stared at Trotti; the left eye squinted, as if taking aim. For a long moment no one moved; then the glance turned unhurriedly towards Pisanelli. To the aluminum crutch.

Neither Trotti nor Pisanelli spoke.

Just the slightest movement of the muzzle.

"Forward!"

The sergeant nodded imperceptibly, lowering his weapon as he gestured the two men onward into the via del Tempio.

Trotti mumbled thanks, his lips dry, his hands trembling.

Pisanelli limped along beside him, the crutch clicking on the pavement.

Tension evaporated into the brightness of the morning as the sergeant shouted in thick Roman dialect and laughed, "Arab terrorist with a bloody walking stick."

There was the glint of teeth beneath the short, military mustache. "Saddam's scraping the barrel."

"No terrorists today, I'm afraid," Pisanelli said, turning back and grinning sheepishly. "Two retired cops."

"God help us." With his free hand, the sergeant made the sign of the cross.

"Friends of yours?" Trotti asked in a whisper.

Pisanelli did not reply, but there was sweat along the premature creases of his forehead.

35: Stairs

THE FRONT DOOR to number twenty-six was open.

Trotti ran a finger down the names of the residents, stuck behind a plate of brass and battered, yellowing Perspex.

SIG.NA GUERRA lived on the top floor.

"Fourteen years since I last saw her."

They entered the hall. The air was chill; spring had yet to reach the interior of the building. A grimy floor of checkered tiles.

There was an elevator cage, but no response to Pisanelli's repeated pushing at the worn button. After a silent wait, the two men began to climb the stairs that rose beside the elevator shaft.

It grew darker inside the building as they trudged their way upwards. The crutch clicked against the steps, accompanying Pisanelli's laborious journey to the top of the stairs.

Trotti was out of breath by the time he reached the top floor. Sweating, he rang the doorbell.

Trotti watched Pisanelli clambering the last set of stairs, and behind Trotti there was the sound of various locks being pulled back, keys being turned, bolts being drawn. Then the ponderous oak door of the sixth floor swung inward.

"I was expecting you," a woman said. Her face was lost in the penumbra.

36: Nucleo Politico

She had changed.

In the photograph taken by the *Nucleo Politico*, Lia Guerra had been wearing a handkerchief round her neck, and the young face had an intense, proud beauty as she pulled back her arm in the act of hurling a missile. Now she was older, twenty years older, the face worn and slightly waxen.

A faded prettiness remained.

"I need to know the truth, commissario. I need to know who killed him—it's the only thing that matters." She spoke in a low voice while her eyes held his. Lia Guerra had poured herself a glass of mineral water. Moisture ran down the sides of the thick glass and onto her fingers.

Trotti said flatly, "Life goes on."

"Not necessarily. What d'you know about Lotta Continua?"

"Very little, I hope."

"Tino Gracchi was a founding member of the movement."

Trotti shook his head. "That wasn't why I disliked him."

"Why did you dislike Tino?"

"Tino?"

The lips broke in a smile that immediately vanished. "What'd you hold against him?"

"Gracchi kidnapped my goddaughter. With your help."

"Not true, commissario."

"In the event, my accusations were proved wrong—but Gracchi was deliberately unhelpful."

"Tino saw himself as the protector of all women and children."

(*"But you blow people up? You admit to that, Gracchi?"*
"If it's necessary."
Gracchi sat with his hairy arms resting on his thighs; the blue jeans were scuffed and patched with white dust. Large plasters on his forehead and temples.
"And it is necessary?"
"A bomb can be a clinical instrument. With fools, commissario, there can be no dialogue.")

"You asked me why I disliked him. I can only tell you how I felt. Gracchi believed a bomb was a clinical instrument."

"He was trying to provoke you, commissario."

"He succeeded."

"He saw you as part of the establishment. But that was in 1978, and already he was changing. We were all changing." She caught her breath. "You know Trapani?"

"I've never been south of Naples."

"And Giovanni Verga?"

"What about him?"

"You've met him?" she asked sharply.

Trotti shook his head. "I know Giovanni Verga set up BRAMAN with Gracchi. I know Verga later got very rich—at about the time he became intimate with Craxi. And at the time the Socialists were in power."

Lia Guerra nodded in sardonic amusement. "Bettino Craxi, our ex-prime minister, who is now hiding in Tunisia."

"Spadano tells me Verga's living in Managua."

Lia Guerra said, "Neither Nicaragua nor Tunisia has an extradition treaty with Italy. A great pity, because both Craxi and Verga know who killed Gracchi."

"You should've asked them."

"I asked Verga."

Trotti's face broke into a smile.

"I spoke to Verga," Lia Guerra said. "I spoke to him often—when he was still the uncontested master at BRAMAN. When I went back to visit the place."

"What did he say?"

"He lied."

"You knew he was lying?"

"I still believed he was Tino's friend." The dark eyes inspected Trotti's face. "When did you first hear about Gracchi's death?"

"It was in the paper."

"What did you think?"

"Nothing."

"Tino's death wasn't important?"

Trotti shrugged. "I didn't make the association between Gracchi's killing and the terrorist I'd arrested all those years ago."

"Tino was no terrorist."

Trotti shrugged.

"You didn't realize it was him?"

"An uneducated flatfoot." He shrugged again. "For many years, I never read a newspaper other than the local *Provincia Padana* when I found it lying around the Questura or on the table in a bar."

"Tino said you were shrewd."

"Gracchi believed a lot of strange things."

"He had his reasons."

"Obscure reasons that are beyond me."

"You didn't care about Tino's death, Commissario Trotti?"

"If I'd cared about every politician or journalist who's murdered in this country, I'd never have had the time to do my job." Trotti set the empty glass on the floor and sat back, his arms folded on his lap. "My job rarely required me to read the papers."

Lia Guerra relaxed, as if Trotti's answers were the right ones to some private examination.

"I loved Tino, Trotti. You realized that when you met me. I tried to forget him. For five years I tried to forget Tino and lived with Maltese. Who was also murdered." Still smiling, she said, "Forgive my stupid obsession. I bring bad luck to the men I love. Forgive me for taking up your precious time.

I know you can't understand why I wanted to see you. You have reason for not liking me, commissario—just as I have many reasons for hating you. But all that was a long time ago, so much water under the bridge. I'd like you to know I'm very glad you came—very grateful to you both."

37: Open City

THEY WERE SITTING on the roof beneath a striped awning propped up by poles. Several wicker chairs and a low table. Beside the table was a wheeled refrigerator, and on a chaise longue, the morning's newspaper lay facedown. Also a dog-eared copy of *Prince* magazine.

The red tiles of the terrace absorbed the warmth of the gentle sun. Potted plants—cacti and bougainvillea and dates—stood along the low wall and incongruously, there was a line of towels and white sheets drying in the breeze.

A black cat slept in the shade beneath the woman's feet.

"Everyone calls me Lia but my real name's Angela. The name of an American actress, I believe, with beautiful legs who'd get undressed in the strangest situations." Lia Guerra laughed, more to herself than to the two men. "I'm not going to undress or anything. At least, I hope not," she said. "Past that sort of thing, I'm afraid."

Lia Guerra wore black tights and a white shirt with long sleeves. She had a small, wiry body, a narrow waist and the hips of an adolescent. There was no spare fat to the line of the thighs.

(*He caught hold of her wrist and with his other hand, Trotti rolled back the sleeve of her checked shirt.*

"*An expensive habit.*"

The arm was scarred and hard where needles had pierced the skin.

Lia Guerra pulled her arm free, fell backwards and crumpled on to the floor. "You bastard," she muttered and she scratched at her arm.)

Perhaps sensing Trotti's thoughts, Lia Guerra put down her glass, got up and went towards the balustrade. She placed her weight on her toes and Trotti wondered if she had been—or indeed still was—a dancer.

She was smiling. She beckoned and the two men obediently rose and joined her.

The view of Rome from the rooftop was breathtaking.

The glint of the waters of the Tiber, the grey of St. Peter's, the round walls of the Castel Sant'Angelo and to their right, the dazzling, white brashness of the Vittoriano.

"One of the better things to living in this provincial place."

Pisanelli said, "Birthplace of Christianity? Seat of the Catholic, Apostolic Church?"

"Rome's never really gotten over its past."

"I wouldn't call the capital of the Republic provincial."

"The artificial capital of an artificial country," she remarked dismissively. Lia Guerra spoke with a Turin accent. She deliberately softened the fricatives, as if to prove that she was an outsider in this city.

Peering over the wall, Trotti glanced down at the street below. The machine guns of the Carabinieri appeared no more sinister than the glinting cars or the occasional passerby in via del Tempio.

"In 1555, Pope Paul the Fourth built a wall around the ghetto and the gates were locked every night for 315 years—until Victor Emmanuel decided to tear the walls down. Then when the Germans took control of Rome in 1943, a Jew called Foà collected fifty kilos of gold and took it as a gift to the German Embassy. The Germans promised him no Jew would be deported from Rome. A few days later, a convoy of a thousand Jews was sent to Auschwitz." A shrug of her shoulders. "Just fifteen survived." As if bored by the subject, Lia Guerra asked, as she moved back into the shade, "Would you care for another drink, commissario?"

On the other side of the road, set back in the synagogue garden, Trotti caught sight of a bearded man with a broad-brimmed hat and a dark coat. He had the bowed, thoughtful look of a priest reading his breviary.

Trotti turned back and joined Lia Guerra and Pisanelli in the shade of the awning.

Pisanelli was grinning like an adolescent.

38: Apology

IT WAS EIGHTEEN years since Trotti had last seen her lover, yet he could recall the hot, fruitless interrogation of Gracchi over Anna Ermagni's disappearance, he could recall the smell of fear and sweat and frustration at a time when the very structure of the Italian republic seemed threatened by mindless terrorism.

"The artificial capital of an artificial country." The words could have been Gracchi's. The same voice, the same arrogant tone.

Lia Guerra smiled. "The general said you'd help."

Lia Guerra's slippers lay on the tiles before her. She had raised her feet onto the chaise longue and set them beneath her thighs.

The cat stirred in its sleep.

"Tino's been dead for eight years. With all this talk of the pubblico ministero reopening the case, I remain cynical—even if they do arrest Chiara Gracchi."

"Nothing's going to bring Gracchi back."

"You don't believe in justice, commissario?"

"I don't believe in wasting time."

"Tino was murdered—and I want to see justice done. I want to know the truth. I no longer have faith in the police or the Carabinieri or the investigating judges. Perhaps not even in Spadano. They have their private agenda—and the truth has little place there." Lia Guerra looked at Trotti. "Spadano maintains you're a man of integrity."

"Spadano doesn't know me."

"Don't jerk me about, commissario." She moved her legs and sitting up, set her feet onto the floor. "I've been jerked around for too long. Jerked around by too many people, too many false promises. I need to know the truth."

"From a retired, ignorant policeman? A retired, ignorant, Northern policeman who threw Gracchi into jail all those years ago? I just happen to be in Rome for a few days. Visiting my good friend Pierangelo Pisanelli." He gestured towards Pisanelli.

The woman's glance went to the aluminum crutch, then to Pisanellis.

"A one-time colleague," Pisanelli apologized, grinning from ear to ear. "Now retired from the police. Thank goodness."

Lia Guerra asked him, "You knew Tino, Pierangelo?"

"A long time ago, in 1978. I met him—and I met you."

She frowned, "In those days you had more hair? You wore aviator sunglasses?"

Trotti interrupted, "Pisanelli and I met Gracchi just once. Not a nice experience for us and probably not for Gracchi, either."

"If you don't want to help, Trotti, I don't see why you came here," Lia Guerra remarked, turning back to face the older man.

"Gracchi's presumed killer now wants to kill me."

"He must have his reasons."

"A man called Beltoni."

"I know all about Enzo Beltoni, Commissario Trotti."

"His brother was tortured, strangled and then his body burned and left for the dogs. Beltoni holds me responsible for a Mafia killing."

"It's to protect yourself you've come to talk to me?"

Trotti looked into Lia Guerra's dark eyes. "Spadano asked me to speak with you. He says I owe you a favor."

She frowned, "Why should you owe me any favors?"

"When you and I met several years after the kidnapping and you were working in Milan at the Porta Ticinese and . . ." Trotti allowed his voice to trail away.

"Yes?"

Trotti was silent.

"Is this your way of apologizing, Commissario Trotti?"

"Spadano asked me to see you."

"You owe me nothing." In the shade of the overhead canopy, the dark eyes appeared to glow. "Someone killed Tino, commissario. Find out who killed him and why. You don't owe that to me. You owe it to Valerio Gracchi."

39: George

"YOU SAID YOU spoke to Giovanni Verga."

Lia Guerra nodded. "Several times. Later I learned to hate the bastard. Just as I learned to hate Chiara." She tried to light a cigarette with a kitchen match, but her hand trembled. Pisanelli produced a lighter from his pocket.

"You believe Giovanni Verga and Chiara Gracchi murdered Gracchi?"

"For years I thought Enzo Beltoni and the Trapanese Mafia'd killed him." The woman inhaled a mouthful of smoke. "So did everybody else. As a young man, Tino'd wanted to save the world. Later he wanted to save Sicily. I had this idea of the gallant Northern knight going to the rescue of the Sicilian masses, downtrodden by the dragon of organized crime. A television camera and a microphone instead of a shield and a lance, but the motive and the nobility of the gesture were the same." The hand that held the cigarette lay on her thigh. "With time, I learned to be less naïve. Not every violent death in Sicily is a Mafia killing."

"So who killed Gracchi?"

"I'd been seeing these people as his friends. Later I realized Tino'd always been alone. Alone because of his ideals. Alone because he stuck to those ideals and, in sticking to them, he made things very awkward for other people."

"For Giovanni Verga?"

"For the kind of people whose motivation was different."
Lia Guerra caught her breath. "I went down to Sicily for the
first time in 1984. It was a joy to be with Tino again, and I was
pleased to see he was happily married. You know, he was not
a serene person—Tino was always running after something,
and his new family'd given him a certain peace of mind."

"Turning up the way you did—that didn't create more
problems for him?"

Lia Guerra shrugged. "He was good to me. Tino got me
a job, and I enjoyed working at BRAMAN. I stayed for over
three years, helping the *guests*—addicts, but also people with
drinking problems." She paused as her glance went from one
man to the other. "I'd had my own encounter with addiction.
What BRAMAN was doing was useful—it was practical. Yet
I could see Tino was bored with the place—this was before
he got the job on television. I created problems for him? Tino
was glad to have me around—somebody who shared so many
of his ideals. He was speaking less and less to Giovanni Verga.
Verga wasn't happy about all the dope Tino was smoking."
Lia Guerra added, "She couldn't stand me."

"She?"

"Chiara Gracchi was pathologically jealous. Not what you'd
call an intellectual, not by any stretch of the imagination. I don't
say she reads *Duemila* or *Vissuto*; she's never had two ideas to
rub together. Not a particularly good mother, either. Lakshmi
spent more time with her father and Giovanni Verga than with
Chiara Gracchi. The woman was like an animal in the way she
wanted to hoard what belonged to her. Absolutely convinced her
husband and I were lovers, and she couldn't believe what existed
between Tino and me wasn't sex. Something stronger, something
better, something quite beautiful. The woman was consumed by
a diseased jealousy. You could see it eating away at her. Chiara's
never understood there's more to a woman than what's between
her thighs."

Trotti frowned. "Chiara Gracchi had lovers?"

"There were a lot of very virile young men at BRAMAN—
and Chiara was boss."

"That's why you disliked her?"

"She pretended to be my friend. Behind my back, she persuaded Giovanni Verga to send me off to Rome."

"Why'd you leave?"

"I felt useful in Trapani—happier and more useful than I'd ever been before. It was good to be near Tino again, but Verga needed someone here in Rome to run the public relations. Someone to deal with the politicians. I gave in." The same hand that held the cigarette brushed back hair from her forehead.

"You weren't in Sicily when Gracchi was killed?"

"I came to Rome just as Tino was starting on television—in July 1987. He had another fourteen months to live."

"You've been back?"

"For the funeral. Several times afterwards. In 1992, I finally spent two months in Trapani. I'd always refused to admit Tino was dead. For years, I'd talk to him as if he were in the kitchen or sitting in the car beside me. We would chat. When at last I brought myself to admit he was dead, I had to know why. I needed to make my own enquiries. The police were getting nowhere, and I no longer believed Beltoni'd acted alone—there were too many contradictions. Since his death, BRAMAN had become a vast international enterprise. So I asked Tino's friends from Lotta Continua to help me. Friends from Trento and Milan. They'd been down to the funeral with me in '88, they'd thrown their flowers on his coffin. They made me their fine promises, but in the end they all had something else, something more pressing to do elsewhere. So I flew down to Trapani alone and started interviewing everybody at BRAMAN."

"What'd you discover?"

"People Gracchi'd loved—people who should've been only too willing to push the police and the magistrates out of their lethargy—these people refused to talk."

"They had something to hide?"

"They talked in riddles."

40: Prime-time

"HIS DEATH BECAME a knot in my belly, getting tighter and tighter. Gradually killing me."

"Let's not exaggerate."

"Pure, deep friendship. Mine was the kind of friendship no other woman could give him. Not his first wife—poor little thing—nor the loathsome Chiara."

There was silence while Lia Guerra looked thoughtfully at him, and Trotti could almost see the face of her dead lover in the eyes and the prominent cheekbones.

"You should have married Gracchi."

"Marriage is a bourgeois convention. I had other preoccupations at the time."

"You didn't want a home and children of your own, signora?"

"The best friend I've ever had. The best and the truest. Tino and I shared everything—including our reticences and our silences. We understood each other, and there was little need for words. Like brother and sister."

"And sex?"

A scornful smile. "We already had everything."

"Gracchi didn't want children?"

"Tino had enough children. Lots of them—and they were just the ones he knew about." Lia Guerra laughed, "At Padua, at the university, Toni Negri was plotting the downfall of the

Italian Republic, but it was my Tino all the girls were bedding."

"Padua—on the American bases?"

"In the mid-seventies. Lotta Continua sent him there, but he never finished the sociology course he was supposed to give. The parents complained—a couple of girls pregnant by Christmas. The rector told him to take the pay and forget about lectures."

"You knew his first wife, signora?"

Lia Guerra leaned back in the chaise longue. "Bettina still writes occasionally. A nice woman—terribly working-class, of course, ignorant and impressed by money. The great, great mistake of Tino's youth, but Bettina worshipped the ground he walked on. Now a grandmother, the woman still talks about Tino as if he's just popped out for a packet of cigarettes. After all these years, after all Tino's women, she still thinks he's coming back."

"Coming back from the grave?"

"Bettina's son worked at BRAMAN for a summer—but he wasn't happy there. He didn't like Sicily and he didn't get on with his father—they were too alike. Jimmy's now married and works for the Banca del Lavoro. I saw them all—grandmother and grandchild—only six months ago when I was in Turin." There was a softness in her voice. "The baby has Tino's looks."

"Why stay in Rome?" It was Pisanelli who spoke. "Signora, wouldn't you be happier in your native Piemonte? Happier in Turin."

"I have to work for a living." She gave Pisanelli a friendly glance. "Until BRAMAN was liquidated in 1994, I had a well-paying job. A job I considered important." She smiled, more to herself than to the two men. "I didn't want to lose the contact with Tino."

"Contact? Gracchi had married. He had a family of his own."

Lia Guerra said dreamily, "Being with Tino was like being with Father Christmas."

"You still believe in Father Christmas?"

She retorted, "I needed to believe in something, commissario." The face had lost its dreaminess. "When I was kid, I used to screw up my eyes and pray that my real mother would come and find me. I never wanted to believe the woman who shared my father's bed was my real mother. I prayed, hoping Jesus would hear me. I believed in Jesus then—but there is no Jesus. And there's no revolution. The revolution, Lotta Continua—they fooled me with their proletariat just as the priests had fooled me with Jesus. The working class didn't need me or Tino—they never had." She added thoughtfully, "It was me who needed Tino. He was my sole reason for living."

Trotti nodded.

"Tino made me feel important—and happy. You see, I was the only woman he ever loved, and we made each other complete—just by being together. In your wretched little town—all those years ago now. We were young and very happy."

"You should've married him."

"Tino wanted to marry me, but in those days I felt my first duty was to the Revolution."

"You'd have saved his father a lot of embarrassment."

"Tino had to be true to himself." She added, "Anyway, Tino wasn't the most important thing in his father's life."

"Didn't stop Gracchi's threatening me with his father's political clout."

"Bravado." Lia Guerra smiled. "He knew you wouldn't touch him—Tino hadn't kidnapped anybody."

"You and Gracchi may've known that—I didn't."

"You met Tino in 1978. Aldo Moro'd been kidnapped and the country was in a state of shock. His father felt Tino'd chosen a foolish time to get arrested."

"All times are foolish for getting arrested."

"Tino'd done nothing wrong. As I remember, Signor Gracchi had a lot of respect for Commissario Trotti."

"His son didn't. I was a Fascist—that's what he called me."

Lia Guerra laughed, her chin tilting upward. The neck was pale, thin and strong. "Tino loved play-acting. More than a journalist or politician or intellectual, Tino should've been an actor. Always playing out some new role. One day he was the cop, the next the robber."

"That's how he ended up playing a corpse?"

Even the sounds from the street below seemed muffled.

"You couldn't understand him, commissario."

"Supposing I wanted to."

"Tino got into television journalism because he loved playing to the gallery. The center of attraction with the cameras pointing at him and, throughout the province of Trapani, tens of thousands of people drinking in his words—that's what Tino loved. *Prime-time*."

Trotti frowned.

"His news bulletin went out three times a day. But it was just after eight that people would leave the other channels, Berlusconi and the RAI, just to see Gracchi berating the local politicians in the evening news. Laughing at the politicians. Baiting the Mafia."

"The Mafia that didn't kill him?"

"Tino was the victim of his own acting. In Trento and in Padua, in your horrid little city and then in Sicily." Guerra tucked her legs beneath her. The cat watched her with sleepy eyes.

"His death didn't come as a surprise to you?"

"As soon as he got in front of the television cameras for the first time—Tino was like a moth trapped in the light. An outsider who thought he could change Sicily? Of course they were going to kill him. Everyone could see it coming—everyone except Tino."

"You warned him?"

"Everyone warned him. In Sicily, there are your friends. And then there are the friends of your friends. The television station warned him. People in the street warned him." Lia Guerra shook her head. "I don't pretend to know who pulled the trigger. I just know that I've been terribly miserable without him. Miserable knowing the telephone will never ring again for me to hear his voice." She took a deep breath.

"A couple of times I took the plane and flew to Trapani for a long weekend. I thought being with people who'd known Tino would make the pain seem more bearable."

Lia Guerra took another cigarette from the packet on the chaise longue.

"The bastards all wanted Tino out of the way. All of them."

41: Parquetry

"I STAYED IN Tino's room in Trapani. A tiny, cramped place a long way from the Dovecot."

"Where?"

"The Dovecot was the management building at BRAMAN. The last three months he slept by himself in the room—I never realized it was his punishment." Lia Guerra paused. "Sleeping in his bed brought me closer to him. It was as if we were together again."

"A bit obsessed, weren't you?"

"Very obsessed," Lia Guerra retorted. "Obsessed and miserable and terribly lonely." She looked at the two men defiantly. "They say time can heal everything. How long do I have to wait?"

"Some pain you take with you to the grave."

Lia Guerra gave the old policeman an appraising smile. "You know about that, commissario?"

Trotti did not reply.

"The only two men I've ever loved—both of them murdered. And I'm still alive—an ex-heroin addict and I'm still alive." Her smile slowly died, but her eyes remained on Trotti's. "I'd sit in the little bedroom at BRAMAN and I could see Tino. I really could see him, you know. Just as I can see you two now. Driving his Duna back to BRAMAN or walking towards me, just as he used to when we were so happy together, commissario."

"Happy together? Gracchi was married—with wife and daughter."

"I gave him something he never found with them."

Trotti asked, "You got on well with Lakshmi?"

"Tino's daughter's never liked me. Her mother gave her everything—and just like her mother, Lakshmi's always seen me as a rival for her father's affection, even after his death. You know what women are like."

"Pisanelli here knows all about women."

Lia Guerra lowered her voice. "In Tino's bedroom one evening . . ."

"Yes?"

"A wooden chest of drawers." Lia Guerra's legs were still tucked under her thighs and for a moment she looked like a girl, small and fragile. All harshness had vanished from her face. "The little chest of drawers his father had made."

The two men instinctively moved forward on their seats.

"I recognized the piece of furniture."

Pisanelli, pale and attentive, held the mobile telephone between his clasped hands. His elbows were now on his thighs.

"Very good with his hands, the architect Gracchi, and he liked to make things—things he'd give away. Tino always said his father found it a lot easier to give things than to give himself."

"It's not always easy to be a father."

Lia Guerra answered, "Not easy to be a child." She took a lungful of cigarette smoke before squashing the butt into an ashtray on the cushion beside her, "Last time I'd seen that chest of drawers was in the seventies, back when Tino'd broken up with Bettina. Tino and I had a little place that belonged to his parents in the city center. In that awful city of yours, commissario, with its fogs and its mosquitoes and its dour citizenry. I can remember the chest well—inlaid with delicate parquetry. Tino'd brought it down from Turin in the old Cinquecento. Fifteen years later, there it was, the same chest standing in front of me in Sicily. Been there the entire time and I'd never noticed."

"Why not?"

"Dusty and badly chipped. The varnish'd flaked off and of course, the parquetry was hidden beneath a lace mat."

Lia Guerra's eyes held the attention of both men. They watched her carefully. Pisanelli's mouth was slightly open.

"It must have been about midnight—around Christmas time—December, 1992—and it was exceptionally cold. I was in his bed at BRAMAN and I couldn't sleep. It was as if Tino was there, as if he needed to tell me something. I'd thrown down the book I was trying to read and as it fell, the book tousled the lace mat." She nodded. "I recognized the old chest."

"And?"

"Fate was guiding me."

"Fate'd taken a long time."

"Despite the cold, I was sweating. Tino was telling me what I had to do. I clambered out of bed—I swear his hand was guiding me. I took hold of the drawer and I pulled at it. It wouldn't budge. Something was stuck to the underside of the drawer, something was wedged there. So I tugged and I tugged. And all the papers came tumbling out onto the floor."

Pisanelli asked, "What papers, signora?" His voice was strained and the Adam's apple bobbed in his throat.

She looked at him. "Sheets of paper, various folders. Everything spilled out all over the floor. And I saw the fax."

"What fax?"

"The first page'd disappeared." She put her head back and closed her dark eyes.

Pisanelli asked again, "What fax, signora?"

When she spoke, Trotti was reminded of a girl reciting her catechism. "*Essentially false, unkind, unsuitable.*" That's what it said. That's what the fax said. "*Essentially false, unkind, unsuitable. And dangerous.*"

"Who said that?"

"*Chiara and I must ask you to vacate your room in the Dovecot and find somewhere else to sleep within BRAMAN. As sign of our disapproval. Chiara can help you move your belongings. With all best wishes, Giovanni.*"

"A conflict between Gracchi and Verga?"

"*Essentially false, unkind, unsuitable. And dangerous.*"
Her eyes remained closed.

"What conflict, signora?"

"Nobody'd ever mentioned anything. Not to me, not for
three years. Just their crocodile tears."

"You shown the fax to anyone?"

Her head was still held back, her eyes were still closed.
"Chiara Gracchi."

"What did she say?"

"Why should I doubt her word—the word of the grieving
widow?"

"What did she say?"

Lia Guerra opened her eyes. "A little squabble between
old friends."

"Squabble over what?"

"She didn't want to say."

"But you found out?"

Lia Guerra tapped the dog-eared magazine that lay beside
her on the chaise longue. "Yes." She nodded. "I found out."

42: Beirut

PRINCE: WHAT IS BRAMAN?

Gracchi: When I was a student at Trento, back in 1968, I lived on a commune with several companions. With people like Antonio Cocco and his wife Alice—altogether there were about twelve of us. One of the marvelous moments in my life.

Prince: But not for long.

Gracchi: Unfortunately not. Antonio's been in prison now for fourteen years as a convicted terrorist, while his wife Alice, so gentle and timid, and a wonderful violinist, was gunned down by the Carabinieri in 1975—Public Enemy Number One because she had sprung the man she loved from jail. All that was to come later—*les lendemains qui déchantent*, as the French say. Antonio and Alice—in those days still practicing Catholics—joined the Red Brigades. Not satisfied with analyzing history, they wanted to speed it up.

Prince: You didn't join the Red Brigades?

Gracchi: I remained a poor hack with Lotta Continua. We went our separate ways, but I never forgot the experience of communal living. Then in India, many, many years later, I lived a similar experience. I found great serenity at the ashram in Poona—but when Guru Anish went off to California and his secretary disappeared to Switzerland with the Rolls Royce and all the cash, I was seriously pissed off. Pissed off and lost. Losing the guru was like losing my father. That's when

Giovanni Verga suggested an ashram in Sicily, where he had this wonderful place. Giovanni started talking to me about his vineyards and olive groves and dovecot in Trapani. A commune based on the same values as Poona and built around Zen philosophy. I agreed immediately. The idea of working with addicts came later.

Prince: You returned to Italy in 1981.

Gracchi: Giovanni and I set up an autonomous commune. My wife and daughter were with me and BRAMAN was a great experience. I'm not somebody who's concerned with material wealth—my first marriage had floundered precisely because I bought my wife flowers instead of a car. In Sicily, I at last found exactly what I was looking for, what I needed—simplicity and purpose.

Prince: And the addicts?

Gracchi: You know, everything's connected. I belong to the baby boom—I was born in 1946—and when I was coming to manhood, like most other people of my generation, I could see Italy was sick. You didn't need a crystal ball to see things had to change. That's why we set up Lotta Continua.

Prince: For the revolution?

Gracchi: The people who came after us, five—ten years younger—they saw that, for all our talk, we'd gone the same way as our parents. Revolution? Lotta Continua had become Stalinist. A hierarchical and rigid structure—and when we voted ourselves out of existence at Rimini, it was precisely because Lotta Continua had failed to recognize the role of the feminists. The new generation—the indiani metropolitani—had none of our beliefs. Nor our ideals. They were anarchic because they were cynical—and central to their anarchy were drugs. Heroin was their revolution. By 1977, the stuff was flooding into Italy from Lebanon where it helped pay for the war, and we began seeing people overdosing in the street. People who were a lot younger than me and Gianni. Even women and young girls. I felt something had to be done. My generation'd lost the revolution—perhaps this was the battle we were supposed to be fighting. I believed addicts could find serenity in much the same way that I had found serenity in India. I managed to convince Giovanni Verga this had to be the purpose behind BRAMAN.

Prince: Yet for years, you advocated mind altering drugs.

Gracchi: If you mean pot, I still do. [*A laugh*.] Fortunately, I know the difference between soft and hard drugs. I know about the effects of heroin—I've had my share of bad trips. I thank God I never fell into that trap. One of the few mistakes I haven't made in my life. As it is, the girl I was going to marry got into the heavy stuff—and addiction.

Prince: That's why you went off to India?

Gracchi: By the time she ended up in a clinic in Switzerland, it was way too late for any talk of a future between us. There were things the drugs had killed for good. Things like innocence and intimacy. Things like sharing. Perhaps that's why I set up the rehabilitation center. My way of making amends to the woman I loved.

43: Aid

"I WAS READING *Prince* last night," Trotti remarked. "I fell asleep."

"The interview gives the impression Tino was the founder of BRAMAN."

"That's what I thought."

"That's what everybody thought."

Pisanelli asked, "What's the problem?"

"Verga was irked by the interview. Giovanni Verga liked to see himself as a guru. Of course, BRAMAN was Tino's idea. Verga's creativity was limited to producing pornographic magazines packaged with gift dildos or magic love potions. That's how he got rich in the seventies. He was the founder of *Prince*—but sold it off in the eighties when he moved on to better things. Better ways of making a lot of money—thanks to Tino. Giovanni Verga needed to be admired. He wanted everybody to think BRAMAN was his idea. You know Sicily?"

Trotti shook his head.

"Sicily is very Victorian. You can murder—but you mustn't divorce. Giovanni Verga understood the mystical longings of his fellow islanders. He needed to put his past as a pornographer behind him. For himself, but also for the sake of his Socialist friends. Giovanni Verga was a political animal who never did anything without carefully considering all the ramifications. Especially political ramifications. He wanted the kudos of a guru, the aura. He needed to be seen as the founder of BRAMAN." Lia Guerra faltered. "There was something else, too."

"What?"

"Tino'd publicly given his support to the legalizing of cannabis." She laughed. "The Region of Sicily—the local Christian Democrats—was footing the bill for BRAMAN. Giovanni Verga said Tino was pissing in the soup." She spoke in a low, hushed voice.

"What soup?"

"The Mafia could never accept the legalization of drugs."

"That's sufficient reason for the Mafia to kill Gracchi?"

"I don't know who killed Tino," Lia Guerra answered in subdued exasperation. "I just know his so-called friends hid the truth from me, just as they hid it from the investigating magistrates."

"Why?"

"They all had something to hide," she said. "All of them, Giovanni Verga, Chiara Gracchi, the inmates. There'd been a bitter quarrel between Tino and Verga, and everybody knew about it. Everybody knew why he'd been banished from the main building, from the Dovecot, but no one ever told me."

There was silence on the terrace, apart from the wind as it flapped at the clothes drying on the line.

"The Carabinieri worked away at their theory of an insider at BRAMAN while the Polizia di Stato blindly followed the line of a Mafia killing. The enquiries were badly flawed—in my opinion, deliberately so. Nobody got arrested and all the while, the newspapers in Sicily screeched about Lotta Continua."

"Why?"

"You've read the article in *Prince*, Trotti."

"I fell asleep."

The briefest smile. "Tino'd finally received the summons from the courts in Milan—the summons concerning the murder of Commissario Pugliese." She added, "Tino was gunned down just six days before his departure for Milan and his arraignment."

44: Window

PRINCE: DID YOU murder Commissario Pugliese?

Gracchi: I beg your pardon?

Prince: Two friends of yours from Lotta Continua have just been arrested for the murder of Commissario Pugliese back in May 1972. You, too, will soon be served with a summons to appear before the investigating magistrates in Milan.

Gracchi: Let's hope so.

Prince: Were you involved in the death of Commissario Pugliese?

Gracchi: Lotta Continua was never a terrorist organization.

Prince: Yet Antonio Cocco is serving a life sentence for murder.

Gracchi: While it is true that several comrades went on to armed action and that several—including Antonio Cocco and his wife—subsequently joined the Red Brigades, it was not as members of Lotta Continua.

Prince: What's the difference?

Gracchi: In 1968, the working classes started making demands on the ruling elite. Lotta Continua, which we—me and Antonio Cocco among others—created in Trento, was merely intended as a mouthpiece for the working masses. It was no channel for violence or political terrorism.

Prince: Yet cofounder Cocco is now serving a life sentence.

Gracchi: That was Antonio's decision—not mine, nor that of Lotta Continua.

The "hot autumn" of 1968 was a time of student unrest in the universities and widespread strikes in the factories. The French had risen in revolt in May, and here in Italy, it was time for change. The country was no longer the poor, backward peasant society of 1945. We'd lived through the industrial miracle, yet there was no change in the way the ruling classes maintained their control. The Church and the Christian Democrats felt threatened and nervously referred everything back to their allies and sponsors, the Americans.

Prince: Reason enough for Lotta Continua to advocate violence?

Gracchi: Lotta Continua never espoused violence—even if, ultimately, all left-wing parties had to confront the problem of violence from the right.

When a bomb exploded at the Banca dell'Agricoltura in Piazza Fontana, it wasn't the act of left-wing terrorism—even if that was the message that was promptly flashed around the world. In Milan, on the twelfth of December, 1969, sixteen people were killed and many more injured. They were murdered by a right-wing terrorist group that was being manipulated by the Italian secret services. We didn't know at the time the Christian Democrats and the military—with the enthusiastic backing of the CIA—had opted for a strategy of tension. Tension that was to last more than ten years and bring the country to the brink of civil war. The PCI was the largest communist party in the West, and the Americans chose to believe Italy could topple into the Soviet sphere of influence, hence the violent repression of the extreme left.

Claiming the bomb in Piazza Fontana was the work of terrorists, the police promptly rounded up all the various anarchists and leftists. While being interrogated by the police, one of these anarchists threw himself out of the window of the Questura and fell to his death in the street below.

It was not Lotta Continua who decided the anarchist had been 'suicided'. It wasn't Lotta Continua who ordered his

presumed assassin, Commissario Pugliese, should be eliminated in an act of proletarian justice.

Sixteen years later, my two ex-comrades from Lotta Continua are in prison and if I myself am to be arraigned, it is
simply because during the intervening sixteen years, since that
fateful day in May 1972 when Pugliese was gunned down
in Milan, the judges haven't been able to find a culprit.
Like drowning men, they now jump at the rope thrown to
them by a pentito—a grass who, for reasons best known
to himself, has decided to accuse my ex-companions. The
same witness has mentioned my name. Yet he's also stated
explicitly I was hostile to any form of violence. How he can
say these things when he and I've never met?

I look forward to any opportunity to speak openly with
the Milanese judges.

It'll be fun to see how they cope with the truth.

45: Metropolitana

"UNFORTUNATELY, TINO CHOSE not to see what was going on."

"What was going on?"

"Giovanni Verga, Chiara Gracchi and Tino were absolute masters. The three of them ran BRAMAN."

"Why was that a problem?"

"BRAMAN changed—and Verga was doing all the changing. When Verga and Tino returned from India, they'd set up a nonprofit association—all very innocent and amateur and highly laudable."

Trotti nodded.

"Verga could always smell where the money was. That's why he went to Poona in the first place—his girlfriend, the daughter of a millionaire Austrian aristocrat, had run out on him and he needed to bring her back to Italy. Once he was in Sicily with Tino, he realized he could do without her. BRAMAN was now his golden goose. Within four years, Verga turned the commune into a foundation. Then, before I was sent to Rome, it became a therapeutic community. That lasted just four years, until 1990. With Tino conveniently out of the way, BRAMAN was made a holding company with nearly thirty rehabilitation branches throughout Italy—and a couple in France. As well as a private yacht for Giovanni Verga—and a plane. Plus, of course, the residence in Milan and the office in Rome, in the via Veneto."

"With Gracchi out of the way?"

"Tino was the short side of the triangle," Lia Guerra said sourly. "Tino didn't play their game. He believed in what he was doing. Unlike Verga or Chiara, he genuinely liked people—he wanted to help them. Tino was a friend—sometimes intolerant, sometimes unfair—but always loyal. Just as he was faithful to his ideals." She added, "Just as he was always loyal to me."

"Gracchi must've seen what was happening."

"In the end, Tino compromised. He hated quarreling with a friend. Courageous in front of the Mafia, he would back down in front of his wife or his daughter or Verga. Tino had never wanted to change out of his Poona saffron—but Verga told him it was a financial necessity and Tino did as he was told. Verga said it was imperative to break with the guru in India." Lia Guerra gave a cold laugh. "The framed photograph of the guru Anish in the main dining hall was replaced with a bigger, better painting of Giovanni Verga, dressed in white and looking wise and benevolent. The great helmsman. With the engraving, 'BRAMAN exists to help all those who dedicate themselves to the mystery of life.'" Lia Guerra gave another snort of mirthless laughter as her glance went from Trotti to Pisanelli. "Tinpot philosophy, completely bogus, but everybody went in fear of Giovanni Verga. Even Tino was in his thrall. Or perhaps," she added, "simply in thrall of all the dope he was consuming."

Pisanelli raised an eyebrow.

"The whole cult of personality remained hidden to the outside world. Too many sects around—Jehovah's Witnesses and Scientologists. Verga realized people wouldn't like to see public money being funneled into anything that resembled a sect, not in the very Catholic Sicily. When BRAMAN was recognized as a therapeutic center—that's when the money really started rolling in. Word of the place began to spread—Club Med for addicts and their keepers. Giovanni Verga, Chiara Gracchi, and Tino lived in the Dovecot, which could've been the Ritz. They were served hand and foot by the inmates—a very far cry from the egalitarian commune that Tino'd intended. Giovanni Verga was the undisputed head, and Chiara Gracchi the administrator. It was Chiara who did all the hobnobbing with the Region of Sicily, then later with the city of Milan that was controlled by the Socialists. Don't forget that in 1986, Craxi and his Socialist clan were in absolute control of the country."

"And Gracchi? He didn't mind?"

"I tried talking to him about the new money, but he'd just give me that little-boy smile of his and shrug his shoulders. Shrug his shoulders and take another drag on his spliff." She added bitterly, "There was so much money—and Giovanni Verga enjoyed spending it. In his heart, Verga's basically a peasant, a Sicilian peasant with an atavistic Sicilian hunger. He can't quite believe he's got money. Only the best will do for Giovanni—expensive, but tasteless and pretentious. Even the chicken run at BRAMAN was luxurious—the inmates called it 'Beverly Hills Coop.'" A smile as she shook her head. "When I went to Switzerland, believe me, the rehab clinic there was no Club Med—although my parents paid through the nose for the pleasure of getting me off drugs."

"Through the nose?" Pisanelli repeated quizzically.

"Heroin in those days," she said.

Trotti asked, "You've never gone back?"

"To Switzerland?"

"To drugs."

Lia Guerra gave Commissario Trotti a thoughtful glance before shaking her head. "I've got you to thank for that. Spadano says a lot of good things about you, but with me, Commissario Trotti, you were an unfeeling bastard."

There was silence. Possibly Guerra was awaiting a reaction from the old policeman.

There was none.

"Switzerland was hell and I hated being there. I wanted to die—I suppose I'd always wanted to die, and heroin was an agreeable way of killing myself. Then one morning I woke up, and for the first time since I was a little girl, I could smell the trees, I could smell the flowers, I could smell the newly mown grass. I don't know quite why, but I was happy. It was like being born again—or being with Tino the first time we met. It was Tino who said that addicts were beautiful. We've visited death—yet I'm still here to talk about it."

Lia Guerra's hand ran slowly down the sleeve of her arm, as if to reassure herself that the scabs and the marks had gone forever.

It was very quiet on the terrace. The wind had dropped and the clothes no longer danced on the line. The black cat slept.

Lia Guerra gave Pisanelli a fleeting glance.

Trotti said, "Pisanelli and I were there in Milan the day you scurried down into the Metropolitana, the day you left for Switzerland, signora. It was Pisanelli who insisted I let you go."

46: Automatic

LIA GUERRA TOOK her third cigarette.

"At the end of 1994, the pubblico ministero asked for the Gracchi dossier file to be shelved. After six years of getting nowhere, there was no point in wasting more public money on the search for Tino's killer."

Pisanelli leant forward to light her cigarette.

"The possible motives—the three possible motives behind the murder had been amply investigated and no culprit had been identified."

"Three?"

"An ex-companion from Lotta Continua, the Trapani Mafia or somebody within BRAMAN wanting Tino out of the way." Lia Guerra stared at her three outstretched fingers; two fingers held the burning cigarette. "Tino died just six days before he was scheduled to give his evidence in Milan. He could have been an embarrassment for his old friends at Lotta Continua."

"They didn't kill him?"

"It's possible Tino knew more about Pugliese's murder—but I doubt it."

"Why?"

"Tino hated violence."

"That would save him from being murdered by his Lotta Continua companions?"

"Sixteen years on—middle-aged, married men who'd lost their revolutionary fervor. Why kill him? They were all friends."

"Friends who are afraid of being sent to prison like Cocco. Friends can do a lot of bad things."

"After so many years, what could Tino tell the judges? Even supposing he knew anything about the murder." Lia Guerra appraised Trotti reflectively. "You are cynical."

"Realistic."

"Chiara Gracchi's convinced Tino was killed by the Mafia. She thinks Lotta Continua was just a way of sidetracking the enquiry."

"She knew the people from Lotta Continua?"

"Not as well as I did. She says the motive of silencing a loudmouth journalist is more convincing than a sixteen-year-old murder enquiry."

"Perhaps the Mafia did kill him."

Lia Guerra shook her head. "No witness has ever come forward to say Tino's death was ordered by the Mafia in Trapani or indeed anywhere else in Western Sicily."

"Which leaves the third possibility?"

"Precisely," Lia Guerra said.

"Your theory of a person on the inside?"

"Person or persons."

"Giovanni Verga and Chiara Gracchi?"

Lia Guerra said nothing; she bit her lip, her glance on Trotti.

"You're saying Chiara Gracchi's support of the Mafia theory was a way of diverting attention?"

"She knew about Enzo Beltoni and she never told me."

"Told you what?"

"Commissario Trotti, a few weeks before his death, Tino received a call from the studios."

Pisanelli interrupted. "What studios?" He was still holding the cigarette lighter.

"The television station, TRTP in Trapani. There were several ex-addicts working as apprentice journalists on his television program. Including the girl Luciana, who was in the Duna when Tino was murdered. In the car when he was shot and she was never touched—not even a drop of blood, and yet there was blood all over the car. Blood and splintered glass."

"Who phoned Gracchi?"

"A TV journalist—a real one, a professional journalist—had found a syringe while rummaging through various pockets for a cigarette."

"The apprentices from BRAMAN were shooting up?"

"According to Giovanni Verga's statistics, eighty-seven percent of the inmates at BRAMAN broke free of their various addictions following treatment. Statistics which so pleased the Sicilian Region and all Verga's chums at Bettino Craxi's court." The mirthless laugh. "Eighty seven percent—and here they were, all these rehabilitated addicts, mainlining under the nose of Tino—not in BRAMAN, but on the outside, out in the real world—in the Trapani studios."

"How d'you know all this?"

"I went to the television station and spoke to the journalist," Lia Guerra replied simply.

"But the journalist didn't tell the police?"

She shook her head. "Too dangerous. When Tino discovered what was going on, he was furious. Hypocritically, really, when you think of the dope he'd gotten through over the years. That same evening he phoned me here. Didn't say why he was pissed off—too proud for that, too proud to admit BRAMAN wasn't working, too proud to admit Giovanni Verga was playing him for a fool."

"What did Gracchi tell you?"

"I told you, Trotti—our friendship was very special. When one of us was feeling miserable, we'd phone the other—and the phone calls could last hours." A drag on the cigarette. "Tino intended to throw several people out of rehab," Lia Guerra said. "Including Enzo Beltoni."

"That's all he told you?"

"In front of witnesses, Beltoni produced a knife and threatened Tino."

"What did Gracchi do?"

"He immediately told Giovanni Verga that Beltoni was threatening to kill him."

Trotti frowned. "Gracchi phoned you in July?"

"Late June."

"Enzo Beltoni was working at BRAMAN at the time of Gracchi's death—in September."

"Giovanni Verga never kicked Beltoni out."

"Why not?"

No answer.

"You knew Enzo Beltoni, signora?"

"You couldn't help knowing Beltoni at BRAMAN. Everybody knew him just as everybody knew Beltoni'd killed a boy in America. He was dangerous—violence waiting to happen. Beltoni was wild—and he wanted everybody to know there was nothing they could do to him."

"Why not?"

"He was Giovanni Verga's favorite. Verga indulged Beltoni, humored him. Which was strange, because everybody else was frightened of Giovanni Verga. Verga carefully cultivated power, and everybody went in fear of him—everybody except Enzo Beltoni. The two men were more like good friends than employer and employee."

"Giovanni Verga protected Beltoni?"

"Tino knew he couldn't kick Enzo Beltoni out."

"Then why did Beltoni threaten him?"

"Beltoni wasn't somebody to control himself."

"Yet it never occurred to you Beltoni murdered Gracchi?"

"Of course it occurred to me—just as it occurred to the magistrates in Trapani. Like them, I was convinced Beltoni was working for the Mafia. It was later I understood he was working for Giovanni Verga—and Chiara Gracchi." Lia Guerra paused. "Spadano says Beltoni was blackmailing Verga. Sexual blackmail."

"Spadano?" Trotti asked unhappily.

"Spadano has reason to believe that homosexuals . . ."

Lia Guerra fell silent. Her dark eyes were wide open.

"What's Spadano got to do with BRAMAN, signora?" Trotti asked, but the woman was no longer listening.

Her glance had turned to the open door of the terrace.

Trotti followed Lia Guerra's glance.

One of the men sharply jabbed the cold barrel of the automatic weapon against Trotti's cheek.

The woman put a hand to her open mouth.

47: Lombard League

THEY STUCK ADHESIVE tape across his mouth. His hands were held by plastic cuffs behind his back, and a bag was pulled over Trotti's head.

Coming down the stairs, his feet scarcely touched the ground, and then one of the men, possibly the man in the beret and bulletproof jacket, jabbed him in the small of the back. As his shins met hard metal, Piero Trotti fell headlong.

Unable to protect himself with his elbows, he tumbled forward, landing on soft fabric.

Trotti realized it was a car seat.

His head was spinning. He had been struck with a butt to the side of his head, and now there was a painful ringing in his ears.

He would never see his grandchildren again.

Trotti was in pain, in dreadful pain. He felt old. He wanted to die. He did not want to be hurt. He did not want any more pain. Blood was trickling down his cheek.

(*Crablike, the man had stepped sideways through the door onto the terrace, a finger on the trigger of his weapon. With the other hand, he had gestured for Trotti and Pisanelli to lie down.*

The man's face was immobile.

For a long moment no one had moved; just the slightest movement of the muzzle. Then without turning his glance, the

*Carabiniere had kicked Pisanelli's aluminum crutch and sent
it clattering noisily across the terracotta tiles.*

*Lia Guerra started to scream before the other man silenced
her.*)

People clambered into the car, pushing Trotti into an upright
position.

Vomit rising in his throat.

The exhaust pipe reverberated distantly as the car pulled
out into the traffic along the Tiber.

Trotti heard the whine of the siren. It came from another
world.

"Friends of yours?"

"Bastard says he's a policeman. Commissario from Milan
or somewhere."

"Let's hope he doesn't arrest us." The man beside Trotti
rocked with laughter and he jabbed something into Trotti's
bruised ribs. "They don't like us southerners up in the North.
Racist bastards."

48: Freed

THERE WAS PURPLE bougainvillea climbing down the warm brick of a wall. Beyond the wall stood a clinic or a hospital.

No one released the handcuffs, but before reaching the hotel, someone removed the cape and Trotti's eyes, by now accustomed to darkness, blinked unhappily.

The car jerked to a stop and the man beside him unceremoniously ripped the tape from Trotti's mouth.

Then he was being manhandled from the car.

The Hotel Toscana was hidden behind a crowd of people and carelessly parked cars. There were a revolving blue light, several policemen in uniform, a crowd of onlookers and as Trotti stumbled forward, held firmly on either side by two Carabinieri—their semiautomatic guns had disappeared—he was caught in the light of flashing bulbs.

He was old and he felt ill, but above all, he was embarrassed by the handcuffs at his back. He tried to turn his head away from the cameras.

Like a common criminal while the photographers continued to take their pictures.

The Carabinieri pulled him through the open wooden door with its ground glass window.

The old man in the Milan AC waistcoat beamed at him inanely. "Commissario Trotti?"

The Carabinieri pushed the man aside and the smile died on his face.

They jostled Trotti through the hotel entrance, past the dining room and up the narrow stairs.

Upstairs to the hotel room. The door was now open.

There was the white brilliance of a spotlight.

Somebody coughed and there was silence as heads turned to stare as Trotti was pushed into the bedroom.

With incongruous relief, Trotti noticed Spadano's coat was still hanging from the back of the door.

Just five hours earlier, Trotti had been watching Fred Astaire on the small television.

Strangers stared at him with cold eyes. Policemen in uniform, policemen in civilian clothes. The dull, olive skin of southerners. A couple of women.

Turning his head, Trotti looked at the bed. Blood had seeped through the clean, white sheets and formed a shapeless dark blot.

A narrow leg and a small foot hung over the edge of the bed.

A narrow, dark leg and a woman's small foot.

49: Mission

"THANK YOUR FRIEND and his telephone," the man said with a self-congratulatory grimace.

"What telephone?"

"How else d'you think we knew where to find you?" The accent was pure Naples.

"Are you going to take these handcuffs off?"

He scarcely looked like the Neapolitan of Trotti's northern imagination. The detective was tall, very pale, and had thin blond hair that had been combed flat across the top of a large domed head. He wore a shabby, crumpled suit. He was smoking an unfiltered cigarette. "Why did you kill her?"

"I've killed nobody."

"You're going to be difficult?"

"Get these cuffs off."

The man had led him into another hotel room, and Trotti now sat on the beige counterpane of the bed while the detective leaned against the jamb of the bedroom door, his back to the hall.

A woman in the uniform of the Polizia di Stato, her arms folded, stood at the door of the bathroom.

There was movement in the hallway.

"The dead prostitute in your bed—nothing to do with you?"

Trotti raised his shoulder in a shrug and there was an angry ringing in his ears. "Give me a glass of water, could you?" He felt nauseous.

"That black girl in your bed? Things got out of hand?"

"A glass of water, please."

"What tricks had you two been up to?"

"I don't feel very well."

The uniformed women went into the bathroom, removed a glass from its cellophane package and poured water from the tap. Trotti, his hands helpless behind his back, drank the proffered glass in a single gulp. He was like a child being fed.

"Thank you," he said; he could smell the policewoman's perfume.

The Neapolitan asked, "The bitch deserved to die?"

"I don't know what you mean."

"Why'd you kill her?"

The policewoman was young, and blonde hair cascaded over the collar of her white blouse and blue serge uniform. She did not acknowledge Trotti's thanks. She returned the glass to the bathroom sill. She was wearing lipstick.

The detective lit another cigarette with the stub of the old one. "You knew her?"

"I met her in Florence."

"A high-class whore."

"I met her outside the railway station in Florence. She was freezing to death."

"You're sick. You know that? Young and ready for anything . . . at a price. You like the black girls, don't you?"

"She's an American student."

"She phoned you this morning and you thought you were in luck."

"She's an au pair in Milan. From Chicago."

(*The word sounded distant and exotic.*)

"The young ones cost a lot of money. Surprised you can afford that sort of thing."

In exasperation, Trotti said again, "Are you going to take these cuffs off?"

"You told her to come here. The call's been traced."

"Then you know she was staying with American friends in Rome. You know she phoned me—wanted to meet me in the city. In the via Veneto."

"When she got here, she wasn't willing to play your dirty games."

"She's not a whore."

"I hear you do things differently up there in the north." A leer. The breath smelled of cigarette and garlic. "Missionary position not good enough for you?"

"Remove these cuffs."

"A pervert."

Trotti caught his breath, knowing he was going to lose his temper. "You know who I am?"

"A pervert."

Raising his voice only made the ringing more painful. Quietly, Trotti asked, "You really believe you can talk to me like this? Take these cuffs off at once."

The detective appeared amused.

"I'd advise you to be careful."

The Neapolitan took the cigarette from his thin mouth and held it between finger and thumb. His lips broke into a smile that transformed the lopsided face. The tip of his tongue darted at a shred of black tobacco.

"I'm Commissario Trotti."

The detective pushed himself away from the door and stood directly in front of Trotti.

"You advise me to be careful?"

"Please take these cuffs off."

The detective struck Trotti across the face with the palm of his left hand. "You're a pervert."

50: Scola

"SHE CALLED ME just as I was leaving my room."

"You waited for her and then you screwed her."

"I screwed nobody. I was with Pisanelli."

"You sodomized her."

"Tenente Pisanelli and I were in the piazza. Santa Maria in Trastevere. Lots of people saw us. Ask the waiter."

"How did the bitch end up in your bed?"

"No idea."

"End up in your bed—raped, battered and killed?"

Trotti's ears were ringing. "The last time I saw Wilma . . ."

"You know her name?"

"Of course I know her name. We traveled down from Chianciano together. She asked me to help her. I gave her Pisanelli's phone number."

It was too painful for Trotti to raise his head. The Neapolitan was standing directly in front of him and Trotti was staring at the man's leather belt, at the crumpled, stained trousers, at the fly zipper.

"You're lying."

"Wilma Barclay. Her name's Wilma Barclay. She's working as an au pair with an American family in Milan."

"Working as a whore in Milan."

There was no reason for the detective to hit him, yet Trotti knew another blow was coming before the man's palm ever struck the side of his head.

Trotti let his body loll sideways. The ringing in his head became intolerable. He wanted to vomit. He wanted to lose consciousness. He wanted to die.

He thought of his granddaughters.

"A pervert."

Piero Trotti stared at the carpet between his feet. Blood was falling from his mouth—or perhaps from his nose—in a continuous stream onto the floor.

"We know about your daughter."

Trotti tried to raise his head. "What about my daughter?"

"We know all about your games."

"Where's my daughter? Where's Pioppi?"

"She stopped eating, didn't she? Your daughter nearly died. We know all about that. Just as we know about the Uruguayan woman you beat up. Broke her arm, didn't you, and the bitch needed fifteen stitches."

"What are you talking about?"

"You're sick."

"I don't know what you're talking about."

"You've always been sick, Commissario Trotti. Can't control yourself. You can't control your obsessions and you don't get better with age." Again the man laughed. "A pervert in charge of a children's center."

The policewoman moved uncomfortably and from the corner of his eye, Trotti could see her flat, black shoes.

"A pervert in charge of a children's center—where he can be alone with all the little girls and boys. Where he can get up to his tricks."

"You're crazy."

"Or perhaps your wife never told you why she walked out on you? Perhaps your daughter never told you why she wouldn't leave you with her children?"

"You'd best be quiet."

"You thought the Scola woman would keep silent about your nasty habits? Nasty little habits with the children—and everybody covering up for Commissario Trotti, the pervert, the child molester, the sodomite."

Between Trotti's feet, the drips were forming a puddle; a puddle of saliva and blood and mucus.

"This time, you're retired and nobody's going to cover for you. You're on your own, Trotti. This time you're going to pay for your dirty little habit," the man said and struck him again. "About time, too."

51: Barbour

THE POLICEWOMAN MOVED away from the bathroom and now stood by the door of the hotel room, her hand on the handle.

The Neapolitan detective had started to shout. "Time you were put away, Trotti."

Trotti was no longer listening.

"You're old and sick."

From beyond the closed door came the sound of people moving along the corridor and the heavy fall of feet down the narrow stairs.

"Can't you get it up anymore?" the detective was saying. "Is that why you play your games?"

Trotti slowly raised his head to look at the woman and their eyes met. Trotti found no sympathy. She could have been looking at an animal or an inanimate object.

With his hands locked behind his back, Trotti felt ashamed. A mistake—his arrest and now the ignominy of being interrogated, it was all a mistake. That did not stop him from feeling ashamed. More ashamed than angry.

"You began sticking things into her."

Trotti tried to raise his head.

"Sticking objects into every orifice." The detective struck Trotti, but this time less harshly. The hand glanced off Trotti's jaw.

"Can't you see the man's hurt?" The policewoman opened the door. Her accent was Roman.

"Close that damned door, bitch!"

On the edge of his vision, Trotti saw the stretcher coming out of the room opposite. He saw two men in white coats and white canvas shoes bearing the black body bag.

Trotti's eyes hurt; they were watering and it was hard to focus.

Several people followed the stretcher. A young man wore a windbreaker, the word CARABINIERI stenciled in yellow letters on the back.

Nobody took any notice of Trotti.

The detective went to the open door, but just as he pulled the handle from the woman's grip—her face remained immobile beneath the peaked cap—there was shouting from the stairway.

Shouting in a foreign language.

The detective tried to close the door but a shoe was firmly placed against the jamb. A large shoe. Then the door was pushed open and a head poked through the doorway.

The intruders' eyes fell on Trotti where he sat on the bed, head bowed and his hands behind his back.

Trotti looked up and their glances met.

The man looked at Trotti and smiled with embarrassed surprise.

(*The place was both warm and empty; no sign of all the tourists.*)

"You crazy, Portano?" The Englishman barged into the room.

(*When the man placed the small camera on the glass shelf, beside the chocolate boxes, Trotti rose and hurried out into the cold of via di Città.*)

"Take those absurd cuffs off Commissario Trotti," the man in the waxed jacket said in Italian. "Take them off at once. Can't you see he's ill?"

Trotti lost consciousness.

52: Ray-Ban

"COMMISSARIO?"

He was wearing an anorak, and he now had a mustache. He looked fatter than when Trotti had last seen him.

"Commissario?"

If Magagna had not been wearing his American sunglasses, Trotti would have had difficulty in recognizing his friend.

"Well?"

He had been sitting on a steel chair; he now stood up and emptied the contents of his pockets on to the bed. "I bought you this." Half a dozen boiled sweets.

"A rich man."

"One of the advantages of working for the Polizia di Stato—easy money and fast promotion."

Trotti winced in pain as they shook hands. The ringing was still there in his head. "Unwrap one of those sweets for me."

"What flavor?"

"Milan, Omicidi and promotion make you forget rhubarb's always been my favorite?"

"I thought perhaps in retirement, your tastes might have matured."

"No risk of that."

Magagna took one of the packets, removed the wrapping and placed the sweet in Trotti's mouth. "Looks as if you've been in a fight." Magagna smiled.

"I walked into a door."

"In Rome?"

"Lot of doors in Rome."

The smile vanished. "The Carabinieri did it, commissario?"

Trotti felt stiff. His shoulders and arms were bruised. There was a pain in his ribs. When he moved his head, he could feel a sharp pain at the back of his skull. "Trying to remember."

"They clearly didn't like you."

"How'd you know I was here, Magagna?" Trotti clicked the sweet against his teeth.

"Pisanelli told me."

"Pisa?" Trotti hesitated, his memory returning.

"I was driving down from Bologna when he called."

"How is Pisanelli? Where is he? Did they hurt him?"

"Pisanelli's at the wedding."

"What wedding?"

"He's getting married."

"Oh, my God. What's the time?"

"You've been under sedation for over twenty-four hours— they thought you had a concussion."

"The time, Magagna?"

The other man looked at his watch, and Trotti noticed it was an expensive Swiss affair in rolled gold. "Half past nine."

"Friday?"

"Half past nine, Saturday morning."

"Christ! Pisanelli's wedding."

"I was hoping you'd forgotten."

"You're going to get me to the church."

Magagna smiled, "In hospital pajamas?"

The white door opened and a male nurse entered.

He was middle-aged with grey hair and effeminate features. He wore a silver crucifix in the lapel of his lab coat. Beneath the coat, there was a white shirt and a khaki tie. "You're not supposed to have visitors." He placed a delicate hand on Magagna's shoulder. "With liquid that could well be spinal fluid coming out of my mouth, I'd make sure I was getting some rest." He spoke in a flat, lisping monotone.

"Commissario Trotti wants to go to church—to his god-daughter's wedding."

"Kill two birds with one stone—go to his own funeral while he's there." The lips pulled tight, as if activated by a purse string.

The nurse turned on his heel and left the bright, hospital room in silence.

53: Déja Entendu

"Papa, is that you?"

"Pioppi."

"Papa, how are you? Are you all right? Where are you phoning from? From a hospital?"

"I'm with Magagna."

"You were supposed to call me. I've been trying to get you for the last twelve hours. Are you all right, Papa? I'm catching the next train to Rome."

"There's no need."

"Anna said you'd been arrested."

"You believe everything you hear?"

"Papa, you must tell me the truth. I'm worried about you."

"It's nothing, Pioppi."

"It can't be nothing if you're in the hospital. Are you hurt? And how long are you going to be there for?"

"A slight bruise."

"Anna said they beat you up."

"I'll be out of here in half an hour."

"Why did Anna say you were hurt?"

"There's really nothing to worry about, Pioppi."

"Of course I'm worried about you."

"There's no need. How are the girls? And how's Nando?"

"Nando's with me now. Tell me where you are. I'm getting the Rome train."

"That's absolutely stupid—I'm leaving for Pisanelli's wedding."

"Nando says it's the right thing to come. And I phoned Mamma in America."

"Magagna's driving me to the wedding."

"Mamma's worried."

"After all these years I'm sure your mother's got better things to worry about than her accident-prone husband."

"Why are you always so stubborn? Why don't you accept any help. I'm your daughter—I want to be with you."

"It's not necessary."

"And the girl?"

"What girl."

"Anna said there was a girl with you."

"Yes?"

"Well, how is she?"

"Dead."

"That's what Anna said. Who is she?"

"Listen, Pioppi. There's no good reason for you to come to Rome. I'm all right. I'll come to Bologna as soon as I can get away from the wedding. And in the meantime, stay at home. Stay with my little girls—because they need you. I'm all right, I swear to you. Don't worry about me—and there's no need to bother your mother. Tell her I'm well. Just look after my Francesca and my Piera. Kiss them for me, Pioppi. I'll be with you tomorrow. Ciao, amore."

54: Tiburtina

MAGAGNA DROVE.

He could have taken the autostrada but it was Saturday morning; there would be the convoys of trailer trucks, panting in the uphill sections and reckless as they lumbered downhill, carried forward by the momentum of the Apennines.

Trotti slept; his unshaven chin had sunk to his chest and he looked, with the bags under his eyes, like a crumpled insect.

Magagna took small, provincial roads, heading north. There was hardly any traffic. A few fishermen, returning on their Vespas from an early morning at the river. They held their rods like aerials and their legs appeared deformed by their protruding wader boots.

The Alfa Romeo came to a bridge and the car shook as it took the bump.

Trotti woke with a start.

It was a clear day and the mountains stood snow-capped against a cloudless sky.

"Sleep well?" Magagna asked. He had developed a double chin in Milan. He was wearing his aviator sunglasses and an unlit cigarette dangled from the corner of his mouth.

"I wasn't sleeping." Trotti rubbed his eyes. "You spoke to Pisanelli?"

"Nice day for a wedding."

"Did you speak to him?"

"I wouldn't worry about Pisanelli, commissario."

"Of course I worry about him. I always have."

"Anna'll make an honest man of him yet."

Trotti emitted a sharp sound of vexation. "Is Pisanelli all right? They didn't beat him up?"

"They?"

"In via del Tempio. The Carabinieri stuck a bag over my head, so I couldn't see much."

"Pisanelli's busy. You'd expect that, wouldn't you, on his wedding day?" Magagna made a gesture of his hand. "Your clothes are in the back, commissario. Pisa said you were threatening to turn up in goggles and a snorkel."

"He's lucky I'm turning up at all."

"That's not what Pisa says." Magagna gave him a quick look of appraisal. "Anything'd be better than those pajamas."

Trotti looked down at the military pajamas of faded khaki. The pajamas were short and Trotti wasn't wearing any socks. On his feet, he had a pair of black conscript shoes that Magagna had dug out of a hospital cupboard.

"You went to the Hotel Toscana?"

Magagna shook his head. "The Carabinieri took everything."

Panic in Trotti's voice. "The wedding gift for Anna, the photo? And the Carabinieri coat?"

"I found some clothes at Pisa's place—I think they belong to his father-in-law. Should fit you—old man Ermagni has a paunch, too."

It was another five minutes before they started to climb, winding between the vineyards, green and neatly terraced. Perhaps because of the fresh air coming through the open window or perhaps because he felt he was awakening from a bad dream, Trotti felt less tired.

"The sedative's losing its effect?" Magagna lit his cigarette. "You were in a bad way when we left the hospital."

"I'm no longer under arrest?"

"Apparently not."

"Never believe the Carabinieri."

"I don't suppose they think you're going to abscond to Tunisia."

"Or Guatemala."

"They know about the wedding. Perhaps that's why they didn't rough up Pisanelli," Magagna said and laughed loudly.

"That's funny?"

"Poor Pisa's already cripple enough." Magagna's eyes were fixed on the driving mirror. He said in a matter-of-fact voice, "We've been followed ever since we left Sant'Onofrio."

"Where?"

"They may have let you walk out of their military hospital, but your Carabinieri friends don't want to lose the commissario from Lombardy. Still convinced you're a lady killer."

"And a pervert."

"I could've told them that years ago."

55: Sapienza

SERA ROMANA

The lifeless body of a black woman was discovered yesterday in a quiet hotel in Trastevere.

Signorina Wilma Barclay, age 21, was found lying on a bed in the Hotel Toscana. She had been stabbed to death with a single blow. The weapon, a knife, had pierced her heart, and death was fast, but not immediate. Bleeding was not profuse.

The young American woman had met her death some two hours before the discovery of the body. She had recently been engaged in sexual activity.

Both Carabinieri and the Polizia di Stato were called to the gruesome scene by a couple of anonymous phone calls. Capitano Rizzi discovered the young woman lying naked on the bed. Although her wrists were attached to the bed, at the time of death she had the free use of all her limbs. There was considerable bruising to the face and on the inside of the thighs.

The hotel room had been rented to Piero Trotti, a retired commissario of the Polizia di Stato. Commissario Trotti who is a native of Lombardy and who for many years served with distinction in his native city, is helping the police in their enquiries.

Commissario Trotti was not in the hotel when Capitano Rizzi arrived. He was later located in an apartment near the Coliseum.

According to informed sources, Commissario Trotti is spending a few days' holiday in Rome.

In his native city, Commissario Trotti headed a children's section, specializing in the detection and prevention of child abuse. Last year, Commissario Trotti retired prematurely and at the time, there were rumors that he had been forced to leave, following irregularities. There were complaints from both children and parents.

The murder victim, Signorina Barclay, had been in the country for little over six months. Following a dispute, she had left Milan and the family she was working for. It is believed that she had been prostituting herself in Milan.

Barclay grew up in Chicago. She told her employers that she was looking for her Italian father. Her mother was once a military nurse serving on the USAF base at Padua.

It is not yet known whether Signorina Barclay was in any way connected with illegal organizations operating in Lazio.

A couple of years ago, the manager of a prostitution ring at Sapienza University was arrested for immoral earnings. He had created a network of foreign students who sold their services to businessmen.

While helping the investigators, Commissario Trotti collapsed and is presently under observation at the Ospedale Militare Sant'Onofrio.

According to informed sources, an arrest is imminent.

56: Sleep

"*LAST YEAR, COMMISSARIO Trotti retired prematurely and at the time, there were rumors that he had been forced to leave, following irregularities. There were complaints from both children and parents.*"

Magagna shrugged.

Trotti sounded hurt. "I retired because I had reached the age of retirement. What rumors? I never heard any rumors. Damn it, I was asked to stay on. The hospital wanted me to stay on. The Questore wanted me to stay on. The mayor wanted me to stay on."

Magagna asked, "And Signora Scola?"

"What about her?" Trotti pushed the newspaper off his lap and onto the floor of the car.

"Pisanelli always said Scola rather liked you."

"Signora Scola's a married woman."

For five minutes, neither man spoke, then Magagna said, "Who killed the American girl, commissario?"

"How would I know? I was with Pisa." Trotti pulled the newspaper back onto his knees and again he read aloud. "*She had been stabbed to death with a single blow. The weapon, a knife, had pierced her heart and death was fast but not immediate. Bleeding was not profuse.*" Trotti turned to his friend. "Killed with one blow, Magagna?"

"Seems unlikely, but if the knife pierced Wilma's heart, it's possible. Normally there'd be blood all over the place because of the pressure that builds up in the heart." Magagna took his eyes from the road, "You didn't see the corpse?"

"Of course I saw the corpse. The face was badly bruised. There was very little blood apart from the staining on the sheet."

"How do you explain that?" Magagna had worked with the Omicidi in Milan for eleven years.

"You tell me, Magagna. You're the expert."

Magagna answered thoughtfully, "Normally, if the stabbing pierces the heart, blood leaves splatter patterns."

Trotti caught his breath, "And death would be quick?"

"Quick but not immediate." Magagna added, "I saw no signs of blood on the walls."

Trotti turned in his seat. "How come the Carabinieri let you into the room?"

"Place was spotless. If it hadn't been for the two men in uniform at the top of the stairs and the scene of crime tape everywhere, I'd never've guessed there'd been a murder. Just the mattress that'd been taken away."

"Why did they let you in?"

Magagna raised an eyebrow. "If the knife pierced the ventricle of the heart where the blood goes from the heart to the lungs, death would've been slower. Blood would trickle out."

"Death wasn't slow." Trotti said querulously, tapping *Roma Sera* where it lay on his knees, "*The weapon, a knife, had pierced her heart and death was fast but not immediate.*"

"The girl didn't try to get up from the bed, so she probably never had time to seek help." Magagna took a drag on his cigarette, then with the cigarette between his fingers, gripped the steering wheel. "It's possible she died of asphyxia long before she ever succumbed to loss of blood."

"Suffocated?"

"Death from lack of oxygen. Quite possible, if the lungs were torn. She'd've drowned in her own blood."

"Drowned in her own blood," Trotti repeated dully.

There was another silence in the car.

"*Death was fast but not immediate.*" Trotti shivered and turned to look through the window of the Alfa-Romeo at the passing countryside. "My God."

(*Wilma smiled suddenly and at that moment, she was so pretty, so young, so sweet, so innocent that Trotti could not stop himself from sharing the smile.*)

Magagna remarked cheerfully, "After thirty-seven years in the police, you didn't know death was gruesome?"

"The long night awaits us all, Magagna."

57: Mani Pulite

MAGAGNA'S EYES WERE raised as he looked at the car's mirror. "You want me to lose your Carabinieri friends, commissario?"

"I want to get to Anna's marriage and I want to get there in one piece. It's the first day of the Renaissance."

"What?"

"That's what the dead girl said—the day Petrarch met Laura and fell in love—somewhere in France. Pisa's wedding day."

Magagna accelerated gently as he pulled the Alfa out of a curve. At the same time he took another draw on his cigarette. "Poor Pisa."

Trotti's ears were beginning to pop as the car rose into the hills. "I don't see why he's poor. Pisanelli's always loved Anna. Ever since she was a little girl."

"That was twenty years ago."

"He's been waiting for Anna to grow up."

"Or your goddaughter was waiting for Pisanelli to grow up."

"She used to be my goddaughter."

Magagna had a brief, bemused smile. "Used to be?"

"I haven't seen Anna in a very long time. She avoids me—Anna's never forgiven me for Pisanelli's accident."

"Pisanelli was doing his job."

"That's not what Anna thinks." Trotti shook his head.

"Now she's got them all to herself—Pisanelli and Pisanelli's pension. The girl ought to be grateful to you."

"Anna's not mercenary." Trotti then asked, "How's your wife, Magagna? How are the little boys?"

"Not so little anymore. They take up a lot of real estate in a small apartment."

"Then go back to Pescara. Get yourself a proper house." Trotti smiled. "Years since I last saw the boys."

"So I noticed," Magagna replied.

"How are they?"

"Strapping teenagers, more interested in basketball than soccer. And more interested in girls than in basketball." There was reproach in Magagna's voice. "Now you're retired, there's nothing to stop you from visiting them. From visiting my wife and me, while you're at it. You still know where Milan is, don't you? Or did you think it'd disappeared with Craxi and Craxi's socialists? With Operation Clean Hands?"

(Trotti had never been a good godfather to Anna, just as he had never been a good friend to Magagna and Pisanelli. Trotti had always been too busy, too caught up in his work. For more than twenty-five years, the only thing that ever really mattered was his job.

It had come as a surprise all those years ago when his driver, Ermagni, asked him to be godfather to Anna. Trotti had accepted more from weakness than conviction. Over the years he had scarcely seen little Anna, though she lived just a couple of blocks from the via Milano.

Then, in 1978, Anna was kidnapped. Just six years old and she had disappeared while playing in the public gardens of via Darsena.)

They were fast approaching a crossroads and a village. A series of billboards announced an AGIP filling station.

"They're still tailing us. Sure you don't want to lose them?"

"Risk my life? Miss the wedding of my goddaughter? Miss the Renaissance? No, Magagna. Let the bastards play their little games. They know I never killed her." Trotti added, "I was with Pisa. Wilma was murdered long after I'd left the hotel."

"She could've been murdered before arriving at the hotel."

Trotti shook his head. "The guy who hit me—he knew she'd rung me just as I was about to leave the hotel."

"Rang you?"

"Wilma wanted to see me, said she had something to tell me. Said it was important. Said she hadn't been totally honest."

"What does that mean?"

"She couldn't have phoned me if she was already dead."

"It's been known to happen."

"How could the body've been taken up the narrow stairs to my room without being seen?"

Magagna squinted as smoke rose into his eyes. "You sure you didn't kill her?"

"Too many people saw Pisanelli and me bickering. I've got a cast-iron alibi."

"Bickering, commissario?"

"Pisanelli was acting churlishly." Trotti sighed. "The stress of getting married."

Magagna asked, "Who killed your girlfriend?"

"She went to my hotel. Alive. Either willingly or under duress. Somebody knew I'd just left and probably took her there. Wilma was murdered there in my room. Murdered so I'd be seen as the culprit."

"It wasn't a sex killing?"

"She was raped, the poor girl, but nobody's going to find my DNA on her body."

"Sure you've got any DNA at your age?"

Trotti shook his head. "It's me the killer's out to get. Wilma was just a tool."

"Why get you?"

"According to Spadano . . ."

"Your Carabinieri friend?"

"What friends do I have, Magagna?" Trotti made an impatient gesture of his hand. "According to Spadano, there's a Sicilian hitman looking for me."

"A hitman should be able to distinguish between an aging, rather ugly white male and a pretty black woman."

"Something went wrong."

Magagna asked, "When'd you last see your Wilma?"

"I was looking for a taxi with Pisa and she was getting into a car. Outside Stazione Termini." Trotti went on, "You've read the paper. There'd been intercourse. That can only mean she got to the hotel, was raped, was murdered, and the police alerted—all within four hours."

"So?"

"Wilma was set up. The patsy."

"Set up by who?"

"Somebody she trusted."

"Who, Piero?"

"No idea. Wilma told me she knew nobody in Rome."

"Then she was lying?"

"I never got the impression she was lying."

"You always believe women. Particularly if they're young and pretty and have small tits."

"Lying or telling the truth, there was no reason for her to be raped on my hotel bed. Enough places in Rome to rape a woman without having to go to the Hotel Toscana."

"She was followed there?"

"Why go to Trastevere. I was going to meet Wilma in the via Veneto. After lunch."

Magagna was shaking his head, "You really believe all that crap about being Gracchi's daughter?"

Trotti laughed without humor, "You're just like Pisa."

"Flatter me."

"Pisanelli claims Wilma was using me."

"She wasn't?"

"She wasn't completely honest with me. She didn't tell me the whole truth. If she'd told the Americans in Milan she was Gracchi's daughter, she must've known her father was dead. And that's not what she told me."

"There'd've been no reason for you to go looking for a dead man."

"Precisely, Magagna."

"Gracchi was the bait. And you rose to the bait, commissario. Your young woman was manipulating you."

"That's not the impression I got."

"Now you'll never know."

"Now I'll never know," Trotti repeated thoughtfully, just as Magagna yanked at the steering wheel. Trotti's body was flung hard against the unyielding seatbelt.

The car swerved and left the road. The Alfa Romeo was traveling too fast for the four wheels to keep their traction.

58: Bordeaux

TWO PUMPS STOOD like forgotten aliens beneath a stout pillar. The yellow and blue sign, with its six-legged, fire-breathing animal advertised AGIP petrol.

Magagna jerked the Alfa Romeo into the forecourt of the petrol station. The rubber treads screeched on the concrete.

In a uniform of the same yellow and blue, a peaked cap pushed back on his head and the pink pages of *La Gazzetta dello Sport* between his hands, sat a young man.

At the squeal of tires, he looked up in surprise.

Magagna braked sharply; without waiting for the car to stop, he threw the gears into reverse.

"Trying to kill me?"

"You mustn't put ideas into my head, Piero."

The rubber screeched unhappily and Magagna rammed the car backwards into the shade of an immense hangar. The vehicle lurched on its springs.

"Now breaking my neck with whiplash."

Magagna pulled the handbrake with theatrical finality.

Trotti's head throbbed painfully; he wondered whether it really was spinal fluid he could taste on the back of his tongue.

Both men rocked in their seats and their bodies were tugged by conflicting momentum.

"Third car back," Magagna said. "After the four-wheel

drive and the black Fiat." He pointed a finger through the windscreen as he cut the motor.

Old bodywork and rusting engines littered the ground.

The following cars could not see Magagna's Alfa Romeo where it was now hidden in the lee of the garage.

"One Cherokee," Magagna said, holding out a finger. He added, "With Rome plates."

The Cherokee immediately flashed past. It disappeared down the road, promptly hidden by the curving row of trees.

"One black Fiat Punto." Magagna held up a second finger. "Plates illegible."

The Punto went past.

From where Trotti sat, he heard the motor rattle as it, too, was soon lost behind the trees.

Magagna grinned expectantly as he now held up three fingers.

"What's so funny, Magagna?"

A fraction of second later, the third car entered their field of vision, just twenty meters from where the two men were sitting.

"One rented Twingo. Bordeaux red, modern plates."

It was midday and the sun was at its spring zenith. Sunlight glinted on the red car roof as the Renault went past.

There was little time to catch sight of the driver.

"Friend of yours, Trotti?"

A young driver, leaning forward. A woman; headgear that looked like a turban.

Just the briefest glimpse of the profile.

"Wilma," Trotti said softly, so softly that Magagna hardly heard him.

Piero Trotti turned very pale.

59: Daisy

MAGAGNA PARKED THE car.

On foot the two men followed an unsurfaced road that ran between swaying fir trees.

(Trotti, still wearing the military pajamas, had bought a disposable razor in the AGIP garage. He had then shaved in the lavatory, looking at his face in the mirror where Luca from Ravenna had scrawled encouragement to Lazio and obscene insults for Manchester, spelled without an H.

"Spinal fluid?" Trotti smiled at his tired and bruised reflection, had then changed out of the pajamas and put on the dark suit from Pisanelli's house.

Magagna had brought him underwear but had forgotten socks and shoes. No choice but to keep the scuffed conscript shoes from the hospital.

Washed and shaved, Trotti felt much better, but cold at the ankles.)

As they approached the church, Trotti had to slacken the pace. The dull ache in his head seemed to get worse when he exerted himself.

Trotti was soon out of breath; Magagna strode effortlessly ahead. Magagna, now in his mid-fifties, looked tanned, well-fed and healthy.

"Wait for me."

"Time you gave up your boiled sweets, commissario."

"I'll worry about sweets when I'm dead."

"The sort of place you're going to, there won't be any sweets to worry about."

The dull ache in his head was made worse by the wind buffeting Trotti's face.

The wind grew stronger as they followed the road. It pulled at Trotti's hair and flapped noisily at his trouser legs, chilled his ankles.

The church stood at the top of a hill and the undulating countryside lay around and below them on all sides, like the background to a Renaissance painting.

Sixth of April—the first day of the Renaissance.

Chiesa Sant'Antonio was at the end of the lane, surrounded by a half circle of fir trees. From a distance the two men could hear the music of an organ.

Trotti's eyes had started to water.

They climbed up worn, marble steps and entered the church, pushing through the large wooden doors and the dark curtain.

Trotti was glad to get out of the wind.

Anna and Pisanelli were standing at the altar, facing a small, rotund priest.

The church was warm and very full; some people had not been able to find a place to sit down. Everybody seemed well dressed. Many of the women were wearing hats.

The air was thick with incense and the perfume of flowers.

Several guests turned to look at the new arrivals. Some smiled; Trotti had the impression they were expecting him.

Trotti and Magagna stood at the back of the church, near a couple of vases that overflowed with lilies.

All the flowers were white.

The pews were hung with chains of marguerites, and two tall lilies stood like trumpets at the end of each pew, lining the aisle.

Light streamed through the stained windows; saints, angels and nuns transfixed with eternal joy in the glass.

Trotti recognized Ermagni.

It was nearly twenty years since he had last seen Anna's

father. Ermagni had aged since the days when he was a taxi driver, had put on weight, but in his grey suit and with his carefully groomed white hair, he looked more like a prosperous banker than a taxi driver from Bari. Ermagni, a white carnation in his lapel, stood proudly beside his daughter.

Trotti could not see Anna's face but from behind, in her white gown, she looked as beautiful as he had always remembered her.

Beautiful and young and as innocent as the day she was kidnapped.

60: Pullman

THE MAN PULLED the sliding door shut—it folded like a concertina—and Trotti approached the small crowd.

Anna was hidden by the people standing in a pool of light. A man was crouching in front of her.

He stood up. "Commissario."

It was Magagna; he looked tired, but gave a thin smile as he approached Trotti.

"I thought you were at home."

"I was sleeping," Magagna said and shrugged his shoulders. He looked strange out of uniform. "So they phoned me." He took Trotti's arm and directed him towards Anna. The crowd—employees of the bus company, men in blue shirts and matching trousers—drew aside.

Anna was sitting on a chair. Her head lolled forward and her eyes were hidden by the fringe of dark hair; her feet just touched the concrete floor.

"She came in on the bus from Genoa. We tried to wake her up but she was sleeping." The bus driver wore neatly pressed trousers and there were large, damp patches at the armpits of his shirt.

Trotti asked the driver, "You called a doctor?"

"We let her sleep."

"When did she wake up?"

"Half an hour ago. Beppe recognized her."

"Beppe?"

"That's me." Another driver, small and wiry, with a friendly face. "I came in on the Piacenza run. I saw the girl sleeping and I recognized her. I used to know her father." The corner of his mouth implied that Ermagni was not a happy memory. He shook his head. "Poor little girl."

Trotti crouched in front of the child. Her eyelids were heavy and there was no flicker of recognition. She was still half asleep. Her body was slumped forward and she had difficulty in keeping her head upright.

"Get an ambulance—quickly."

Magagna was standing beside him. "It's coming, commissario."

For a while, nobody moved, nobody spoke. Trotti stared into the young, drugged eyes. Then in the distance, he heard the wail of the ambulance.

Trotti stood up.

61: Schubert

THE MONKEY-LIKE PHOTOGRAPHER danced and squatted and clicked, moving from the altar to the nave and back. He had various instruments that hung like necklaces at his throat. His camera flashed incessantly.

Trotti felt a pull at the sleeve of his jacket.

Two maids stood behind Anna, minute replicas of the bride but in short dresses. White shoes, white ankle socks. They had bows in their hair and they demurely held their hands behind their backs.

Pisanelli was wearing a frock coat. His thin hair, normally so unkempt and uncombed, had been trimmed at the collar. He looked taller, straighter and happier than he had appeared in Rome.

Pierangelo Pisanelli could not contain his joy. Whenever Pisanelli turned his head, Trotti was dazzled by the wide smile that split the middle-aged face. The crutch had disappeared. The groom leaned on a malacca cane.

The rotund priest mumbled, his voice relayed indistinctly from a microphone, as the couple were joined in holy matrimony. There was an exchange of rings, an exchange of smiles and a long kiss.

Then high above Trotti's head, the pure, clear voice of a boy sang Ave Maria.

Everybody seemed to be smiling, including Trotti and Magagna.

Trotti remembered his own marriage. He remembered Agnese and how beautiful she had been. He remembered how in love he had been, how full of hope. How happy they both had been.

Agnese now lived in America, probably still working for the big pharmaceutical company. They never spoke to each other; an occasional message relayed by Pioppi.

Again Trotti felt a tugging at the sleeve of his jacket and realizing someone needed his attention, he stepped back.

The girl was wearing a turban.

Trotti had been right all along about Wilma: she had not been lying to him.

The girl was pretty, young, and white; she smiled and at that moment, Trotti could not stop himself from sharing the smile.

62: Benacus

LAKE BRACCIANO WAS small; a mere pond, Trotti thought disparagingly, as he looked through the panoramic window.

(*"You'll be impressed by my lake."* One of the last things Trotti had said to the girl on the train.

"Your lake?"

"You must come and visit me at the Villa Ondina. Garda's beautiful and very big. More like a sea than a lake."

"Big lake, commissario?" Wilma giggled then, just as the Petrarca *was pulling into Rome. "You really don't know Lake Michigan, do you? You must come and visit me and my lake in Illinois."*)

The reception was being held in a hotel overlooking the placid waters. Trevignano Romano stood at the foot of the Sabatini mountains.

It was still too chill for the summer season. Within a month or so, visitors would return to throng the thirty kilometers of villages along the shoreline. There would be music and bronzed bodies lying at the lake's edge, clear skies and a warm sun.

For the moment, there was peace.

Sailing boats rocked gently beneath their stretched winter tarpaulins while birds picked their way through the mud on long, articulated legs.

Trotti heard his goddaughter's laughter.

Anna was surrounded by family and friends and he could hear the unrestrained happiness. She had chosen to ignore her godfather and he, in turn, had decided to keep out of the way.

Flowers—white peonies—everywhere and everybody seemed very happy, sharing in the couple's joy, touching each other, talking, laughing, drinking.

On the spotless white of the tablecloth stood a folded card with the neat, handwritten inscription: *Piero Trotti.* Another hand, writing with a different pen, had added: *The best policeman in the world.*

A woman's handwriting.

Trotti had been allocated a place at a small table, with his back to the groom, the bride and her family.

There was champagne—not Italian stuff, *méthode champenoise,* but the real thing—good, French and certainly expensive. After a first toast from Ermagni, everybody sat down expectantly for the meal.

"I'll be back," Magagna whispered in Trotti's ear and disappeared.

The food was excellent, and Trotti realized that he was very hungry after two days of saline drip. He ate greedily while the waiters danced in attendance. Between dishes, Trotti spoke with a young man from Somalia who worked with Anna at the FAO.

From time to time, a quartet of musicians set down their plates of food, took up their violins and broke into a romantic air from Verdi or Puccini or Donizetti.

"A most lucky girl," the man from Somalia said, showing a long, thin smile beneath a long, thin nose. His teeth were spotted with dark discoloration. His voice was wistful. "Quite beautiful and marrying the only man she's ever loved."

Trotti ate in silence and nodded politely while the man went on to talk about his own wife and family in Africa.

Speeches were given from the central table, more toasts were made, and the champagne and grappa and brandy and marsala ran free.

Sitting opposite Trotti, a buxom woman took little sips of Fiuggi water; she ate nothing but sometimes cleaned her teeth with a frayed toothpick. She dabbed at her ample chest and necklace with a napkin.

Soon the bridesmaids and the little boys in bow ties were running between the tables and playing hide and seek. They shrieked gleefully and ignored their parents' demands of silence.

The Somali man was right. Each time Trotti turned to steal a glance at his goddaughter, he was struck by Anna's luminous beauty.

It was hard to believe this was the same face as all those years ago, in his provincial city. The drugged child at the bus station.

Anna was no longer a little girl and her body, her dark eyes and the lustrous hair with its tiara, announced the fullness of her womanhood.

She smiled radiantly at the guests around her; her hand rarely left her husband's shoulder or his sleeve.

Pisanelli grinned foolishly. Confetti now speckled the lapels of the frock coat. The malacca cane had disappeared.

The newlyweds' happiness was almost tangible, and Trotti bitterly regretted the accident, regretted ever having asked Pisanelli to drive him to Alessandria that winter's evening in 1993.

As soon as it was politely possible, he rose, excused himself, left the table and taking the Esportazione cigarette that his African neighbor had proffered, Trotti stepped out through the large French windows. Out into the cool air and the failing light of evening.

Trotti had drunk too much champagne and the pain in his temples had got worse.

He made his way down the stairs—between the date trees and the hidden garden lights—to where the lake lapped gently at the shore.

"Commissario!"

Trotti turned and recognized the tall figure coming down the steps towards him.

63: Bongusto

"COMMISSARIO!"

Trotti, realizing there was no escape, gave a weary smile.

"Been having a few problems?" Ermagni said. "I heard you were in prison."

"In a military hospital. The Carabinieri like to play their games."

"Games, commissario?" In Ermagni's mouth, the title was curiously formal.

"Call me Piero. I'm retired now."

The two men met and shook hands on the wooden pier that jutted into the lake.

"I want you to talk to her, Piero."

It was getting dark and the air was cold against Trotti's bare ankles. The conscript shoes were thin and scruffy.

A few other guests had left the dining room and were chatting on the lakeside steps where they laughed, ate ice cream, or drank coffee or brandy and smoked.

"She still thinks the world of her godfather."

Trotti ran his tongue against the packed, dark tobacco of the Esportazione. There was a smell of impending night, of the lake's water, of perfume and of coffee.

The landing light of the jetty had come on; a couple of boats rocked gently on the lake's surface. Wind worried the masts, rattling the ropes. The reflection of the green lamp danced on the water's rippled surface.

From the reception came soft music. *Una rotonda sul mare.*

"Smoking now?" Ermagni held out an expensive lighter.

"I need something comforting."

"You used to be so abstemious."

Trotti brushed the flickering lighter away.

"Come." Ermagni pulled at Trotti's arm. "It won't take long."

Trotti tried to shrug off the large hand. "I've got to get back to Rome."

"Rome? You're booked into the hotel. And I want you to speak to my daughter." Pulling him by the arm, Ermagni led Trotti back towards the steps.

"Anna thinks it's all my fault."

"My daughter knows how you helped me."

Firmly held by Ermagni, Trotti reluctantly went up the steps, up to the brightness of the French window.

They entered the dining room and Trotti again tried to throw off the heavy hand.

He shook his head defiantly.

The floor was littered with crumpled napkins, cigarette stubs, crushed flowers, champagne corks, spilled water. The air was heavy with cigar smoke and mingled smells.

Only the white peonies were fresh and cool; the heat had opened them to their full extent.

Empty plates were strewn across the table. Anna had placed her head on her husband's shoulder. She appeared to be smiling to herself as she admired her finger and the wedding ring.

"Your daughter doesn't want to talk to me, Ermagni. You understand."

"Of course she does."

"She's busy."

"You must talk to her, commissario." Ermagni's eyes were strangely innocent; though his breath was heavy with grappa, he was not drunk.

"I think I've done enough."

"That's why you must talk to her."

"I nearly killed the man she loves. What more d'you want? What d'you want me to say?"

The large eyes looked at Trotti: large, bloodshot eyes that failed to understand the reluctance in Trotti. "You're her godfather, a policeman. Tell her the truth." Ermagni tapped his chest. He was wearing a suit of linen and a silk tie. "Since her mother died, she's been so good to me. My Anna loves you because she loves me."

"Nothing that I can say." Trotti pushed the hand away and at the same time placed his left hand on Ermagni's shoulder. "The most important day in her life. She doesn't need me."

"Commissario, you're part of the family."

Trotti turned and walked back towards the steps and Lake Bracciano. "I'm sorry, Ermagni."

"You've always been a good godfather." A voice that trembled on the edge of doubt. "A good man. A good friend."

Trotti stepped out into the evening. Clouds had come up from the west. The rippling waters had turned black.

Ermagni stood with his mouth open and his feet apart as he watched Trotti walk away. He moved towards the top of the steps.

Trotti did not turn.

"It'll only take you a minute."

Trotti continued down the steps, between the terracotta vases, towards the jetty.

"Please." A different voice—a softer voice. "Please, Piero."

Trotti stopped.

"You've always been our friend."

He smiled and turned.

Ermagni was still there, standing at the top of the flight of stairs, his large hands hanging at his side.

Anna held her father's arm.

"You're not going to kiss the bride, Piero Trotti? Not going to kiss your favorite goddaughter on the happiest day of her life?"

Signora Anna Pisanelli smiled, the smile bright in the darkness.

A smile that lit up the night, that lit up Lake Bracciano, that lit up the Apennines, that lit up Trotti's weary heart.

64: Polgai

"WHAT'S WRONG?"

"A pain in the side of my head."

"You didn't stop smiling all evening."

"That's a nasty accusation."

"Driving up in the car, I thought you were still in a coma. Or dead."

"Wishful thinking, Magagna."

Soon it would be dawn.

"You're cheerful, commissario. It's all rather unexpected and a bit frightening."

"What happened to you? You disappeared."

"I had things to see to," Magagna replied enigmatically.

"In Bracciano?"

"You never stopped smiling at Anna. I don't think I've ever seen you so happy."

"I was happy because my goddaughter's happy."

"I never knew you could dance, commissario."

"I can't."

"You danced enough with Anna. And with her pretty stepmother, the delightful Signora Ermagni."

Trotti did not feel tired although, as the reception progressed, he had drunk a considerable amount of local wine.

Smiling?

Thanks to the ballo liscio, for the first time since his return to the Hotel Toscana, Trotti had been able to think about something other than Wilma's death, something other than the bruised young body beneath the sullied sheet.

Magagna gave a muffled snort of laughter. "Sure you're not in love with your own goddaughter?" His large hands were folded behind his neck on the large pillow.

"Beautiful, isn't she?"

"Signora Pisanelli's always been beautiful. That's part of the problem."

It was a small room overlooking the lake. Comfortable beds, wooden paneling and a large bathroom with large mirrors.

"Problem?"

The two men lay parallel to each other in separate beds. From downstairs came the sounds of muted music, of furniture being rearranged, of tables being cleared.

Magagna said, "Anna's always known exactly what she wants."

"Thank goodness for that."

"It's going to be hard for Pisanelli."

"Marriage's hard for everybody—you're supposed to assume responsibilities."

No reply.

"Your wife, Magagna?"

"What about her?"

"I've been promising myself I'd drive up and see your wife and the boys."

"You have other priorities."

Trotti turned to look at his friend, but Magagna did not move.

"I thought with retirement I'd find the time to do the things I've always wanted to do. Instead, I do nothing and I see nobody. I seem to spend my afternoons looking at old films on the television. Watching films while my cousin talks to me about Holland and her neurotic grandchildren."

Light was coming from between the curtains as dawn arrived in the east.

Trotti asked softly, "How is she?"

"Who, commissario?"

"The last time I came, your wife gave me some Abruzzi

honey. Isn't it about time you took her back to Pescara? What sort of life is it for her, living with two boys in an apartment in Sesto San Giovanni? The boys need elbow room at that age."

"You think I like Milan?"

"I don't know anybody who does."

"There was a time when a woman could walk alone at night and not be afraid. Now there are Albanians and Yugoslavs everywhere. It's not even our Mafia; criminals and prostitutes from Eastern Europe. I take the boys to school every morning and I bring them home at lunch. I don't want them picking up syringes in the gutter—or worse."

Trotti asked, "Why not go back to Pescara?"

"Too late."

"I don't see why."

There was no reply.

"You've put in the mileage, Magagna. You could get a posting to the Abruzzi if you wanted. Get a job at the new POLGAI. Why stay in Milan? Foggy and damp and you no longer need the promotion."

"POLGAI? You think I have friends in high places?" Magagna rolled on his pillow, glanced briefly at Trotti. "Nobody owes me any favors." He pulled the blanket up to his ears and turned away.

"A couple of days in Milan would do me good. It would be good to see you all. We could even go to a basketball game— see Olimpia Milano. I suppose the boys want to be policemen like their father?"

Silence.

Trotti waited but Magagna did not answer.

More furniture being moved and then the music was turned off. *Una rotonda sul mare.*

To be policemen like their father—Trotti was tempted to ask his question again, but his jaw felt heavy and the words would not come to his lips.

Trotti was dropping off into sleep. A sleep free of blood-stained bedsheets, of pain, of saline infusion.

He dreamt of confetti and white peonies.

65: Wealth and Happiness

THE LAKE MUST have been volcanic in origin, for it appeared to be lying in a crater and was perfectly round. On the far side of the calm waters, woods ran down to the lakeside.

"I like the turban."

A sailing boat slid across the flat surface of Lake Bracciano.

"It's not really a turban." Lakshmi ran a hand through her loose black hair. "A scarf I wear when I'm driving."

"It suits you."

"I tie the knot at the front, in the style Papa liked. He had a fondness for everything Indian." She paused, lowered her head and raised her eyes to look at Trotti. "You realize India was all your fault, commissario."

Trotti found himself frowning and smiling at the same time. "I don't see why."

It would soon be midday, but the wedding guests were still taking a late buffet breakfast.

Pineapple and croissants on a spotless tablecloth. The smell of coffee and fresh bread rolls. The dining room was flooded with the spring sunshine. Last night's spilt champagne and confetti had vanished.

"You threw him in prison. Just a couple of nights— but long enough for Papa to realize he'd been going in the wrong direction."

"He needed me to tell him that?"

"Without those nights in prison, he'd never have left for India."

"Glad to have been of use."

"He belonged in India. Papa was an outsider, always looking for an alternative. Piemontese in Sicily, Sicilian in Piemont. A terrorist for the bourgeois, a middle-class poseur for Lotta Continua."

"Why poseur?"

"He wasn't willing to take up arms. That's why he broke with Lotta Continua. It'd become a recruiting ground for the Red Brigades and Papa loathed violence."

"Your father once told me the machine gun could be a clinical instrument."

"*Épater la bourgeoisie*, as he used to say." The girl smiled. "Papa spent over a year in India—at a place called Poona." She added reflectively, "He should've stayed there."

"He'd still be alive?"

She shrugged. "Giovanni Verga owned an old olive-growing estate in Trapani, and together they agreed to turn it into a commune. A transcendental meditation commune. So of course, back in Italy, Papa wore saffron—which didn't go down at all well. Sicilians don't like anything different. They don't like anything—or anyone—foreign."

"Not sure they like each other very much."

"You're Sicilian?" the girl asked in surprise.

"A peasant from the hills of Lombardy, signorina."

"Sometimes Papa'd put a little red spot on my forehead. A caste mark. It never occurred to him he was being sexist. Just as he couldn't see that wearing saffron and chanting his mantras in Sicily was patronizing. But then, I don't think Papa saw people as being different. He saw all humanity as one. He wanted to take the best from each culture. From each individual."

"Except me. Your father told me I was a fool—a dangerous fool, the worst kind of Fascist."

Lakshmi laughed happily. In the bright light of day, she no

longer looked like her half-sister. Lakshmi had a thin, pale neck. The long hair accentuated her Sicilian origins. An olive complexion. She was younger than Wilma, Trotti thought, probably a little over eighteen. Her body had the same structure of wide shoulders and narrow hips.

She was wearing jeans and a Benetton polo shirt. A gold medallion nestled in the hollow of her throat. An Indian goddess with many arms and legs.

"How old are you, Lakshmi?"

"Old enough."

"Old enough to hire a car?"

She smiled.

"What are you doing here?"

"Talking to you, commissario?"

"I don't imagine you were invited to the wedding."

"You can help us, commissario."

"How'd you know I was coming here?"

"I didn't." The set of her lips reminded him of Wilma. The same mixture of shyness and self-assurance. "My mother's been accused of aiding and abetting in the murder of her husband."

Quite suddenly, the oval face crumpled and tears began to run down her cheeks.

"Get her out, commissario. Get my mother out of prison."

"What on earth do you think I can do?"

"Everything." Lakshmi Gracchi produced a beige folder and tapped it. "Papa always spoke so well of you."

66: Ronald

VISSUTO, PALM SUNDAY EDITION
"I simply seek the truth."

Chiara Gracchi speaks in a calm voice, but it is clear that she is a woman in anguish.

"The pain I carry within my heart can't disappear. I merely hope the wounds will lessen in time. Living here in Turin, where my husband grew up, is helping me find new meaning to my life."

Does the sostituto procuratore really believe Signora Chiara Gracchi is guilty of aiding and abetting the killer who gunned down her husband as he was driving back to BRAMAN?

"The wretched man thinks I'm Clytemnestra. He thinks I murdered my husband just as Clytemnestra murdered Agamemnon."

Chiara Gracchi lights a cigarette. "The accusation of murder is not something you can shrug off. Yet if my imprisonment means at last there will be a trial, if my imprisonment means there's now a genuine desire to get to the bottom of my husband's death, believe me, prison's a cross I'm more than willing to bear. For myself, for the memory of Tino and above all, for the happiness of our daughter, Lakshmi."

Chiara Gracchi pushes her large glasses up onto her forehead. "My husband was murdered at a time when things were getting better for him, when his life—and the life of our family—was approaching an important turning-point. I was four months pregnant—and the evening of his murder, I miscarried. In just twenty-four hours, I lost the two most important men in my life—my husband and my son. Since that day, I've spent eight years going over Tino's death, going through all the documents coming out of the Trapani Palace of Justice. I've hardly slept, thinking of Tino, thinking of our son. I have constantly been searching for the elusive clue that'll unmask the assassins of my husband and my child. Eight years of nightmare. Fortunately"—and here Chiara Gracchi finally smiles from behind a cloud of smoke—"I have Tino's daughter beside me. Lakshmi's been a tower of strength. An adult when she was still just a little girl. Tino's murder has robbed her of her childhood, just as it has robbed her of the baby brother she dreamt of."

A mere nine years old at the time of her father's death, Elena Gracchi—Lakshmi to her friends—is now at liceo classico in Turin, where she is a model pupil. Her ambition is to become a television journalist, just like her beloved father.

"'Don't cry, mamma.' That's what she's always told me. It's Lakshmi's strength I'll miss if I'm put behind bars. Prison will change little else; even as a free citizen, I've endured every indignity our Italian justice can mete out to a woman. If the worst comes to the worst, if I'm permanently silenced, Lakshmi will continue the battle to clear my name, continue the battle to bring the murderers to justice. I'm not Clytemnestra—but like Electra, Lakshmi will avenge her father's death."

For eight years, the Trapani judges believed the murderer of Gracchi was an inmate of BRAMAN: Enzo Beltoni, an ex-addict who had been recruited by Giovanni Verga to help in the running of the commune.

The judges knew about an acrimonious quarrel between Enzo Beltoni and Valerio Gracchi just a week before his death. Gracchi accused Beltoni of selling heroin to the BRAMAN inmates. He also accused Enzo Beltoni of being in the pay of the Trapani boss, Roberto Palermeri. In anger and in the presence of witnesses, Gracchi threatened to have Beltoni arrested. Enzo Beltoni replied by threatening to kill Gracchi.

Following an initial interrogation in October 1988, Enzo Beltoni chose to abscond. He hastily left BRAMAN, Trapani and Sicily. It was believed at the time that he returned to the United States, where he had spent much of his childhood and where in his youth he had murdered a man.

According to this, the official theory, Gracchi was killed by Enzo Beltoni with the help of the Trapani Mafia.

Valerio Gracchi, one of the founding journalists of Lotta Continua when it was a fledgling political tract in Trento, had taken it upon himself to attack the Mafia on television. The local boss, Roberto Palermeri, no longer able to tolerate the daily attacks that Gracchi mounted against him—and against the wealthy politician Mario Agrate—ordered Enzo Beltoni to silence Gracchi for good.

Over the years, frequent and insistent dissenting voices have claimed that Gracchi's death had nothing to do with Palermeri, Mario Agrate or the Mafia in Western Sicily. Indeed, the investigating magistrates have never found any corroboration from pentiti. No criminal giving state evidence has ever spoken of a link between Roberto Palermeri and Gracchi's death.

For many, the true motive behind Gracchi's death is to be found in BRAMAN. The Guardia di Finanza continues to look into the murky accounting at BRAMAN—and more importantly, into the nature of the ties that held Gracchi, his wife Chiara and Giovanni Verga together.

Chiara Gracchi promptly dismisses such theories. "It's true my husband and Giovanni Verga disagreed—at times almost violently—about the nature of BRAMAN. Yet there can be no doubt in my mind Tino was killed by the Mafia. I bear no grudge against the sostituto procuratore. He has his job to do; I am convinced of his good faith. A job that's difficult elsewhere becomes impossible in a place like Trapani—a city backward in outlook, yet thoroughly modern in its criminal methods. The globalization of the drug trade and the

Trapani ramifications of this trade—that's what my husband denounced on the very evening he was slain."

Chiara Gracchi pauses, inhales more smoke from her German cigarette. "I find it incredible anyone could possibly believe I was involved in my husband's death. I was carrying his child in my belly." She pauses before continuing, weighing her words carefully. "My loathing of Giovanni Verga, my husband's associate and alleged friend, is total. I have no idea who Giovanni Verga thinks he is. All I can say is he's a person I despise intensely. I have not seen him in a very long time—and I thank God for that."

After eight years of enquiry, in Trapani, in Palermo and even in Nice where BRAMAN ran a French rehabilitation commune, still very little is known about the death of Valerio Gracchi other than that he was shot with eight bullets to the head and body as he was driving back to BRAMAN in a Fiat Duna on September 26, 1988.

For the last couple of years, the Trapani magistrates, aided by the enquiries of the Guardia di Finanza into the finances at BRAMAN, have been taking a hard look at the relationship between Gracchi's widow and Giovanni Verga.

Like Clytemnestra, was Chiara Gracchi in love with another man? Like Clytemnestra, did she feel her husband had become an obstacle to her happiness? To her happiness and the happiness of Giovanni Verga? Was Gracchi really the father of the child she was expecting? Had Gracchi's role as the scourge of the Mafia become a threat to their power at BRAMAN?

Verga, originally from Trapani, was a good friend of various Socialist politicians in Milan. Meeting with Gracchi in India, he decided to set up a rehabilitation center in Sicily. Before long, considerable financial support was pouring into BRAMAN.

At a time when Bettino Craxi was prime minister and Craxi espoused the hard-line position of President Reagan on the drug trade, Giovanni Verga's stand against all forms of drug use was appreciated by Craxi's inner circle.

BRAMAN received a significant amount of financing,

not just from Craxi's Socialist government but also from the autonomous region of Sicily.

Drugs were certainly a cause of conflict between the two founders of BRAMAN. On the one hand, Giovanni Verga, the Sicilian businessman with close ties to the government in Rome, needed to show his pro-Socialist loyalty by endorsing Craxi. On the other, Valerio Gracchi, the eternal outsider, the Sicilian from Turin, the ex-university lecturer, the ex-journalist of *Lotta Continua*, the convert to Indian religions who could see no harm in a joint, had become a serious embarrassment. Gracchi's "hippy" libertarian views constituted a threat to the steady flow of subsidies.

The widow lowers her cigarette. "People say Giovanni Verga and I were lovers. Nothing could be further from the truth. Although there was a time when I admired Giovanni Verga profoundly, and although there were periods of great stress in my married life, my first concern's always been for the happiness of our daughter, Lakshmi. Despite his failings, Gracchi was a good father. I could never have loved another man as I love Tino."

67: Oenone

"MY MOTHER'S NOT Clytemnestra."

Trotti shook his head as he set the *Vissuto* magazine down on the beige folder.

"Solenghi thinks my mother killed my father."

"Who's Clytemnestra and who's Solenghi?"

"The sostituto procuratore in Trapani—he's from the north. Solenghi hates my mother, and now he's had her arrested and put in prison."

"Why?"

"Because she killed Papa."

"Why'd your mother kill your father?"

"Of course she didn't kill him," Lakshmi retorted. "Mamma loved him. And Papa always loved her in his own way. Ours was a happy family—a very happy family—until Papa was murdered. Solenghi needs to show he's in charge. After waiting eight years, he's suddenly decided he's found Papa's murderer."

"Why wait eight years?"

"You tell me," Lakshmi said, and again she started to cry.

Trotti leaned forward and squeezed her hand where it lay on the beige folder.

"He's now decided my father wasn't killed by the Mafia." Lakshmi repressed a sob.

Guests at the neighboring tables turned to look at the old policeman and the unhappy adolescent.

"Clytemnestra's from BRAMAN?"

The girl smiled through her tears. "You never studied mythology?"

"I left school at the age of fourteen." Trotti released her hand. "A long time ago—in those days, not everybody could stay at school. Work to be done in the fields. There was Mussolini. There was the war. War in Africa, in Spain and Greece and Russia. Then there was the war with Hitler and the Repubblichini." Trotti breathed in. "Just an ignorant peasant, I'm afraid."

For a moment, she looked at Trotti's hand where it rested beside hers on the folder. Very briefly, she touched the knuckles of his finger. Then, taking the fork, she prodded her slice of pineapple.

She blushed. "I'm sorry, commissario," she said without raising her eyes.

In the large, bright dining room, Trotti had the feeling they were alone together, just him and the girl, and that the lake was some picture projected onto the panoramic window. Lake Bracciano and the chattering guests at the other tables had nothing to do with either of them.

They were alone.

"Solenghi maintains my mother killed her husband, just as Clytemnestra killed Agamemnon."

"Please explain, Lakshmi."

She jabbed a slice of pineapple, "Agamemnon was the king of Mycenae and commander of the Greek army in the Trojan War. Helen was the most beautiful woman in all Greece. She was courted by almost every prince in Greece, but in the end she married an old man."

"What possible interest could a beautiful young woman have for an old man?"

"Menelaus—the king of Sparta—happened to be the richest of the suitors."

"Helen was in it for the money?"

The girl gave a nod, "At least, until she met a handsome prince from Troy called Paris, and Paris fell in love with her."

Trotti laughed.

"What's funny? You don't believe in love at first sight, commissario?"

"Not with a married woman."

The girl brushed away a tear with the back of her hand. "Paris was so smitten by Helen that he left his girlfriend and abducted Helen. Left Oenone and ran off with Helen to Troy."

"Where they lived happily ever after?"

"Happily ever after for ten years. Menelaus wasn't thrilled about losing his young bride, and he persuaded his brother Agamemnon to organize an expedition of all the Greeks against Troy. That's why Agamemnon and the Greeks set off and for ten years besieged the city of Troy. The impenetrable, walled city of Troy."

"The young man didn't get bored with the stolen wife?"

She said in irritation, "You don't believe in the power of love?"

"Life's not very romantic by the time you reach my age."

"Nobody's too old for love."

"You'd be surprised."

"Nobody's too old for love—not even you, commissario."

"Tell me about Clytemnestra."

"The Greeks built a horse and left it in front of the city gate before finally sailing back to Greece. The Trojans assumed the horse was a gift and dutifully hauled the thing inside Troy's walls—and that, of course, was their undoing. Greeks hiding in the horse jumped, burned down the city, and massacred the Trojans. After ten years, Helen was reunited with her rightful husband."

"Soiled goods by that time."

"Helen's considered to be the daughter of Nemesis because she caused such unhappiness."

"Unhappiness?" Trotti poured himself another cup of coffee from the plastic beaker. "Unhappiness is not being able to drink and eat what you like." He spoke to himself rather than to the girl. The coffee was strong and bitter and Trotti winced as he drank. "What's all this got to do with your mother?"

"While Agamemnon was away at war, besieging the city of Troy with his army, his wife Clytemnestra had taken a lover."

"Ten years's a long time for a woman just as much as a man."

"You know about these things, commissario?"

"I attained peace of the senses years ago."

"The lovers decided to kill Agamemnon." Lakshmi said. "Actually, Clytemnestra had another reason for wanting to kill her husband. When the gods had refused a favorable wind to the Greek fleet, a sacrifice seemed the best way of appeasing them. Agamemnon had sacrificed their eldest daughter, Iphigenia. Ten years on, when her husband got back, Clytemnestra welcomed him, but that same evening, as Agamemnon was taking a bath, Clytemnestra murdered him." Lakshmi stopped.

"A dysfunctional family?"

"Most families are, commissario." Lakshmi sighed. "That left the problem of Electra—Clytemnestra's daughter. According to the papers, I'm Electra and I persuaded Orestes."

"Orestes?"

"My brother."

"You just told me you were your father's only child. You're confusing me, Lakshmi, with all your talk of Agamemnon and Clytemnestra and Electra and Orestes."

"Not me, commissario. It's the newspapers." The girl's hand lay atop the magazine. "They say my mother murdered my father."

"She didn't?"

"You're being deliberately obtuse?"

"It's not deliberate. If you're Electra, you seem to think your mother's innocent."

The pale skin was turning red. Lakshmi put down the fork and raised her glance to meet Trotti's. Her breath smelled of pineapple.

"My mother's innocent."

68: Uncle

TROTTI POINTED AT the magazine. "It says you hope to be a journalist?"

"Journalist or novelist—I take after Papa. Mother's the realist, thank God for that. In many ways, I think she should've married Zio Chicchi. She had more in common with him than with Papa. Papa was a dreamer and an idealist. Like me."

"Zio Chicchi?"

"I always called him Uncle Chicchi."

"Him?"

"Giovanni Verga. When I was a kid, he was like an uncle."

Trotti was surprised, "You liked him?"

"Always very kind to me. And it was nice to have somebody a bit more realistic around the place, somebody with his feet firmly on the ground. There was a time—I was still very little—when Papa lived on a cloud—a cloud of dope. Unlike Papa, Zio Chicchi'd grown up. He'd moved on to making important friends and lots of money. Zio Chicchi was set on turning BRAMAN into an empire—but Papa wasn't interested in power. Papa always saw himself as a thinker."

"That's why there were rumors about your mother and Giovanni Verga?"

The smile vanished from her face. "You're not going to start talking rubbish, are you, Commissario Trotti?"

"They had an affair?"

"Of course not."

"But they liked each other a lot."

"My mother loathes Giovanni Verga."

"Your mother liked him at the time your father died."

The girl said nothing. She raised her head and turned to stare out of the window.

"Your mother liked Giovanni Verga at the time your father died—even though she was pregnant."

69: Waterloo

AT THE OTHER tables, the guests were rising, preparing to leave for the long drive back to Rome.

"I couldn't have asked for a kinder or gentler father. I used to curl up in his arms and fall asleep. Those were the happiest days of my childhood: the smell of his clothes, of his lavender soap, and just a hint of a smoked joint. I felt safe." Lakshmi laughed before adding, "Now that I'm a woman, I can see how selfish Papa was."

The young woman stopped and looked at Trotti. Her fingers touched the *Vissuto* magazine where it lay open on the table. "Look," she said pointing to the photograph beneath the title in large red letters.

Trotti reached across the table and picked up the magazine. A color photograph taken at BRAMAN.

Trotti held it out at a distance to get the page into focus—he had left his glasses in Rome, at Lia Guerra's. He studied the text beneath the blurred picture:

A GROUP OF PEOPLE AT BRAMAN.

According to the magazine, the photograph had been taken a year before Gracchi's death—June 1987. Men, women and a couple of children who stood or sat in the Sicilian sunshine, beneath an olive tree.

Gracchi and his wife Chiara were on the left of the photograph, standing hand in hand, smiling at the camera.

Gracchi was dressed in a white linen suit with a matching Panama hat.

"The clothes are an improvement," Trotti remarked. "When I knew your father, he wore flared jeans and tight-fitting shirts."

"And listened to Abba and watched *Saturday Night Fever?*" Lakshmi smiled fondly. "He liked to show me the old photos. He was so thin in those days. He always said those were the best years of his life. As he grew older he put on a lot of weight. And stuck to the Indian robes."

In the photograph, Chiara Gracchi was almost hidden beside her husband. She held a smoking cigarette in her hand. She was not looking at the camera, but smiling at the little girl at her feet.

Lakshmi, dressed in a saffron dress, sat cross-legged on the ground. Trotti had no difficulty in recognizing her; there was a red spot on her forehead. The dark hair was hidden by a turban. She eyed the camera and the cameraman inquisitively, with her head to one side.

Lakshmi tapped the photograph. "Papa never loved her."

"Never loved who?"

"It wasn't Mamma he loved. Despite the big smile."

"That's not what your mother says in the article."

"They were friends—more than friends. Papa didn't love her."

"They were husband and wife. And later she got pregnant for a second time."

"Papa tried as best he could to assume his responsibilities—it was more from love of me than for love of my mother. It would've been better if I'd never been born. Without a child, they could've drifted apart. Very amicably, of course, but that would've been better for everybody."

"Then why did she get pregnant again?"

"I kept them together. They were about to divorce when she discovered she was carrying his child. In time Mamma would've drifted into Zio Chicchi's bed." Lakshmi said, still smiling. "With him, she knew where she stood."

"Your mother loved Giovanni Verga?"

"Papa never gave Mamma the attention she deserved."

"There was an affair between Giovanni Verga and your mother?"

"Several—but never consummated. More a meeting of the minds. It couldn't have been easy for Papa—that's why he hid behind a cloud of dope. That's why he was so depressed—until he rediscovered himself as an investigative journalist."

"He knew Giovanni Verga was screwing her?"

She looked at him coldly. "My mother's never loved anyone other than Papa."

"But Papa didn't love her?"

Silence.

"The short side of the triangle?"

"Commissario Trotti, there was nothing physical between Zio Chicchi and my mother."

"But there was another woman in your father's life?"

"Mamma could put up with anything—she still does. It was for me she set her foot down. She insisted Papa be present for me. A woman always knows when she's not desired—she could live with that. It was for my sake Mamma couldn't accept a divorce."

There was a long silence until Trotti repeated his question. "There was another woman in your father's life?"

"There'd always been other women."

"At the time he was murdered, was there someone else?"

A small nod. "Someone who could never love him as Papa wanted to be loved."

"Who?"

A brief silence.

"Who?"

Lakshmi stretched her finger and pointed to the upside-down photograph that Trotti was holding away from his eyes. Her finger pointed to the right side of the photograph, to a woman sitting away from the others.

Trotti tipped his head slightly to get a better look.

The woman was staring at the camera with dark eyes.

Her legs were demurely crossed at the knee, and one hand lay loosely on her lap. She was wearing tights and a black cardigan.

Unlike the other people in the photograph, she was not wearing white. Unlike the other people in the photograph, she was not smiling. The strong, regular features appeared devoid of emotion.

"She'd told father years before she could never love him. Him or any other man."

"Lia Guerra?"

70: Baritone

"I WANT YOU to take this."

"What?"

"This folder—there are some photocopies. And my phone number." From the beige folder she took a cassette. "This, too. It comes from a program Papa was working on."

"What do you want me to do with it?"

"Listen to it—that's what people usually do with audio tapes."

Trotti frowned.

"If you intend to help my mother, you might find it useful. It was recorded not very long before his death. Papa intended to do an autobiographical video and this was going to be the soundtrack."

"What made your father want to do anything autobiographical?"

"His idea of a testament." Lakshmi shrugged. "Staying alive would have been the greatest testament for me. I told you—Papa was selfish without realizing it. He loved people—but he never understood loving means having to make personal sacrifices." The girl caught her breath. "He found it a lot easier to be a martyr to the cause than a good father. Papa never gave a second thought to the years of loneliness for Mamma and me. Loneliness and now prison."

"Your father knew the people who wanted to kill him?"

"Everybody wanted him killed—that wasn't what mattered."

"What mattered, Lakshmi?"

"His appointment with destiny. Or so Papa said. Twenty years earlier, in Trento, he thought his destiny was political. Those were the days when he believed Lotta Continua would change the world. By 1988, he realized the only way to change the world was by telling the truth. Papa liked to see himself as an educator. He was so happy with his new job as a television journalist—and he knew he had to die for it."

"He knew he was going to die?"

Lakshmi gave a sad smile. "A priest came to TRTP on one occasion. Like a black beetle, he spent a day sitting on the settee at the studio, waiting to speak to Papa in private. The dusty little cleric must have gotten up early that morning and driven in from some forgotten Sicilian parish in the hills just to tell Papa he was talking too much."

"The warning had no effect?"

"You could never tell Papa what to do." Lakshmi lowered her voice to a baritone imitation of her father: "The true revolution's here in Trapani."

Trotti laughed.

In the same deep voice, the girl continued her imitation. "Our struggle in 1968 wore the threadbare clothes of the cultural revolution, the clothes of Marxist ideology. In Lotta Continua, we were incapable of inventing new terms, a new language. What I now see here in Sicily is not a revolution, it has nothing to do with Marxism. It's something much more important: life itself. It is the right to dignity. It is the fight to the death against the forces of evil, against the Mafia. It is the battle I wanted to fight twenty years ago. The fight for justice."

There was a moment's silence before Trotti realized she had started crying again.

"When the papers talk about Papa, they talk about the courageous enemy of the Mafia. The fighter, the hero. In Trento, where it all began, where he upset the first of many

apple carts, there's even a memorial museum in his name."
She looked at Trotti. The tears had started running down the
soft skin of her cheeks.

"Please don't cry."

"All I ever wanted was a father." Lakshmi dropped the
cassette into the folder and hurriedly stood up. "Not a bloody
martyr."

She did not look at Trotti, but turned and walked fast
towards the door of the bright dining room.

Trotti's troubled glance followed her.

Two men were standing in the doorway. One was in a black
uniform; the other held an unlit cigarette between his lips and
was leaning against the door.

Lakshmi brushed past the men without sparing them
a glance.

The men were looking at Trotti. An officer of the Carabinieri and the tall, dome-headed Neapolitan detective.

Portano was smiling.

71: Tributary

"THANK YOUR FRIEND and his charming young bride,"
the man said with a self-congratulatory grimace as he pushed
away from the doorjamb.

"What are you talking about?"

"How else d'you think I knew where to find you?"

"I said I was coming to my goddaughter's wedding."

"You should have stayed in the hospital, Trotti. You'd
have saved me a lot of bother." The voice was grating. "And
yourself. Perhaps you think I enjoy chasing you halfway
across Italy."

The thin blond hair had been ruffled by the wind off the
lake. Portano was wearing the same shabby, crumpled suit.
His white shirt was grubby and at the collar, his tie was askew.

"You want to put the handcuffs on?" Trotti held out his
wrists. "You're going to beat me up again?"

"You're not under arrest, commissario." The officer of
the Carabinieri held a peaked cap under his arm. "No need
for handcuffs," he added, in a soft Ligurian accent. He gave
Trotti a reassuring smile. "Your presence's required in Rome
and I know I can count on your cooperation. There shall be
no violence."

Trotti looked at the officer. He was young, not yet out of
his twenties, with long lashes and dark hair. He was wearing
gloves. He looked like something off a recruiting poster.

The Carabiniere said, "Perhaps you'd care to collect your things so we can make a prompt departure."

"Just the clothes I'm standing in."

The voice was firm, the glance unwavering. "Best get your things now, commissario."

Lakshmi had disappeared, but from a distance, several guests were watching the three men. The music—Tony Renis— had been turned down. No noise came from the kitchen.

Trotti's glance was on Portano. "You haven't called me a pervert yet?"

The detective was lighting another unfiltered cigarette. "Going to be difficult, Trotti?"

"While Commissario Trotti fetches his stuff, get yourself a drink, Portano." The Carabiniere took Trotti by the arm. "Come, commissario."

The detective exhaled a stream of smoke from his narrow nostrils. Portano smiled knowingly and entered the dining hall.

The officer, without letting go of Trotti's arm, accompanied him upstairs. Trotti put up no resistance.

Pierangelo Pisanelli and his young wife were standing at the top of the stairs. Pisanelli was wearing jeans and there was a blank smile on his face. Neither Pisanelli nor Anna spoke as Trotti brushed past them, but when their eyes met, Trotti was aware of the anxious look on Anna's young face. She, too, was wearing jeans and a pullover.

They were about to leave on their honeymoon.

Walking purposefully, the young Carabiniere went along the corridor, his hand on Trotti's sleeve. A maid scuttled out of the way as Trotti entered the hotel room.

"I don't have any baggage." Trotti sat down on the rumpled sheets of the bed. "Just the pajamas they gave me in the hospital."

The officer closed the door and leaned against it. He let out a sigh while throwing his cap onto the table.

"My goddaughter now thinks you've arrested me."

The officer looked at him. The young face tried to smile, "I needed to get you away from Portano, commissario."

"You think I'm running away because I killed the black girl?"

"Portano's mad."

"He enjoys hitting people," Trotti observed.

"He's mad," the Carabiniere repeated and he tapped the side of his head. "Certifiably mad. An obsessive man."

Trotti could taste the coffee at the back of his throat and he felt giddy. For a moment, he glanced through the window. Several sailing boats moved across the lake.

It occurred to Trotti that there was no river running in or out of Lake Bracciano.

From beyond the closed door came the sound of people walking along the corridor and the heavy fall of feet down the stairs.

"I want to say goodbye to my goddaughter properly—wish her luck on her honeymoon. Would you mind waiting just a few minutes?"

The young officer looked sadly at Trotti. "You've got to go now."

Trotti raised his shoulders in a shrug. "Give me a glass of water, would you?" The taste of coffee rose unpleasantly at the back of his throat.

The uniformed officer moved into the bathroom, took a glass from its cellophane wrapping and poured water from the tap. Trotti drank the proffered glass in a single gulp.

Like a child being fed.

"Thank you," he said. He could smell the policeman's cologne.

"Let's go now."

"I've got no luggage."

The man in uniform paced across the hotel room and opened the window. "Go."

"Go where?"

"Take the Alfa. Get out of here. Go down the fire escape— without being seen. Take Magagna's car."

"Take me back to Rome."

"Head north, Commissario Trotti, and don't get caught speeding. I can deal with Portano."

"I want to go to Rome."

"Later you can go wherever you want, commissario," the young officer said and pushed the retired policeman through the window onto the sunlit verandah. "Go north and . . ."

"What?"

"Be careful."

"Careful of what?"

"Careful of Portano. You might not get another chance."

72: Trash

STEPS RAN DOWN the side of the building. For a moment he hesitated; almost beneath him, the boats danced on the lake's surface where they were tied to the jetty.

He followed the stairs carefully, gripping the iron rail, wondering whether he was visible from the dining room.

Once Trotti reached the terrace, he realized that to get to the parking lot, he would have to go past the dining room's panoramic window.

To do so meant running the risk of being seen. Portano had only to be looking in the direction of the lake to catch sight of him. The detective was probably at that moment taking his coffee and smoking his cigarette. Trotti thought he caught a fleeting glimpse of the man through the glass.

Trotti pressed his back against the wall. It was warm in the sunshine. He was sweating and his heart was beating much faster than it should do when you are sixty-eight years old, when you have taken your retirement and when you should be at home, basking in the warmth of your family with your Dutch cousin, your daughter and your two granddaughters, watching television and relaxing.

He could not walk past the window without being seen; there was no choice but to go left, following the wall of the dining room. Past the whitewashed flower pots standing on their stumpy, chipped columns.

There were windows along the side of the building, but they

were at waist height and unlike the panoramic window that faced the lake, there was a thin lace curtain.

Bending down as far as he could, Trotti followed the warm, concrete passage between the dining room and the balustrade. The conscript shoes creaked unpleasantly.

On the other side of the passage, there was a sharp drop. The hotel's cellar was probably beneath Trotti's feet.

Trotti was too old for gymnastics. It was painful to bend over, and he was short of breath. He advanced as fast as he could, trying to muffle the sound of his feet on the concrete.

He felt stupid and Trotti knew he was unfit—since retiring he had taken very little exercise.

"Going somewhere?"

Slowly, very slowly, Trotti straightened his back.

"I asked if you were going somewhere, commissario?"

Portano was standing in the doorway, one hand casually in his jacket pocket and the cigarette smoldering in his mouth. A broad smile. With the other hand, he shielded his eyes from the midday sun.

"I get the feeling you don't want to come to Rome." He was standing in front of the door to the kitchen. Portano's white shirt was even grubbier in the sunlight, and his tie appeared further askew.

A grey refuse bin stood beside the doorway.

"I really was hoping I wouldn't have to use the handcuffs." Portano took his hand from his pocket and held up a pair of American cuffs. "Silly me—thinking you were going to be reasonable, Commissario Trotti. A funny lot, you Northerners. Must be all that polenta you eat."

He beckoned for Trotti to hold out his wrists but before Trotti could react, before he could even massage the hurting muscles in his back, Signora Anna Pisanelli appeared at the kitchen door.

The Neapolitan turned and as he turned, Anna struck him forcefully in the groin with the malacca stick.

There was an explosion of escaping breath, and then Anna hit Portano a second time, this time directly between the legs.

The man grunted as he crumbled to the ground.

73: Wojtyla

IT WAS A long time since Trotti had driven a car. After Pisanelli's accident, he had been wary of cars, and in the last summer months at the Questura before retirement, he had frequently cycled to work. A friend in automobile maintenance restored the Ganna that had been gathering dust in the cellar for the last twenty years; Gerolamo had baked a grey coat of enamel onto the old frame and he had replaced the sprung saddle for something rather sporty in leather—"a Brooks," Gerolamo said with pride.

Several months later, when Anna Maria arrived in via Milano, she started complaining about not being able to get out to the new shops. "If you want me to do the cooking, Rino, I've got to have something to cook," she said in a querulous voice that kept the trace of fifty years in Holland, fifty years of bullying her Dutch husband. "You do understand." Trotti dutifully promised her he would get a new car.

In the end, it was Anna Maria who found an old Seicento and it was she, sitting perched on cushions behind the steering wheel, peering through her Count Cavour glasses, who drove Piero about the city on the Po.

Trotti now headed north in the rental car.

The tank was full and the engine was powerful. He took the minor roads.

It was a pleasure to be on his own again, the first time, Trotti realized, since meeting Wilma in Florence.

Midday and hardly anybody on the road from Bracciano—a truck of refrigerated meat, the occasional farm vehicle crossing the road.

Trotti could find no map in the glove compartment so decided to follow the signposts to Viterbo. He turned on the radio. Easter Sunday and religious music from the RAI.

The second day of the Renaissance.

(*"Take care of yourself."*

His goddaughter had hurriedly accompanied him to the parking lot and to the Fiat. The car was not locked and the key was in the ignition.

"Whose car is it?"

"My father rented it for the honeymoon—another of his presents."

"What are you going to do without it?"

"We'll use Papa's."

"I can't take your car. Not today of all days."

"Take it and go. Stay with your daughter, stay out of the way. That man wants to hurt you, zio."

"And the car?"

Anna placed a finger on his lips and Trotti reluctantly smiled. Then she pushed her godfather into the driver's seat. A few guests were leaving the hotel, but nobody seemed to be taking any notice of Trotti and his newly married goddaughter.

"Go to Bologna," she said, kissed him on the forehead and watched as Trotti turned on the powerful engine. She did not wave.

He pulled out of the parking lot. A last glance in the mirror and he saw Anna holding her hand to her mouth.)

Trotti appreciated the assisted steering. He enjoyed the way the car responded to his touch. The driving seat was comfortable. The music reminded him of the years when Pioppi sang in the church choir.

After twenty minutes, the sun disappeared behind clouds and it started to rain.

A Volkswagen Golf?

Trotti switched on the headlights in the gathering gloom while the car's single wiper beat a relentless rhythm. He made good time despite the rain that grew heavier and bounced off the road's surface. Taking the ring road around Viterbo, he continued northwards towards Lake Bolsena.

He should not have drunk the coffee. He no longer felt sick, but he needed to stop. After a long ascent, Trotti reached a village in the hills. It was almost lost in the low clouds.

Trotti had left his Bancomat credit card in Rome along with his wallet and his glasses. All he now had were the few thousand lire that Magagna had given him at the AGIP station.

He parked the car in a wet piazza and ran to a small bar. After the heating inside the car, the mountain air was cold.

As Trotti entered, a bell rang somewhere and the barman seemed taken aback to have a customer. Above his head, a silent television gave the early afternoon news.

The Pope, visibly old and trembling, was blessing the crowds before St. Peter's.

A deer's head looked down glassily at Trotti from the wall and a lethargic fish swam in a glaucous tank. Humorous postcards punctuated a long, cracked mirror.

"Not from these parts?" the barman asked pleasantly. There was a mole on his nose. He was smoking.

"Milan."

"All that fog?" The barman laughed, amused by his own wit. "Sooner you than me."

Trotti moved away from the bar to a bare wooden table. With a smile lingering on the crumpled face, the barman smoked placidly while watching the rain from behind his coffee machine.

Trotti drank mineral water served in a chipped glass and ate a stale *panino* of tomatoes and mozzarella, but without any pleasure. He was in a hurry to get back on the road.

Trotti glanced at the broadsheet that lay scattered across the table top.

The front page of *Sera Romana*.

With a cold shock of surprise, he recognized the photograph of himself, looking younger and healthier. A photo that had been taken when he set up the child abuse unit.

Retired policeman last person to see murdered American woman. A ring of student call girls in Lazio. Police keeping the body for further analysis.

Trotti grunted on reading that he had been a highly respected policeman. Highly respected and pioneering.

The article added little new information—other than that the retired Commissario Trotti was now in Bracciano for the wedding of a close relative.

"*Arrivederci!*"

"*Arrivederci,*" the barman responded, surprised by the sudden departure and by Trotti's generous tip, all the money from his pocket.

Trotti walked hurriedly back to the car, almost unaware of the cold rain. He climbed into the driving seat.

"They know my movements, the bastards."

Trotti's hand was trembling as he placed the key in the ignition. The wheels screeched on the wet tarmac and the rented Fiat pulled away from the misty piazza.

74: Tube

TROTTI DROVE FAST and did not stop again for over an hour. Half an hour after San Quirico, with the car cruising downhill, the lowering clouds finally began to draw back and a watery sun made its appearance.

The Volkswagen.

Trotti had noticed it before, on the Viterbo ring road.

His eyes returned to the mirror at regular intervals—at a crossroads or when pulling out of a town. The car was always there, about a kilometer back, traveling to the left, on the crest of the road.

A Golf, too far behind for Trotti to read the plates.

It disappeared at Quinciano and Trotti laughed aloud.

In a poor imitation of a Neapolitan accent, Trotti said, *"Thank your friend and his charming young bride. How else d'you think I knew where to find you?"*

Trotti laughed, and it was then that he remembered Lakshmi's tape. He retrieved it from the folder on the seat beside him and fed it into the car's tape deck.

I arrived in Trento in October, 1967.

I was totally lost. Turin and my family were behind me. My old life was behind me. I had no idea where I was heading—just the feeling there was no turning back.

I was twenty-one years old, once married, the father of a little boy and now divorced. I had worked in Germany and I had worked in London.

Trento was a revelation—and a joy.

I found myself surrounded by exciting, intelligent people. They spoke of St. Thomas and Plato and Marx. Their learning came from books, while mine came from the Turks in Frankfurt and the Jamaicans in London, from the capitalist machine. I was interested in Weber and Protestantism and the trade union movement. I'd had firsthand experience of emigration, of the problems of the Turks, the West Indians and the Southerners working at Fiat in Turin.

For the first time in my life, I found people who were genuinely interested in what I had to stay.

Trento was a heady place to be in 1967.

I enrolled at the university and began preparing a degree in sociology.

We were all so motivated! Young, innocent and convinced that if you looked hard enough, there was an answer to all life's questions.

We read late into the night, we exchanged ideas in the lecture halls and in the beer cellars of that peaceful Alpine town. History was on our side. We knew we were preparing the Counter Counter-Reformation.

Then 1968.

Italy was unprepared for 1968. The students rioted in Paris, and suddenly in Italy the status quo—the accepted dogma of postwar reconstruction and the Italian miracle—was threatened by the revolution, by our revolution. We were working like ants to change society. We were not going to miss our appointment with history.

My ex-wife in Turin had remarried and she no longer needed money. I was economically free and I felt that Trento could change the world.

Trento—and Lotta Continua—radically changed me.

For some reason, I was perceived as the intellectual of the party—we were all intellectuals, we were all clocking up full marks in our sociology and psychology and politics examinations at the university.

Some companions asked me to produce the weekly newspaper. It was a challenge I could rise to—more satisfying than putting down rails at Notting Hill underground, where the slightest slip of your foot could turn you into frazzled bacon.

I produced and edited the paper and it was a huge success.

Before long, friends were contributing what little money they had and as much time as they could spare. The weekly paper became a daily. Before long it was being distributed outside our Alpine city. Within a couple of months it was being read in Cagliari and Brindisi.

I was doing something I enjoyed. Something that satisfied my need to produce, my need to feel useful, my deep-felt need for recognition.

I was happy and fulfilled. But no longer was I aware of my happiness than it began to elude me—just as three years earlier, the happiness of our honeymoon in Capri had turned into the nightmare of sharing a run-down flat with a histrionic wife and a bawling, shitting baby.

"Those comrades who hope to bring about the Revolution should not belong to any political party. A party constrains you and demands you should conform to all its incoherencies. You become a perfect pupil, quoting Marx and Mao but you lose your own vision, your own interpretation, your own humanity, your own part of God. In the end, you become an apparatchik and you lose your very soul."

Understandably, that didn't go down too well with the party.

Lotta Continua was becoming a machine, a bureaucratic machine. The more it bureaucratized, the more I was called into question. The party didn't like the cheap necklace I wore—two hundred lira from the local UPIM supermarket. They didn't like my long hair. Above all, they didn't like my smoking illegal substances and my temerity at not hiding the fact.

I knew the protestant north of Europe. For all the revolutionary cant, for all the utopia, Lotta Continua was Latin and parochial—good little Catholics marching to the revolutionary catechism. Like hypocritical priests, they said I was not concerned with the good of the working class. They said I was unreliable, that I set a poor example of party discipline. And while Lotta Continua was growing more regimented and military in its outlook, I was turning westward to English and American models of the revolution: sex, drugs and rock and roll.

I helped Lotta Continua organize a rock concert in Milan. An underground group from New York. At the last moment, Lotta Continua's politburo was afraid it'd turn into an Italian Woodstock, with people blown out of their minds and women showing bare chests and sharing free love.

Lotta Continua gave a couple of hundred free tickets for me and my friends on the understanding I would behave myself. I immediately went to the stadium and handed them out.

There was a riot.

My most recent girlfriend had gone off to Paris, I was feeling miserable and when the police turned up, I was looking for trouble. I was doing a lot of Tai Chi at the time and was very fit.

The police arrived in their vans and charged us with batons. Lotta Continua, but also a lot of the dross of Milan, small-time delinquents from the hinterland around Milan. This was before the days of the P.38, at a time when police-baiting was still fun, when it was still a point of honor to spend a night or two in a cell. In the worst of cases, your parents would turn up to bail you out.

That evening, I managed to throw a few cobbles at the Celere without getting arrested. I hid behind a tree. A couple of my companions were caught and bundled off, but I was safe behind my tree.

The police withdrew, and when I turned round, I was surprised to see a girl standing behind me.

One of the two companions was her boyfriend. Together we went to the Questura and we waited for his release until four in the morning. The police released everybody except him.

Lia Guerra was sixteen years old. I took her home and we made love.

That was the beginning of my troubled love affair with Lia. It was also the beginning of the end of my troubled love affair with Lotta Continua. The party, in its moralizing and bigoted conformity, decided my behavior was immoral— I was sleeping with a child.

I was banished to Palermo. It was supposed to be a punishment, but Lia came with me.

I had lost one love and, for a time at least, I had found true love.

It took me several years to realize Lia Guerra was incapable of loving anybody.

Not me, not herself.

75: Let It Be

THERE WAS A short hissing in the car and the tape stopped. Then it started again as the spools whirred and reversed their movement.

I could no longer believe a revolution would change the world.

And I couldn't bear the anti-American obsession. It was as if Timothy Leary and Abbie Hoffman and Jerry Rubin had never existed. Lotta Continua was so puritanical, so rigid. I had reached the stage where I couldn't give a toss about Lenin or Marx or Mao Tse-tung. I was more concerned with the Stones and the Beatles—and like the Beatles, I'd got interested in meditation. I was nearly thirty years old, and the heady philosophy of the University of Trento had become a new doctrine that had spilled over from the Alps and poured down the Peninsula.

I could no longer go along with any of it. I saw things differently. The answers to life had to come from within, not without.

From the individual, not from the party.

I was in love with Lia, but that only made

me more dissatisfied. Somehow I could never give the woman I loved what she wanted. I disappointed her, and although we spent nearly five years living under the same roof, we never belonged to each other. We were never really close.

In her eyes, we were good friends and after a while, we slept in separate beds.

By the mid-seventies, I was smoking a lot of grass. I'd done speed, I'd done cocaine—in fact, I'd done virtually everything—but it was dope that helped me tick over. I just couldn't stand the priggishness of my companions anymore, and dope seemed the only way I could turn their strident voices down.

I stuck with Lotta Continua for as long as I could—but after 1976, I took nothing seriously.

Sex, drugs and rock and roll. Well, at least drugs and rock and roll.

The final break with my past, with politics, with Lotta Continua, with my bureaucratic comrades—and above all—with my desire to set the world to rights came in 1978 when Aldo Moro was kidnapped.

The country was paralyzed. Hundreds of kilometers to the south, a politician had been kidnapped, but throughout Italy, anybody and everybody could be a terrorist and a murderer.

A little girl was kidnapped in the quiet university city where my father was now working as city architect. For some reason that was never made clear, the police believed I was involved in the child's disappearance. Perhaps it was my hair and the UPIM necklace that frightened the forces of order.

It is quite possible I knew more about the little girl than I revealed to the police. It is certain I was promptly arrested and interrogated in the Questura.

That's when a man called Piero Trotti, a sweaty policeman with a nasal accent, threw me in jail for a couple of nights.

Two nights that were to change my life.

76: Tim

ANOTHER THIRTY KILOMETERS to Siena, and Trotti thought he heard a buzzing noise. It came from within the car and it sounded like a telephone.

He fiddled with the radio, but the sound continued. He ejected the cassette from its slot and the Fiat swerved off the road. The car behind honked angrily. Trotti hastily pulled into a lay-by, beneath a leafless chestnut tree and turned off the engine.

The buzzing continued.

He rummaged in the glove compartment in front of the passenger seat. The ringing continued.

Piero Trotti unbuckled his belt and, leaning forward, ran his hand under the seat. Then, as he slid his fingers beneath the passenger seat, they met a light object that moved.

The object was blinking.

Pisanelli's blue mobile phone.

Trotti had a loathing of gadgets; he was not mechanically minded, and even something as simple as bicycle gears were, for him, baffling.

He pushed the green button with an icon of a receiver.

"Piero?"

Surprised by the nearness of the voice, he replied, "Trotti here."

"Thank God you're answering."

"Answering what?"

"Trotti, I've been trying to call you for over an hour."

"Didn't hear anything."

"Where are you? Put the phone to your mouth, I can't hear you properly. And pull out the aerial."

Trotti did as he was told; the voice became clearer.

"Where are you?"

"Where do you think, Magagna? I'm in Pisanelli's hired car, in the driver's seat and I'm speaking to you over the phone."

"What road are you on?"

"North."

"Heading where?"

"Florence and then Bologna."

"You're on the autostrada?"

Trotti said, "I suppose Pisa wants the car back?"

"You were thinking of keeping both the car and the telephone?"

"Nice car," Trotti remarked.

"You're going to your daughter's place?"

"I don't have any money."

"You don't need any money—Pisanelli tells me the tank's full. For the honeymoon that was. Your goddaughter likes you a lot more than is good for her. I suppose you're delighted to be the subject of the first quarrel of their married life."

"Pisanelli would never be able to drive the car with his stiff leg. What happened to Portano?"

"What made you do that to Portano, Trotti?"

"Do what?"

"You struck him in the balls. He's seriously hurt."

"The accent got on my nerves."

"I didn't realize you were so violent—not with people stronger than you."

"What's Portano going to do?"

"Kill you."

"He knows I'm going to Bologna?"

"Nobody was imagining you were running away to Rome." There was a pause, the sound of muffled talking. "Pisanelli says there should be some cash in the trunk—in one of the bags."

"Pisanelli hasn't left for his honeymoon?"

"When you've got all his wife's clothes? Trotti, there should be an electric cable beneath the driver's seat. Plug it into the phone and put the other end into the lighter socket. That way you can recharge the telephone—and I can call you back later."

"What's Portano going to do?"

"Don't worry about Portano. Get to Bologna—and leave the phone on. I'll be calling you later. I don't want you getting hurt."

"Good of you to keep an eye on me."

"It's not Portano you've got to worry about, Trotti," Magagna said tersely.

"What do you want me to worry about?"

"Pisanelli's marriage."

77: Trotti

TROTTI DID AS Magagna had asked.

While traffic rumbled past him on the road to Siena, he found the cable and plugged it into the blue telephone. Immediately the screen lit up. A written message, large black letters on green. Trotti held the phone away to get the blinking letters into focus: BATTERY CHARGE IN PROGRESS.

He was about to put the telephone down on the seat beside him and drive off when inadvertently Trotti touched another button, a different icon.

A number jumped onto the screen of the telephone. Squinting awkwardly, he recognized Pisanelli's home number in Rome.

Trotti was both amused and puzzled.

There was a cancel button; by punching it, the number disappeared. He then found that if he typed the letters P and I, Pisanelli's number reappeared.

Again he cancelled.

When Trotti typed A and N, Anna's home number jumped onto the screen.

There was, Trotti realized, a list of numbers stocked somewhere inside the mobile phone's memory.

Trotti chuckled, pleased with his own intelligence.

"Anna Maria."

It was time Trotti contacted his cousin. He could call Anna

Maria now, tell her he was all right. Tell her he was alive and
well and he was missing her Dutch cooking and her hector-
ing. It was just past four o'clock and she was probably in the
kitchen by now, digesting one of her biscuits, accompanied by
a generous glass of Bols after a generous Easter lunch.

He had not called her since Bologna. Something else she
would hold against him.

He found the letter T. It took Trotti several minutes before
he realized that he had to punch the same key for the second
letter.

T and then R.

To Trotti's disappointment, it was not his number, but the
telephone started to ring. It was not his home number, not a
familiar code for northern Italy. Instead a number that he did
not recognize, something that Trotti had never dialed before.

"Blast," he said under his breath.

Trotti was starting to panic, but before he could unplug
the phone, the ringing ceased and Trotti's call was answered.

"Trapani," a nasal voice said.

"Trapani?" Trotti repeated in surprise.

"Nucleo anti-Mafia."

Trotti pulled the jack from the cigarette lighter just as he
heard the distant voice ask him what he wanted.

A Sicilian voice.

78: Minox

(*"BE CAREFUL, PIERO. An awful job to get the blood-stains out. Take care of my coat even if you won't take care of yourself."*)

The afternoon sky was blue and cloudless. The snow had gone back to Siberia, the recent rains had drifted east, but out of the sun, the air remained cool. The warm coat had been left in Rome and now, no doubt, was in the hands of Portano and his friends. Without the Carabinieri coat, Trotti felt the chill.

In a week, the weather had improved. In the same week, Trotti had been beaten up twice and accused of murdering a young woman. Arrested and put on a saline drip. Trotti had also made peace with his goddaughter.

He parked the Fiat near the station, placed Lakshmi's folder in the trunk, locked the car and walked up the long hill to the center of the city. In his hip pocket he held the small wallet and fifty thousand lire that he had found in a woman's bag in the car. The blue telephone bumped against his thigh.

Despite the crowd of tourists, a wind scurried across the Piazza del Campo. Easter Sunday and the bars and cafés were doing excellent business. Tourists, both Italian and foreign, sat on the terraces in sweaters and overcoats as the air warmed with the late afternoon sun.

Trotti felt exposed in the piazza and was in a hurry to cross the open square.

(*"Don't worry about Portano. Get to Bologna—and leave the phone on. I'll be calling you later. I don't want you to get hurt."*)

Trotti had the feeling that he was being watched, being followed. He did not like open spaces and he did not like Siena. Trotti was in a hurry to get home, back to his house, back to via Milano and Anna Maria's stodgy cooking. But there were things that still had to be done, questions that had to be answered if he was to stay out of prison.

The clock in Piazza del Campo chimed half past four. Trotti turned away from the piazza and went up one of the alleys. A moment later, walking briskly, close to the wall, ignoring the strolling tourists, Trotti passed the café in via di Città.

Picturesque?

Trotti smiled wryly as he remembered the couple in the bar; they had laughed and Trotti had raised his head. Trotti had heard the word "pittoresco" pronounced in an English accent. The woman laughed again and the man produced a black object. Trotti realized it was a camera only when the Englishman opened up the front lens.

(*"They know my movements, the bastards."*)

Trotti walked towards the cathedral, through the twisting streets of the upper city.

"Spadano?"

"Who?"

Trotti still imagined that most flatfeet were called Quagliarulo or Scognamiglio and spoke in Sicilian or Calabrian dialect. This accent was Tuscan, patronizing and refined.

"Spadano."

With a remote, patrician smile, the uniformed officer leaned forward.

"I wish to speak with General Spadano," Trotti said slowly.

A frown, condescending and amused. "I'm afraid I can't help you."

"I was here last week." Trotti nodded his head. "I spoke to you."

The man seemed puzzled. "To me?"

"You took me to see Spadano."

"You must be mistaken."

"You took me to see the general."

"What general?"

"Spadano—Egidio Spadano."

The man placed a hand on Trotti's arm and with hardly any pressure, maneuvered him towards the exit. "Really?"

Trotti retorted angrily, freeing himself, "I've got to speak to Spadano. I've got to speak to him now. It's important."

"Perhaps you'd like to show me your ID. How did you get past the door?"

(*"I don't work for our cultural heritage, Spadano, nor do I have your pretensions to being cultured and using long words."*)

"I'm Commissario Trotti of the Polizia di Stato, retired."

"I think you should leave, commissario." There was iron in the thin voice.

"General Spadano of the Tutela del Patrimonio Artistico." Trotti said, "He's in charge of protection of cultural heritage. He lives in Siena. I must see him." Inanely, Trotti added, "You have a swimming pool here."

"My advice would be for you to go to Florence. No Tutela del Patrimonio Artistico here in Siena, I'm afraid. Never has been. Or perhaps you didn't know that?" A faint smile, as the man softly added, "Commissario."

79: Retaliation

HE WAS NOT Enzo Beltoni.

Trotti had assumed that the man following him—the man who had knocked him to the ground in Siena, the man in the scruffy suit with the Vespa and the gun at his shoulder—was trying to protect him. A guardian angel that Spadano had sent to keep an eye over Trotti. To protect him from Beltoni.

(Trotti would have recognized Enzo Beltoni anywhere. In eight years, Trotti had not forgotten the twin brother. He had not forgotten the face. Ever since finding the corpse on the edge of the city, that face had come to haunt Trotti's worst nightmares. Beltoni—addict, drug-dealer and police informer. Thirty-five years earlier a mother's baby, and now mutilated and burned to death because of Piero Trotti.)

Trotti had not seen the man who had sent him sprawling to the ground in via di Città, but the following day in Trastevere, Trotti instinctively knew it was the same man who approached the gypsy children in the piazza.

Enzo Beltoni would not have followed Trotti from Siena to Rome. Enzo Beltoni would have killed Trotti. At the first opportunity, with the sole intent of inflicting as much pain as possible. Enzo Beltoni was a Sicilian, and he would honor the ancient codes of retribution. An eye for an eye, a sliced tongue for a sliced tongue.

The clumsiness had to be a ploy.

The fellow in via di Città was a professional, and he had wanted Trotti to know that he was being followed. To warn Trotti—or to frighten him off. For the same reason, in Rome he had deliberately placed himself near the terrace table, and both Pisanelli and Trotti had seen the gun beneath the scruffy jacket.

Why would Enzo Beltoni bother with walkie-talkies? Why would Enzo Beltoni lurk in doorways, pretend to read the newspaper while speaking into his lapel?

Enzo Beltoni was Spadano's invention. General Spadano who now no longer existed.

Pisanelli's phone rang in his pocket; it vibrated against his thigh. This time Trotti knew how to open the phone, pull at the aerial and speak into the plastic flap.

"Where are you, Piero?"

"Here."

"Here where?"

"Siena."

"I thought you were going to Bologna?"

"You're in a greater hurry than I am?"

"Go to Bologna."

"I need to buy some socks. My feet are frozen."

"I don't want you hurt."

"Portano's out to get me?"

"Portano's gone back to Rome—in an ambulance. No need to worry about Portano. The word's out you're in the clear."

"In the clear over what?"

There was a brief pause before Magagna said, "The Carabinieri have found Enzo Beltoni's prints."

"What prints?"

"In the Hotel Toscana." He laughed. "You're not the murderer of the American girl."

80: Merino

"LET THE BASTARDS watch me," Trotti muttered to himself, "I'm in no hurry."

Socks, reading glasses and the latest edition of *Vissuto* were scattered on the seat beside him. And Pisanelli's telephone.

It was warm inside the car, and he would wait an hour before the drive north. Wait until the sun had set and there was less traffic on the superstrada to Florence. Wait until the darkness when he could lose the Volkswagen.

Trotti put the second tape into the player and unwrapped a rhubarb sweet before taking the woolen socks out of their packet.

> "Last week I quarreled with Giovanni Verga. It is with sadness that I realize he is no longer my friend.
>
> It is sad that after nearly a decade of collaboration, there can't now be the same feeling of camaraderie and common purpose which inspired the early years of our being together.
>
> I will always be grateful to Giovanni. At a time when I was at a loss what to do, at a time when I didn't know whether I should stay in India or give in to my wife's demand that we return to Italy, Giovanni's offer of a commune came at just the right moment.

For nearly ten years, Giovanni Verga was a good and loyal friend.

When did things start to go wrong between us? Was it when the regional government began putting money into BRAMAN? Was it when Enzo Beltoni came to the commune, first as a client, then as a trustee? Or was it when I sensed that Giovanni Verga had replaced me in the affections of my wife?

Those first years in Trapani were wonderful. The three of us were so enthusiastic. Unlike me, Giovanni Verga had never had any truck with communism. I, on the other hand, had never really thrown off the need for structure to my existence. As a child, I'd been a good Catholic. As a young man, I'd been taken in by the religion of Marxism.

Dopo Marx, Aprile.

It was with Giovanni—and probably thanks to him—that at the age of thirty-three I put Marxism behind me and entered the springtime of my life. Wife, daughter—they only took on their true meaning once we arrived in BRAMAN. Before then I had been play-acting—always play-acting.

Within a couple of years we began to diverge, Giovanni Verga and I. Nothing dramatic, simply the difference in our philosophies began to make itself felt. He had never made a secret of his desire to be rich. Just as I had never made a secret of my idea of the revolution: sex, drugs and rock and roll.

I loved my family—and I always will—but there are times when I need to escape. People often call me 'the lieutenant.' I have never wanted to wield power, and I've always been happy to be the second in command. By standing back, by distancing myself I've tried to keep my sense of perspective—and my sense of humor. Grass helps me to relax, but unfortunately, when you're running a rehab center and when a lot of important people are placing great hopes in you, it's not a good idea to appear permanently stoned.

A lot of hopes and a lot of money.

Things started going wrong in 1985. Until then, Giovanni Verga managed to tolerate my behavior. Three things changed all that.

In 1985, BRAMAN got its first check from the Region.

Until then, we'd been mucking through as best we could. My wife and I felt we'd embarked upon an adventure of self-discovery, and I had no reason to think that Giovanni Verga saw otherwise. He was good to us—and a wonderful surrogate uncle to Lakshmi. They would spend a lot of time together, my friend and my daughter, and there was a strange symbiosis. She had a calming effect upon Giovanni—whenever he saw her, his face would light up. And he was, no doubt, a substitute parent for her.

I wasn't always the best of fathers.

Once the money came in, there was a shift of vision—and because I was living on my little cloud, I was slow to see what was happening.

BRAMAN ceased to be a commune, a continuation of the adventure I had started with Giovanni Verga and Chiara. We were now running a business and we needed to show we were worth the investment important people were making in us. Giovanni Verga renewed his contacts with his friends in Milan and with Bettino Craxi's Socialists. He needed to be seen as a businessman selling a product. Giovanni Verga was concerned with quotas and statistics and success rates. In this, he was supported by Chiara. My wife took to the management of BRAMAN like a fish to water. After managing our family singlehandedly, running BRAMAN was an easy step for her.

In 1985, we were sent our first customers from prison. I was delighted and I would make my speech—all very Jean-Jacques Rousseau—about how society created criminals. It took me time to snap out of that liberal claptrap—and for that, I must thank Enzo Beltoni.

I liked the man.

I knew Enzo Beltoni had murdered someone a long time ago, but I could see he was intelligent. At first, I didn't notice the power he held over Giovanni Verga. I wasn't even surprised when he was made one of the trustees and given his special room in the complex.

Then I started hearing rumors of his having seduced various women—but of course, BRAMAN had been set up in a firm belief in free love.

Peace and love.

Just like the saffron robes we had once worn, peace and love were soon relegated to the rubbish bin of lost dreams. After all, we were in Sicily, and there can be nowhere in the world—with the possible exception of Afghanistan—where men impose their moralistic values upon the women with such a heavy and hypocritical hand.

Women inmates were soon telling me they'd been forced to spend the night with Enzo Beltoni.

I mentioned this to Beltoni. He simply laughed and gave me a conspiratorial wink.

By now, Giovanni Verga was the grand guru, the uncontested leader of BRAMAN, and he was often away on business. When he came back from one of his trips to Rome or Milan, I told him what the women had been saying.

Giovanni Verga dismissed my fears—he said he had absolute faith in Beltoni's integrity.

I put the problem out of my mind. Anyway, I had something else to worry about: after a silence of nearly six years, Lia Guerra had suddenly reappeared in my life."

THE TAPE FELL silent except for the gentle hum of the magnetic field.

Trotti picked up the magazine, checked the index and turned to page sixty-five.

81: Prince

VISSUTO, EASTER EDITION
After eight years of frustration, the Carabinieri can at last begin to breathe more easily. With the imminent arrest of Chiara Gracchi, the sostituto procuratore in Trapani appears to be giving belated credence to the first Carabinieri enquiry. That initial report arrived at the Trapani Procura on 26 November, 1988, just two months after Gracchi's death.

In it, Colonel Mario Nazareno wrote:

> *The theory of a Mafia killing, so enthusiastically endorsed by the media, can, in our opinion, be little more than hypothesis. Such a theory may suit certain political lobbies, but it is not in accordance with the facts as we know them.*
>
> *We would be derelict in our duty if we were to overlook the possibility of a vendetta within BRAMAN.*
>
> *BRAMAN receives large sums of money from various organizations, both in Sicily and on the mainland. In our opinion, the size of these sums may well explain why Gracchi was murdered. While not renouncing other lines of investigation, we continue to look into the ties that bound Valerio Gracchi and Giovanni Verga.*

It is our belief that Gracchi had become a dissident partner in the financial organization of BRAMAN.

The glaring discrepancy between two eyewitness reports gives further weight to the Carabiniere theory that someone within BRAMAN was the murderer.

On the evening of his death, Gracchi was driving home to BRAMAN in the company of a young woman, Luciana Fiorini. Signorina Fiorini, an ex-addict from Milan, had spent the day with him in the television studios at Trapani. In a signed statement to the Carabinieri, taken just hours after the slaying, Luciana Fiorini states:

"We had got onto the unsurfaced road that leads to BRAMAN. It's the only way into the commune. On the journey from Trapani I had never had the impression we were being followed. We were traveling slowly, at about thirty-five kilometers an hour—but then, Gracchi always drives slowly. When we got to the double bend, I heard three or four explosions.

The windshield was blown apart. At first, I thought something had happened to the car engine. But then I saw the red stains on Gracchi's sweater—on the right upper arm. He was motionless. I asked him if he was all right. "Nothing to worry about," he replied. "You'd better hide." He believed his attackers were going to go away.

I got down between the two seats and buried my head and face into the floor of the car. There was a long wait and all I could hear was Gracchi's difficult breathing. I think he was choking on his blood. Then I heard two or three shots, this time a lot louder than before. I was terrified,

*I couldn't move—they must've seen me, but I
hadn't seen them, so they knew they had nothing
to be afraid of. Only later—a lot later, when I
heard the sound of a car door being slammed—
only then did I dare raise my head. I looked at
Gracchi, I saw his head lolling against the head-
rest and his eyes were wide open. I knew he was
dead. I got out of the car and went running off
towards the entrance of BRAMAN."*

The autopsy on Gracchi's body, carried out at the hospital
in Trapani, openly contradicts Fiorini's sworn statement.

According to the autopsy, Gracchi was killed with two
firearms, a .38 pistol and a .12 rifle. He was shot eight times,
in the head and in the back. There were bullet holes in his
hands. After the first hail of bullets, Gracchi must have tried
to protect his face with his hands.

All the shots were fired from a distance of at least two
meters. There were no signs of burns on the corpse. Nobody had
got close to Gracchi to finish him off with a bullet to the head.

Equally in conflict with Fiorini's evidence is the evidence
of another young girl.

At the time, Carla Serra was thirteen years old. By midnight
on the evening of Gracchi's murder, she was at the Carabinieri
barracks, giving evidence.

*"I was sitting on the steps of the church and I
saw the car of Valerio Gracchi go past. I know
Signor Gracchi well; he always wears a Panama
hat and he has a big beard. Normally Signor
Gracchi drives very slowly, but this time he was
going exceptionally fast. He was being followed
by a blue Fiat Uno. The blue car was about fifty
meters behind Signor Gracchi's vehicle. Because
of the two bends, both cars had to slow down.
As they got onto the unsurfaced road that leads
to the entrance of the commune, I rose from*

> *where I was sitting to watch the cars disappear behind the double bend.*
>
> *I later heard the several short explosions. I thought it was a car backfiring. It later occurred to me that a car doesn't backfire half a dozen times within the space of a few seconds. About five minutes later, I saw the Fiat Uno come back down from the double bend and disappear in the direction of Erice. It was traveling very fast. I saw just one person—the driver. A thin man with dark hair.*

If this young eyewitness is telling the truth, then Signorina Fiorini must be lying when she says that Gracchi was driving slowly.

Why should a member of BRAMAN choose to lie about the founder's death?

It did not escape the attention of the Carabinieri that Signorina Luciana Fiorini was never hit by any bullet, although at least fifteen rounds were fired into the car. Furthermore, no trace of blood was found on her clothes, even though the interior of the Duna was liberally splattered with Gracchi's blood and splintered bone.

The day following Gracchi's murder, officers from the Carabinieri barracks discovered the burnt-out carcass of a Fiat Uno in a cave a few kilometers from Erice. On the chassis, the construction number was still visible; the car had been stolen the previous day in Messina.

This discovery alone tends to prove the veracity of the young Carla Serra's statement. Likewise it suggests that Luciana Fiorini, inmate of BRAMAN, was lying when she made her statement.

Why?

On the backseat of Gracchi's bloodstained Duna, the Carabinieri retrieved a sweater, some money in lire and dollars, a packet of cigarette papers, an empty videotape, and a copy of Niccolò Machiavelli's *Il Principe*.

On the book's flypaper, there was a dedication, handwritten in neat, blue ink.

'Highly recommended reading, dearest Chicchi. With my fondest wishes, Bettino Craxi.'

Chicchi is the nickname of Giovanni Verga, who along with Valerio Gracchi founded BRAMAN in the late seventies. He and Bettino Craxi were friends.

82: Siam

"Craxi."

Trotti put down *Vissuto* magazine on the seat beside him and stared absentmindedly through the window of the car. A few tourists—young people, mainly backpackers—were heading towards the entrance of the railway station. It was fast getting dark, and the pale streetlights were already turned on.

There was no sign of surveillance, nobody lurking in a doorway and talking into a lapel—or a mobile phone. No sign of a Golf.

Trotti's thoughts were elsewhere.

Bettino Craxi. The leader of the republic's longest-lasting government, a government that managed to bring inflation down from 16 percent to 4 percent, a government that gave Italy four years of unprecedented political stability.

Bettino Craxi, Italy's first Socialist prime minister, now in Tunisia, disgraced and condemned in absentia to ten years' imprisonment for fraud and the misappropriation of public funds.

Trotti was not a political animal. Since the end of the war, he had followed politics from a wary distance. There had been times when the politicians had angered him with their indifference or their corruption, with their posturing and their verbosity, yet Trotti never got involved. As a functionary of the state for thirty-seven years, Piero Trotti had faithfully observed that allegiance. His own idiosyncratic allegiance to an absentee state.

Like most Italians, Trotti had mixed feelings about Bettino Craxi. Craxi had ushered in an era of political stability, but Trotti disliked the man, possibly slightly more than he disliked most politicians.

Bettino Craxi, with his bald head and jutting jaw and his arrogance, was reminiscent of Benito Mussolini. Like Mussolini, Craxi had run the country as if it belonged to him, run the country with the help of a few well-placed friends and relatives. Growth and stability were only part of the Craxi heritage; there was also a huge public deficit, there were all his refinements to a corrupt system when he made his alliance with the Christian Democrats.

Bettino Craxi was eight years younger than Trotti. Born into a family of Sicilians, the young politician had first taken control of his local party in Milan. Then, in 1976, at a time when the Communists were edging uncomfortably close to power, when Aldo Moro was envisaging his 'Converging Parallels,' Craxi presented the Italian Socialist Party as a viable alternative to the sclerotic monotony of the Christian Democrats. A party on the left that espoused Europe and the free market. A party that promised reform, but that was totally free of Moscow and Marxist rhetoric. A party with its origins in the partisan war against the Nazi invader. A party of the left that the Italian people, Catholic and conservative, could trust.

CAF—Craxi, Andreotti and Forlani.

Throughout the eighties, three men ran Italy—two of them Christian Democrats, Arnaldo Forlani and Giulio Andreotti. Craxi was the late arrival, but in many ways, he surpassed the older men in both cunning and in his freedom of movement. Bettino Craxi had carefully studied Machiavelli. Craxi did not have to back down before the trade unions at home; he was unhindered by emotional ties to the Vatican. Craxi could speak to the Americans on equal footing. Craxi understood and controlled Italian politics.

Bettino Craxi chose his friends carefully—not least, his

businessman friend from Milan, Silvio Berlusconi. Berlusconi and Craxi were the Siamese twins of the new regime, of the new Italy of the 1980s. Bettino helped Silvio build his media empire; in return Silvio used his television channels to bolster Bettino's reign. A reign that should have lasted forever.

Trotti smiled to himself.

(*"The classes controlled by the Christian Democrats and kept in power thanks to the covert support of the Americans. And of the Mafia."*

"Not simplifying things, Spadano?"

"Piero, all the north—with the exception of the Veneto—and all the center of the country were on the left. It was the South that kept Andreotti and Forlani and all the rest of the Christian Democrats in power. In power for forty-seven years while they pillaged our country."

"You sound like a Communist."

"Like a man who's been taken to the cleaners."

"You're not forgetting the Socialists, Spadano? Or perhaps they weren't on the left?"

"CAF—Craxi, Andreotti and Forlani. The Socialists were worse than the Christian Democrats. They tricked us. They gave us hope of something better—and in the end, they betrayed both our ideals and our innocence.")

It was almost night as Trotti turned on the interior light and picked up the magazine again.

Now, with the new glasses perched on his narrow nose, he resumed reading the article.

Siamese twins.

The picture took up a full page—the same picture that Lakshmi had shown Trotti in the Bracciano hotel that morning.

A group photograph taken at BRAMAN, but this time it had not been cropped.

According to the magazine—Trotti had bought the copy fresh off the newsstand in the station—the photograph had been taken a year before Gracchi's death, in June 1987. Men, women and a couple of children who stood or sat in the Sicilian sunshine, beneath an olive tree.

Gracchi and his wife Chiara were on the left of the photograph, standing hand in hand, smiling at the camera. Gracchi was dressed in a white linen suit with a matching Panama hat. Behind the full beard, he was grinning happily.

In the photograph, Chiara Gracchi was almost hidden beside her husband. She held a smoking cigarette in her hand. She was not looking at the camera but was smiling at Lakshmi who sat cross-legged on the ground in front of her. The little Lakshmi eyed the camera and the cameraman inquisitively, with her head to one side.

Trotti nudged his new glasses, grateful that even in the poor light of the car, the picture was correctly focused.

Lia Guerra's dark eyes were looking at the camera. Her legs were crossed at the knee and one hand lay loosely on her lap. She was wearing tights and a black cardigan.

The strong, regular features appeared devoid of emotion.

Perhaps because it was a better enlargement or perhaps thanks to his new glasses, Trotti now recognized the small man standing behind Lia Guerra. Even out of Carabinieri uniform and a decade younger, there was no mistaking the short hair and Spadano's grey, penetrating eyes.

Egidio Spadano was smiling.

83: Triestino

HE NEEDED TO know why he had been lied to.

Trotti was angry and he discarded the unfinished article, throwing it onto the passenger seat beside him. The answer to his question was not in the magazine.

Find General Egidio Spadano.

Trotti took Pisanelli's telephone from his trouser pocket and gingerly opened the protective flap. With his tongue between his teeth, he entered the Bologna code. Thanks to the glasses, everything was unusually bright and clear.

(*"Highly recommended reading, dearest Chicchi. With my fondest wishes, Bettino Craxi."*)

The screen announced it was nearly eight o'clock; Trotti pressed the green button and the telephone began to ring in his ear.

"Pronto?"

As well as the glasses, with Pisanelli's money, Trotti had purchased a pair of woolen socks in the farmacia. At least his feet were now warm, even if his body still hurt, even if there was still a sharp pain in his temple. Trotti needed to rest. Tomorrow was a public holiday, tomorrow he could sleep. If he took the superstrada now, there should not be too much traffic and Trotti would see if he was being followed.

"Pronto?"

Perhaps he should drink something before leaving Siena.

There would be no stopping on the journey; many, many years before, Trotti had been hijacked on the road between Brescia and Milan.

"It's me, Pioppi."

"Where are you phoning from, Papa?"

"How are you, Pioppi? How are my girls?"

"Okay."

Trotti frowned, surprised by the unexpected terseness. "You don't sound okay."

"Of course I'm okay."

Trotti pressed the receiver against his ear. "How are my granddaughters?"

"In bed." She asked, "Where are you, Papa?"

"Siena," Trotti replied. "I should be leaving in a few minutes and with a bit of luck, I could be home before midnight."

"Pomagaj!"

"What?"

"I can expect you for midnight, Papa?"

"You don't sound very keen to see me."

"How was the wedding?" his daughter asked in a flat voice.

"Everybody enjoyed it. Anna was marvelous." Trotti laughed. "Poor old Pisanelli, he looked just like a bald penguin."

"I seem to remember Pierangelo used to have a soft spot for me."

"He couldn't take his eyes off the beautiful bride."

"That's how all marriages start out, Papa."

Again Trotti frowned. "Are you all right?"

"Tata, ljubim te."

"I love you, too, Pioppi."

"You'll be careful?"

"You're a wonderful daughter and I'm proud of you. And proud of my beautiful girls. Are they asleep?"

"I'm about to read to them."

"Tuck them in and give them a big hug from their grandfather. I'll see them in the morning. Tomorrow evening, it's me who gets to read them a story."

His daughter spoke more softly, almost in a whisper. *"Pazi."*

"Of course I'll drive carefully. You haven't been talking to your mother again, have you?"

"No."

"How's Nando?"

"I'm alone with the children."

"Where's Nando?"

"My husband left for Munich this morning."

Trotti was surprised. "You never said Nando was leaving."

"I didn't know."

"I thought we were all going to the restaurant tomorrow." Trotti added, "I thought you were taking me."

"Something came up."

"Are you sure you're all right, Pioppi? You sound very strange."

"*Pazi.*"

"You sound like the nonna. D'you want me to give you my phone number? I'm using Pisanelli's mobile."

"The number's on the screen in front of me."

"You're sure you're all right?"

"Of course I'm all right, papa. *Pazi.*"

"Why's Nando left?"

"I can expect you about midnight?"

"Why are you talking like your grandmother?"

"*Pomagaj!*"

Puzzled, Trotti repeated, "*Pomagaj?*"

"*Tata, ljubim te.*" His daughter hung up.

Trotti frowned unhappily at the receiver.

84: Axis

"AN UGLY LITTLE *child you were then, Piero Trotti—Italo and I used to joke about you. Thin as a rake—with your long, sharp nose and those awful ears of yours. And your darned trousers and wooden shoes that were two sizes too big for you. You were not a very attractive child."*

Trotti could hear the woman's rasping voice.

The smell of war came back to him: the smell and the taste of the coarse maize bread that had been Trotti's staple diet through the long winter of 1944, through the long winter while the allies were stuck behind the Gothic Line.

Italo had always been his hero. In his uniform, Trotti's older brother was handsome, and Piero had looked up to him. In those days, Trotti was still a boy and he believed all the propaganda. Everybody in Santa Maria did—they believed in Fascism just as they believed in Mussolini.

Then Italo went off to fight. First to Abyssinia, then Spain and then to Greece. Instead of a wooden rifle, he was given a gun and he was sent to kill the enemies of Fascism.

Trotti never saw his brother for seven years. There were just the letters that Italo would write—funny, reassuring letters or an exotic postcard of a black face, of a dark-eyed Spanish beauty. Then one day Mother received a letter telling her that Italo had been sent to Russia.

Mother—who had never been particularly devout—went

every morning to the village church to pray and in the end, her prayers were answered: Italo was coming home.

Trotti knew when he accompanied his mother to the station in Voghera that his brother had been wounded. But seeing Italo again came as a terrible shock. Gone the smart uniform of the Alpini, gone the smooth, untroubled complexion, gone the self-assurance and the optimism of youth. Italo Trotti looked like an old man. He had lost his front teeth and all the toes on his left foot. He could hardly speak. The intelligent eyes had lost their focus.

For more than forty years, Trotti was often to wonder whether the Fascist had not done a favor when he put the gun to the back of Italo's head and pulled the trigger.

Inside the Fiat, the dashboard clock ticked softly. The superstrada was almost empty and Trotti drove fast, without dipping the main beams that lit up the surface of the tarmac before him.

Mother had taken risks that winter, had taken foolish risks to save her son's life. She needed to keep Italo away from the wagging tongues and the spies in the village. With the sour-faced English taking their time to push north and with the Germans counting more and more on the Repubblichini to do the dirty work, you could not trust anyone. Mother lived in fear of Italo's being recruited into the Repubblichini. Although Italo was wounded, she knew she had no choice but to hide him. Mother gave him plenty of warm clothes and then one day the priest delivered her elder son to the partisans in the hills.

The smell of war came back to Trotti: the smell of wet clothes, the smell of the cold earth, the smell of fear. The smell of rotting flesh.

One afternoon in the January of the last year of the war, Piero Trotti was coming home from the fields when he saw a couple of mules outside the house. There was also a Wehrmacht car, parked in the middle of the road. Taken by surprise, Piero felt fear rising in his belly. He broke into a run, his clogs hitting the surface of the village street.

As he got nearer, he could hear the sounds of shouting and laughter.

Mongols.

Mongols—they had been seen recently in the hills around Santa Maria. Nobody quite knew what they were supposed to be doing. Small, fearsome men from the heart of Asia who had been taken prisoner on the Russian front and who had now chosen to fight alongside Hitler's army.

They were said to carry no arms; they were capable of murdering a partisan with their bare hands.

Trotti had a knife in his pocket, a knife that he had been using to cut wood, a penknife with a curved, sharp edge. As he ran, Trotti pulled the knife from his pocket and gripped it firmly in his right hand.

It was his mother's voice that he heard first.

Trotti burst into the house to find his mother sitting in the warm kitchen, surrounded by a crowd of a dozen men. Some sat on the table, several were on the bed. Their round, foreign faces were wreathed in smiles. Their red cheeks glowed. Several held tin mugs and Trotti's mother was laughing in a way she had not laughed in years.

"Poor souls," she said, after the last soldier had left. "They can't speak German, they can't speak Italian. I saw them in the road and they looked so lost. So wretched. I invited them to drink some *Ruski caj*. With my Slovene and their primitive Russian, we could talk a bit. Poor, lost things." She added sadly, "They told me about their mothers."

Russian tea? Where on earth had his mother been hiding Russian tea?

Piero Trotti's mother had been born in the limestone hills of the Carso, north of Trieste. She came from a small farming village where the people made teran, a dark, sharp wine. As a little girl she had spoken Slovene but just before Trotti was born, her schoolteacher father left the Carso. At that time, Mussolini wanted to impose Italian purity throughout the nation—Trieste had been Austrian until the end of the Great War. In the little village school, her father was replaced by a

swarthy schoolmaster from Catanzaro. The Fascist government relocated Trotti's grandparents to a village near Parma.

Italo had been born in the Carso. By the time Piero Trotti
came into the world, his mother and Enrico Trotti, a silent,
hard-working man from the flatlands of the Bassa Padana,
were already living in the hills beyond the Po.

Trotti's mother never spoke to her children in Slovene.

Perhaps at a time of Fascist conformity, she wanted to
show that she was a good Italian. That was why Italo was
given his Christian name. Unlike Trotti's father, an ignorant
and dour peasant, his mother spoke and wrote Italian well.
It was Trotti's mother who had taught the little Piero to read
and write before he had been sent off to the village school.

There were times, after the departure of her first son, when
Trotti would hear his mother talking to herself in Slovene.
Alone in the Apennines beyond the Po, perhaps she believed
that no one other than God would understand her prayers
for the safe return of her first child. Or perhaps it was the
only language that allowed her to express her deepest wishes.

Italo was murdered in February, 1945 and Trotti's mother
reverted to talking her native Slovene. When her only grandchild was born fifteen years later, the nonna would often take
Pioppi and look after her for weeks on end. At that time,
Agnese was sitting her exams to become a doctor.

Pioppi learned to speak Slovene at her grandmother's knee.
Sometimes she and her grandmother would chatter for hours
in the language and Trotti felt unpleasantly excluded.

"Your daughter has taken the best part of me."

It was when the nonna died, that Pioppi stopped eating.

In 1986, Pioppi and Nando spent their honeymoon with
distant relatives in San Daniele del Carso—in Stanjel, as
Pioppi insisted upon calling the place. Even now, Trotti would
sometimes hear Pioppi—married to Nando and living in Bologna—talking Slovene. To herself or to the little girls.

Tata, ljubim te.

I love you, Papa.

Pomagaj!

Trotti drove fast, without dipping the main beams that lit up the surface before him. The road slid beneath the car as he raced towards Bologna, raced towards Pioppi and his grand-daughters who needed him.

Pomagaj!

Help!

85: La Grassa

THE DASHBOARD CLOCK ticked softly.

Trotti was making good time. He got off the superstrada and onto the autostrada at Certosa, but it had been raining in the Apennines and there was a landslide. Blinking lamps and unsmiling Polizia Stradale forced the northbound traffic into a single file and then to a halt.

At the bottleneck, Trotti saw soldiers in protective clothing and keflar helmets. Beneath floodlights, there were several armor-plated vehicles and a bulldozer.

Probably another unexploded Allied bomb from the war brought to the surface as the water-logged soil slid downhill.

The smell of war came back to Trotti, the drone of the American planes flying north to flatten Milan. Then the cars in front spread out into three lanes and he could pick up speed again.

It was nearly midnight by the time Trotti pulled right into the slip road for the Bologna Sud exit. He released the pressure on the accelerator and the Fiat ran smoothly towards the lights of the Fat City.

Before the little girls were born, Pioppi and Nando had lived in an apartment in the heart of Bologna, near the university. From the bathroom, they had a breathtaking view across the city roofs to the Asinelli and Garisenda towers. The office where Pioppi worked was just five minutes' walk from her front door. For six years, she and her husband had led the existence of superannuated students—working during the day and in the evenings hanging out in the local bars. Pioppi seemed determined to catch up on the student life that she had missed as an undergraduate in her dour native city. Here in Emilia, everybody seemed slightly mad, and the madness was contagious. Pioppi's happiness in Bologna was tangible, the same happiness she had as a little girl, before Agnese decided she wanted a job, before the nonna died.

On a couple of occasions, Pioppi and Nando had taken her father to a smoke-filled place in the student quarter to hear guitar music and drink strong wine. Trotti was far from happy about the marijuana that everybody seemed to be smoking or the tablets they were taking. Being among young people made Trotti feel even older than he was.

"Like a peasant, you've never learned how to enjoy yourself."

It was when Francesca was born that Nando decided they should leave their apartment and move out into the suburbs. He wanted his daughter to have a garden to play in. By now, Nando had a good job working for a cheesemaking association; he also had a German car and needed somewhere to park it.

Pioppi gave up her office job and became a housewife and mother. She took readily to the new calling and was, Trotti realized, a better mother than Agnese had ever been. But then, Nando was a lot closer to his girls than Trotti had allowed himself to be with Pioppi.

Trotti always got lost on the way to his daughter's house.

It was Easter Sunday, almost midnight, and everything was closed. He recognized the unlit Q8 service station and then took the first turn to the right. Trotti had driven another couple of kilometers before he realized that he would have to turn back. Here on the edge of the city, there was a vast industrial zone, and TIR trucks waited silently in the brightly lit parking lots.

"Blast."

Trotti backed into the parking lot of a modern church, almost hit a bus stop overhang with the rear bumper, and then headed north again. A few moments later, a car went past him in the opposite direction. Trotti knew it was the Volkswagen Golf but had to wait until it drew level before he could see beyond the blinding headlamps.

Looking in the mirror, he saw the car execute a neat turn in front of the church.

Trotti was tempted to call his daughter, tempted to call Magagna again. He was scared.

This time, he found the proper turn but instead of going left, he continued north towards Bologna. When the road curved, Trotti pulled sharp right into a side road and turned off the lights.

He slid his body down in the seat. He had parked awkwardly between a couple of large cars and from somewhere there came the smell of baking bread. Stretching his neck, he could use the mirror to see the road he had just left.

Almost immediately, a car went past the top of the road. He could not see whether it was a Golf, but he had the impression the car slowed, as if the driver was looking to his right, searching for Trotti's rented car.

Trotti waited more than five minutes while his thumping heart returned to a more reasonable rhythm. Then he turned on the lights and started the engine. Rather than reversing up to the main road, he decided that he could drive round three sides of the block.

Trotti was in luck. He looped back to the main road and the turn he should have taken was immediately opposite him.

Five minutes later, Trotti reached the villa.

He turned off the headlights before allowing the car to quietly coast to a standstill.

The lights of the house were all off, except for the porch-light. The night air was silent.

Pioppi's house stood behind an iron fence. The house was surrounded by a garden and half the basement had been transformed into a garage. Trotti could not see if Pioppi's car was there. He could make out the shape of Francesca's bicycle leaning against the wall.

Trotti unplugged the phone from the dashboard and slipped it into his trouser pocket.

Magagna had not bothered to return Trotti's call.

Trotti got out of the Fiat, closed the driver's door silently, and walked the twenty meters to the gate. The gate came open under pressure and Piero Trotti sensed that something was wrong.

He stopped in his tracks and waited.

Trotti remembered his training in Padua. His eyes needed to adapt to the darkness and he could feel that he was being watched.

Somewhere a cat meowed. There was the sound of water in the garden fountain, and Trotti wondered why the pump was working in the middle of the night.

Here in Emilia, the air was chill, probably ten degrees at most. Spring had not arrived in the Po valley and he was glad he was wearing socks. Trotti pushed his back against the gatepost, allowing his breathing to slow, allowing his sight to adapt to the darkness.

No noise came from the house; there was no familiar flickering of the television from beyond the blinds.

Perhaps he should call Pioppi on Pisanelli's mobile.

After a brief wait, Trotti stepped forward, heading towards where the girls' bicycle leaned against the wall. He placed his feet carefully, not wanting to disturb the gravel. He walked on tiptoe, bent forward, crouching slightly.

An old man in scuffed army shoes tiptoeing across his daughter's garden. Trotti told himself he was being foolish, that Pioppi had probably gotten fed up with waiting for him. She knew that he was a slow driver.

Pomagaj!

He stepped past the bicycle and had his foot on the step that led up towards the kitchen entrance. There was a scraping beside him and Trotti turned.

Trotti hit the wall and something was placed over his mouth as he lost consciousness.

86: Renault

HELL WOULD HAVE proper lighting, neon strip lights as well as all the flickering reflections of the eternal fire.

This could not be hell, and Piero Trotti was not dead yet.

Buried but not dead.

As consciousness returned, Commissario Trotti resented the stubborn beating of his heart; death should have brought him release from the pain and Trotti was in pain, terrible pain. He wanted to die now; he needed deliverance. What use was a coffin if he was not yet dead? His hands were behind his back. He could hardly move them and his right arm, the arm he was lying on, had gone numb.

Alive for how much longer?

He must have been drugged, there had been a strange smell in his nostrils and a burning in his eyes. Now there was just the smell of gasoline and car exhaust.

Trotti had no idea of the time, but he reluctantly realized he was in the trunk of a car and that the car was moving fast. The vibration of the wheels was transmitted directly to his head where it lay on cold rubber.

On three occasions in sixty-eight years Trotti had almost left this world, yet until now, he had never felt the desire to be free of his body. There had always been restraints to his taking the final step: things to worry about, people to care for, bills to pay. Now Trotti desired death wholly; he desired an escape from the pointless suffering. Nobody could share his pain and the pain was unbearable. Everything hurt.

Carbon monoxide.

His head was wedged against something hard and metallic—a car jack, perhaps—that pushed a sharp edge into the skin of his scalp. His face was held downwards and his chin almost touched his chest. His ear was against a rubber mat.

A fetal position, with his legs bent—but what fetus was ever held in handcuffs?

He wanted to die, but Trotti tried to think of his life, tried to find reasons for living. He thought of Pioppi, of Francesca and Piera, but all he could feel was the intense pain. No fear—just the desire to put an end to the pain.

The peace of the senses, the long night.

Death, be gentle.

If he swallowed enough of the poisoned air into his burning lungs, Trotti could speed the final journey.

Perhaps he lost consciousness again; when he opened his eyes, he was aware of the jabbing in the hip that he lay on. His leg had gone numb, and the hurt was caused by Pisanelli's telephone pushing hard against the flesh.

Never see the girls again, never see little Pierangelo Pisanelli Junior, never see the luminous smile of Signora Anna Pisanelli?

They knew where he was. Magagna, Pisanelli, the loathsome Portano—they all knew where he was. Trotti had not turned the telephone off and as he lay in the dark, the phone was silently blinking its message to the world of sanity beyond the steel womb of the car.

The telephone was in his right pocket, and they would find the lifeless Piero Trotti curled up like a baby, lying in the trunk of the Golf. Just like Aldo Moro, a bullet through the head and abandoned in the back of a foreign car.

Converging parallels.

Trotti's cuffed hand could not reach forward to the pocket but slowly, carefully, Trotti pulled at the fabric of his trousers—another present from his daughter. No doubt now covered in grease, and Pioppi would be angry when she saw the macabre photo in the newspaper: "Papa never looked after his clothes, even when he was alive. I always told him you're judged on the way you dress. He wouldn't listen. My father was a very stubborn man. I think he enjoyed embarrassing me."

Trotti put his weight onto the shoulder, and although his right hand was completely senseless, the fingers of his left hand began pulling at the cloth and he could feel the pocket and the telephone shifting hesitantly towards his back.

The left pocket moved towards his belly.

The fumes of gasoline and exhaust burned his nostrils, and Trotti gagged as acid rose in his throat.

The telephone was no longer beneath him. The slit of the pocket moved sideways, and in the darkness of the car trunk, Trotti tried to push his fingers into the opening.

Nearly seventy years old and you can depart in peace—Piero Trotti's Nunc Dimittis.

The index finger touched the plastic casing of Pisanelli's mobile telephone.

87: Sulphur

CONSCIOUSNESS RETURNED WITH fresh air as Trotti realized he was no longer in the car. He lay on the ground and it was cold. There was damp sand on his cheeks, sand in his nostrils and sand stuck to the corners of his lips.

Trotti's head ached badly and his tongue was dry and swollen.

Rain had started to fall, thick drops that fell onto the sand and onto his face. Trotti did not understand why he was still alive.

He had breathed lungfuls of the carbon monoxide and still he was alive—despite the headache.

There was somebody hovering over him. Trotti could not make out the face; all he could see was the blurred silhouette as the man moved purposefully and efficiently.

Beyond and above the man's head, there were clouds in the sky, tinted at the edges with an orange flush.

The man had removed Trotti's handcuffs and was now tying the wrists. He did not speak. The glow of a cigarette and an occasional grunt. He worked well, and Trotti could smell the man's sour odor, an odor of smoke and sweat and anger.

Trotti hoped that his own demise would be fast. No more pain.

Beltoni's tongue had been cut out; Trotti wondered if the twin brother, now tying Trotti's feet, pulling the cord tight against his ankles, would dutifully repeat every detail.

An eye for an eye.

Piero Trotti was not a man given to mysticism; he had little time for anything that was not common sense. Yet at that moment, Trotti was aware of escaping from his bruised body. He was aware of being an onlooker, of hovering a couple of meters above the ground and looking down on what had once been himself, Piero Trotti—son, brother, father, grandfather, policeman. Many years earlier his mother's baby, and now soon to be reunited with her.

No more hunger or thirst, no more desires, greed or pride. The true peace of the senses. Tortured, strangled and burned to little more than a cinder lying in the dust.

Beltoni grunted as he yanked Trotti's head backwards, holding the thin hair in one hand and with the other, running rope around his neck.

"You choke to death as your leg muscles can no longer resist the tension."

The first light of dawn on Trotti's last day on earth.

As his head was pulled back, as the rope burrowed into his skin, Trotti finally knew where he was and smiled at the irony.

The smell of sulphur, the low clouds tinted by the street lights: an ugly place, the edge of the city where the old houses gradually fell away and where the surfaced road became a cart track, running parallel to the river—a no-man's land inhabited by a thin phalanx of plane trees. Beyond them the allotments, then the textile factory, its smokeless chimneys and the satellite apartment blocks.

The man let go and Trotti, head pinned back by his bent legs, could see nothing other than the first light of morning on the waters of the Po.

Coming home.

Trotti bent his legs. He did not have the courage to throttle himself. He was afraid of pain, but he was also aware of the man standing beside him. Aware of his own fear.

There was the glint of a knife blade.

The rain was now falling heavily, running down Trotti's face, seeping through his clothes.

Mutilated, strangled and burned to little more than a cinder lying in the dust beside the river Po.

No more pain, no more pain, Trotti prayed silently.

Somewhere towards the city, there was a distant whine of a siren.

88: Sacristan

WILMA WAS BENT over him and she was kissing him; not the kisses of love, but fierce kisses that hurt his bruised parched mouth. Trotti ran his tongue along the edge of his lips and tried to pull away. In irritation, Wilma muttered something and as she spoke, her place was taken by the Uruguayan whore. There was garlic on Eva's bitter breath; garlic and too many cigarettes. Trotti could feel all the strength in Eva's arms. As she held her mouth to his, Trotti wondered if Eva was brutal with all her clients. He wondered how much she would charge to be more gentle.

Eva and Trotti had always haggled over money.

He raised his hand to caress the woman's black hair, but Trotti's hand was brushed away and he fell into a deep sleep.

Later he could hear the sound of the women's voices.

He was coming out of a dream and the voices were talking to him, but when Trotti opened his eyes, he was alone. He could no longer recall the dream but he recognized the voices.

He saw the sky and the wind pulling at the curtains. The shutters were not completely closed; beyond the window the clouds were grey. It was raining.

Trotti climbed out of the bed.

His bed.

The old body ached, his tongue was still swollen, his head was spinning, and with difficulty he managed to keep his balance. Carefully he moved towards the bedside chair and put on the dressing gown that had been draped over the armrest.

His dressing gown.

Taking small and careful steps, Trotti made his way towards the voices, towards the familiar smells.

He had to lean against the wall.

"Buongiorno."

They turned and smiled hesitantly, like two girls caught by the sacristan while gossiping in church.

"I thought I smelled coffee," Trotti said.

Anna Maria was solicitous. "You're still alive?"

"In a hurry for an answer?"

"A nice bruise, Piero."

"Several nice bruises, and they all hurt." He lowered himself onto the kitchen chair.

"Which only serves you right for gallivanting halfway across the country," Anna Maria remarked with her habitual severity.

"I wasn't gallivanting."

"Why go to Rome? Have you suddenly decided in your old age you don't like this part of the world anymore? You don't care for your family? You don't like via Milano?"

"I was in Rome for my friend's wedding."

"That's how you nearly got yourself killed? Doesn't sound very civilized."

Trotti asked, "What time is it?"

"The doctor gave you something to make you sleep." His cousin gave him a perfunctory kiss on the forehead and a reassuring tap on the shoulder. "Would you care for something to eat, Piero?"

"I'm starving."

"You take these stupid risks. You honestly think you're still a young man with a full head of hair. The nice policeman says you spent the night in the trunk of a car. I'm surprised you're still alive."

"Sorry about that."

Simona Scola had been drinking coffee. She stood up from

the table—there was the parish newssheet and Pisanelli's mobile phone on the formica top—and moved towards him, concern on her face.

She brushed her fingers against his cheek. "You hit your head, Piero?"

"Somebody hit my head."

"Why?"

"Somebody hit my head, somebody hit my back, somebody trussed me like a pig and tried to throttle me to death." Trotti shrugged. He could smell her perfume, he could see his reflection in the bright, dark eyes. Gentle eyes. "I lost consciousness. It's my head that hurts." Trotti moved away from the touch of her cool fingers. "The last thing I can remember was lying on the ground by the river. It was raining and I was cold and wet."

"Your man called half an hour ago." Anna Maria nodded in the direction of the old clock above the refrigerator. It was nearly ten o'clock. "He wants you to ring back."

"What man?"

"With the Abruzzi accent."

"Magagna?"

Anna Maria added, pointing a thin finger at the mobile phone, "Your daughter hasn't stopped phoning since you got here."

"How's Pioppi?"

"Worried about you."

"Pioppi's all right? The girls are safe?"

"The girls are safe, Piero Trotti. Which is more than can be said for you."

"Pioppi started talking in Slovene."

"You and Agnese always spoiled her. That young lady knows how to look after herself." Anna Maria rose from the table—she no longer wore her Dutch slacks, but the shapeless, somber clothes of an old woman from the hills beyond the Po. At seventy-six, Anna Maria was an old woman from the hills. "You'd care for strong coffee with your sugar, Piero?"

Trotti noticed a conspiratorial glance that passed between the two women.

Signora Scola smiled, coughed and said, "Your cousin called me as soon as the Carabinieri brought you here."

"Carabinieri?"

Anna Maria remarked, not without pride, "Even as a little boy, Piero Trotti was always getting into trouble. A stubborn, headstrong child—affectionate and sweet but very, very stubborn."

"Really, Piero, apart from that nasty bruise, you look fine. In fact, for once you don't look tired."

"I must've slept round the clock." He had once loved the woman.

"Is there anything that I can do to help?"

Trotti did not answer Signora Scola's question.

Anna Maria busied herself with the coffee. She poured fresh milk into a saucepan. Her back was towards Trotti and Scola.

(*"Perhaps you thought the Scola woman would keep quiet about your nasty habits?"*)

"Is there anything I can do for you, Piero?" Scola asked again.

"Best if I'm left alone, for the time being."

"I can nurse you."

"Nurse your husband, signora. He needs you—he's in a wheelchair."

"You're angry with me, Piero?"

"You don't need to look after me, Signora Scola."

"I want to help."

"You know all about my nasty little habits."

Signora Scola frowned; standing in front of him in the kitchen of via Milano, she looked slim and graceful and very feminine. "Habits?"

"My nasty little habits with children."

"I don't think I understand."

"You understand, Signora Scola."

She shook her head.

"You know how everybody's been covering up for Commissario Trotti."

Scola shook her head a second time.

"Commissario Trotti, the pervert, the child molester, the sodomite."

Her mouth fell open. Trotti saw the pink triangle of her tongue and the white, even lines of her teeth.

"I need a hot shower," Trotti said. "I'll drink the coffee later."

89: Solihull

CLOUDS HAD COME south from the Alps, and it was now raining along the Po valley: heavy, fat drops that fell noisily onto the tarmac.

Trotti sat behind the wheel of the old Seicento. He went over the bridge and the buildings grew more scattered as he reached the open, flat countryside north of the river.

The Seicento gathered speed.

The heater was on and it was stuffy in Anna Maria's car. Beyond the windscreen, the countryside was still bare with the scars of winter. In the distance, the long line of plane trees was tinged by a shadow of green. At last, the promise of spring.

At Gravellino, he turned left and went through the new residential areas, inhabited by people who had moved out from Milan; people who commuted daily into the metropolis just thirty kilometers to the north.

In the village, Trotti parked the car outside a small café. It was one of the few original buildings, old stables that had been transformed many years before. A rain-washed ochre façade that still carried the script of a Fascist slogan.

Better to live a day as a lion than a hundred years as a lamb.

The other houses were low buildings that imitated the style of the farmhouses that they had replaced.

Gardens were hidden by high privet hedges, and the cypresses demarcated well-kept barriers between neighbors.

In one garden, Trotti saw a fountain—water that spouted enthusiastically into the damp afternoon air.

It had stopped raining.

For a moment, Trotti stood by the roadside, breathing in the air of the countryside—a bittersweet mixture of rich earth, dung, fertilizer, and rain.

Trotti had not been back to the house in eight years. It was still there at the end of the unsurfaced road. The trees in the front garden had grown and the hedge was thicker. Two cars stood in the garage, a spotless Range Rover and a mud-stained Volkswagen.

He went through the gate and rang the bell.

It was a while before the woman answered.

Signora Bianchini was wearing a pair of jeans that accentuated the flatness of her belly, and on her feet, she wore small yellow slippers. She must be nearly fifty years old, and it was not the first time that Trotti had seen Bianchini without makeup, but he was surprised by the freshness, by the youthfulness of her face.

And by the radiance of her smile.

"Piero, how nice to see you!" She stepped back and Trotti could see the pleasure was not feigned.

"Surprised you're not in Tuscany, Signora Bianchini."

"Tuscany?" She laughed in surprise. "What do you want me to go to Tuscany for?"

"Or Sicily."

"Come in, commissario, and stop talking your foolishness. And my name is no longer Bianchini. You know I've been married for eight years now."

"Is your husband with you?"

She laughed happily. "My husband's got nothing to hide."

She had left her native Caserta as a teenager, had come north and had done a lot of degrading jobs before marrying the wealthy Bianchini. She had lost all trace of a southern accent and now she spoke in the flat accent of the Po valley.

"He's certainly been hiding from me."

"You, commissario, who's the recluse. You never leave

that lair of yours in via Milano." Watching him carefully, she added, "Somebody was telling me you've got a girlfriend now."

"My cousin."

She shook her head mockingly, turned lightly on her toes and led Trotti into the house.

The living room was dark and smelled of varnish and cigar smoke. A grandfather clock stood in one corner and a vase of freshly cut flowers stood on the polished credenza. The furniture looked unused.

There was a portable computer, and two men were facing each other from either side of the polished table. They had been staring at the computer's blue screen; they looked up in false surprise as Trotti entered the room.

Both men nodded, but neither smiled.

The woman invited Trotti to sit down. "Gentlemen," she said, "perhaps you'd care for a drink."

Trotti took the chair and his glance went from one man to another.

"I'm sure Commissario Trotti would like some wine—genuine wine from the OltrePò." Then Signora Spadano turned to her husband—to the man she had married after the death of Bianchini, "You, Egidio, what would you like? You're not really supposed to touch alcohol if you want to lose weight. And you, Signor Portano? Some wine and some homemade salami for you, too?"

90: Disney

"YOU LIED TO me."

The Sicilian shook his head.

"You lied to me, Spadano. Why?"

"Why what?"

"Why'd you lie?"

"Why does anybody lie to you, Piero? Because you're arrogant, because you must always be right, because you only believe what you want to hear. Because you won't take any advice from anybody."

"That entitles you to risk my life?"

"I've never risked your life."

"Watching the killer bundle me into the trunk of a car—that wasn't risking my life?"

"You risked your life the day you allowed Beltoni to die. It wasn't me who murdered Beltoni. I never told Enzo Beltoni to come out of hiding in America and avenge his brother's death. I never told him to kill Commissario Trotti."

"You wanted to get your hands on Enzo Beltoni and you used me."

Spadano shrugged. "A lot of people want Beltoni."

"I became your bait—your unwitting bait."

"You already were his bait, Piero."

"You put me on the front page of the paper—on the front page of every damn paper."

"Enzo Beltoni wanted his revenge whatever I did."

"You handed me to him on a plate—without telling me."

"I told you Beltoni was out to kill you."

"Thanks to you, he nearly succeeded."

The Carabiniere shook his head wearily. "Sooner or later, some fisherman was going to find your charred remains on the banks of the Po."

"The decent thing would have been to tell me the truth."

"I warned you Enzo Beltoni'd left America and was back in Italy. I told you he was looking for you. What more could you want?"

"You didn't tell me you were using me."

"You never listen, Piero."

"Who says I wouldn't have listened?"

"Piero, Piero," Spadano said unhappily. "Don't pretend you don't know what you're like."

"Like?"

"Stubborn and opinionated and contemptuous."

"Stubborn and opinionated and contemptuous when a friend's risking my neck for the sake of his own advancement?"

"Bit old for advancement, aren't I?" Spadano laughed in feigned disbelief. "In Siena, you talked all your rubbish, your peace of the senses. You told me you'd lived out your usefulness." Spadano snorted derisively. "Piero Trotti's *Nunc Dimittis*—or have you forgotten?"

"In Siena, I believed you were a general of the Carabinieri, Spadano, and I thought you were doing me a favor."

"I am a general of the Carabinieri and I *was* doing you a favor, Piero Trotti. A big favor."

"By sending me to see the Lia Guerra woman?" Trotti had started to raise his voice. "For heaven's sake, Spadano, the man nearly killed me."

Spadano gestured with the cigar towards Portano. "If Harry hadn't intervened, you'd now be dead meat down by the river."

Trotti glanced briefly at the other man.

"Burnt steak. You've got a lot to thank Harry for. Not least the mouth-to-mouth resuscitation."

"Harry?"

Portano was wearing his shabby, crumpled suit. The Neapolitan had been sitting at the varnished table, smoking his cigarette, never taking his eyes off the computer. He was very pale. Now a smile worked its way across the long face as he removed the cigarette from where it hung at the corner of his mouth.

"Harry Portano of the DEA."

Trotti said to Spadano, "I thought your Harry was in the hospital with a case of mumps."

"Drug Enforcement Agency," Spadano said. "Harry's people in Washington have been helping us look into BRAMAN."

"Perhaps I owe you an apology, commissario," Portano said.

"Washington." Trotti gave a whistle.

Portano's head moved slowly as he turned to face Trotti. "I owe you an apology, Commissario Trotti. I overreacted."

"Hitting an old man? Striking him across the face when he's handcuffed. Knocking him senseless when he's unarmed? Insulting him when you know he's innocent? Accusing him of murder? Of pedophilia and incest?" Briefly returning the American's glance, Trotti softly asked, "What makes you think for a minute you were overreacting?"

Spadano said, "My fault, Piero."

Trotti turned back to Spadano, "Your fault this bastard knocked me senseless?"

"We wanted to piss you off a bit."

"You told this shitbag to beat up an old policeman? Is that what you're saying, Spadano? You wanted me spitting spinal fluid?"

No reply.

"My good friend General Spadano of the Carabinieri was deliberately pissing me off?"

"Not always easy to be your friend, Piero."

"I was your friend, Spadano—whatever you say. Twenty,

twenty-five years we've known each other, twenty-five years I was your friend. And then you tell this bastard from Naples, you tell this piece of shit from the FBI or the CIA or from Disneyland, you tell him to beat the shit out of your old friend?"

"It seemed the best thing to do at the time."

91: Arma

"WHAT DO YOU really want?"

"You'd bite any hand that feeds you, Piero."

"Use me as a decoy? That's feeding me?"

"Enzo Beltoni had to be stopped and you stopped him, Piero."

"It was your idea to get the Gracchi woman thrown in jail, wasn't it? Without her, Enzo Beltoni'd never have returned to Italy."

"The sostituto procuratore has sufficient reason for arresting Chiara Gracchi."

"You know she's innocent."

"Of course Chiara's innocent."

"You and your American friends need to get your hands on Enzo Beltoni. So you put the Gracchi woman in prison. And then you expect the real killer to come out of the woodwork because Enzo Beltoni thinks he's off the hook, no longer the suspect."

"Enzo Beltoni's been in Italy for a couple of months, but I'm flattered you think I can control the Italian justice system."

"You control the Carabinieri. You told me you were a general. You told me you worked for Tutela del Patrimonio Artistico. You even had your own little office with Byzantine frescoes."

"I am a general."

"You don't work for our cultural heritage."

Spadano was silent.

"After all these years, you couldn't trust me with the truth, Spadano?"

"What truth?"

"What you were after?"

Spadano tipped his head, "You would have said no."

"Damned right I'd've said no."

"In your surly, self-satisfied way, you always do what suits you, Piero. You could never understand there are things more important than Piero Trotti."

"More important than General Egidio Spadano?"

"More important than both you and me."

Trotti had begun to perspire. "Your need to get Craxi back from Tunisia—that's more important than me and you? More important than our friendship—the friendship and collaboration and trust, built up over the years?"

"Craxi?" Spadano laughed as he took a packet of American Toscanelli from his pocket.

"You've got Enzo Beltoni—and through Enzo Beltoni, you now hope to get hold of Giovanni Verga and Craxi."

"I know nothing about Craxi."

"Lying again, Egidio?"

Spadano said nothing.

Trotti made a gesture in the direction of Portano. "Your Americans want Enzo Beltoni? A blackmailer and cheap murderer? They fly in their best operatives from Eurodisney because Enzo Beltoni's public enemy number one? No, Spadano, I won't buy that."

Portano moved his cigarette in his mouth and with a tense smile, leaned forward. "Commissario Trotti, perhaps I should . . ."

"Best if your American friend shuts his ugly mouth before this old man rips his balls out—what's left of them." Trotti did not pause. "Spadano, what was so important?"

"Piero, Piero, Piero."

There was an untouched glass of wine on the table before him and sitting back, Trotti took a long draught.

"I wanted to save your life, Piero."

"You wanted to get Enzo Beltoni and all you risked losing was your nice Carabinieri coat."

Spadano sighed. "You really don't get it, do you?"

Trotti clicked his tongue contemptuously.

"The Socialists and the Christian Democrats are gone. It's no longer 1988—and the country's changed in eight years, Piero. When in Trapani, they allowed Enzo Beltoni to escape to America, it was because that's what the politicians wanted—the Third Level."

"Don't talk to me about your Third Level."

"Those same Socialists are now a spent power and our ex-prime minister's a common criminal in hiding in Hammamet."

"You want Craxi?"

"Of course not."

"What the hell do you want? What's so important that you leave me to die like a dog?"

"You were never left to die," Spadano said evenly. "You never saw the Volkswagen, Piero? You never saw the car that's now standing out there in the road?"

"I was lying handcuffed in the trunk—I wasn't looking at the countryside. I was breathing the carbon monoxide."

Portano remarked, "You'd never be safe while Enzo Beltoni's a free man."

"Have I got to rip his American balls off once and for good?"

"Harry's right, Trotti. The carbon monoxide was a risk worth taking."

"Harry can go and sodomize himself."

Spadano shook his head. "Harry wanted you out of that car. He wanted to arrest Beltoni in Bologna, but I was against it."

"You needed to see me trussed up? See me poisoned?" Trotti asked incredulously.

"Look at the long term. By the time you reached Bologna, Beltoni'd been holding your daughter for nearly twelve hours."

"So?"

"Beltoni wouldn't have hesitated a moment to hurt your

daughter or the girls if it suited him. He doesn't have feelings. Once you fell into Enzo Beltoni's trap, there was no longer any need for him to hurt the children. Or rape your daughter, for that matter. I knew you were in the trunk—as did half the Arma between Bologna and Milan."

"For all the good it did me."

"You could've died from poisoning—I won't deny that, Piero. But you're alive and your family's safe. Pioppi's safe. The children are safe—now and for the foreseeable future. You wouldn't have done the same as me?"

"I didn't know what you were doing."

"I should have arrested Enzo Beltoni for attempting kidnapping?" Spadano studied the tip of the unlit cigar. "He'd be out of custody in less than a month—six months at most." Spadano moved away from the table. "Instead Enzo Beltoni's facing attempted murder, Piero. While you're alive and safe. A bit of discomfort in the back of the car's a small price to pay for Piera and Francesca's safety—don't you think?"

Trotti did not reply.

"Enzo Beltoni will get at least eight years." Spadano produced his lighter and held it to the tip of the Toscanelli; acrid clouds of smoke rose into the air. "That'll give you and your daughter some breathing space."

"Your motives are noble, Egidio."

"Your sarcasm's not funny."

Trotti tapped his chest. "Let's forget for a moment Donald Duck here slapped me around. Let's forget I've been accused of murdering an American girl. Let's forget my best friends Magagna and Pisanelli lied to me."

"Pisanelli never lied to you, Trotti."

"Let's forget you manipulated my friends. Let's forget I've been lied to and used, let's forget my life was put at risk, let's forget that the girl was stabbed to death." A dismissive gesture of Trotti's hand. "What's in it for you? What are you after? What can justify your playing at God? Justify your risking my neck while you're sitting in your nice, safe little Volkswagen?"

"I told you—I wanted to protect you."

"Don't give me that shit." Trotti's voice had risen, and he had turned pale. His finger was pointing accusingly at Spadano, and Trotti had started to tremble. "Tell me what you really want, Spadano?"

There was silence in the room.

Beyond the window, the dark silhouette of a cherry tree was tipped with the first green buds of spring. The clouds were moving south and the sky was blue, not the misty blue of summer when humidity hung like a damp towel over the plane of Lombardy, but the clear blue of a beautiful spring afternoon.

Winter was coming to an end and Trotti was still alive. He was stiff, he had difficulty in staying upright, but he would get better. The headaches and the giddiness would go, the pain in his temples would go. In a few weeks, he would be well again.

Spring was returning to the Po valley and instead of relief, Trotti was trembling with rage.

"What the hell do you want, Spadano?"

Spadano looked at Trotti before softly saying, "For years, I never thought one day I'd have a wife and a child of my own."

Trotti held up his hand. "Spare me."

"I never gave marriage or a family of my own a second thought. The insignia of the Carabinieri were tattooed into my flesh—into my soul. That's what you used to say. Into my soul."

"You fooled me, Spadano."

"Ever since he and I first met thirty years ago, Valerio Gracchi was like a son to me. A son and a good friend."

"So bloody what?"

"Before I retire, I'm bringing Valerio Gracchi's killer to justice."

92: Bierkeller

"I WAS SITTING in an Alfetta. It was a cold night, early in February and for some reason the heating wasn't working properly. I had a rug that I'd thrown over my legs, but I was cursing the job and I was cursing my own folly for ever having volunteered. Thirty years ago, Piero, and in those days I was ambitious. Working in the Political Section seemed the best way of moving up."

"Arma burned into your flesh?"

"Older and wiser, no doubt, but I still believe in serving my country. In Siena, you asked me if I was becoming a communist. I now see I've always been a crypto-communist—but that's not the word I used in 1968."

"Thank goodness for that."

"Piero, we're both peasants, you and I. We come from a class of people who've been exploited throughout history. You in Lombardy and me in Sicily. But for all its failings—and goodness knows it has enough of them—this Italy is our Italy, this republic is our republic."

Trotti raised an eyebrow.

"Don't jeer. This republic, morally bankrupt and chronically cynical—it's all we've got. At most, we can hope to improve it." Spadano gave a slow smile, and his grey eyes looked at Trotti from behind a thinning cloud of smoke. "You pretend to be cynical, Piero, but I know you've made your sacrifices. We can't change the big things, but we can try to improve the little things. You and I have shared values. Moral values in a vast moral void."

"Shared values?" Trotti gave an unhappy laugh and Spadano held up his hand.

"Don't rush to judgement."

"Beaten, bruised, humiliated and suffocated—a small price to pay for our shared values?"

Spadano moved towards the table and stubbed out his cigar into the overflowing ashtray.

There was a bottle of red wine from the OltrePò and a plate of salami, but the three men had not touched the food that Signora Spadano had set out before them.

"I was shivering to death in the car and he was there with his friends in the beer cellar, in the warmth. You know Trento, Piero? You know what winter can be like in the Alps. God, I was cold but I had to keep out of sight. And I couldn't run the engine—we didn't want Lotta Continua thinking they were being watched. This was in 1968 or 1969, and on both sides we were fairly unsophisticated. The years of lead were to come later. They weren't expecting surveillance—Lotta Continua was still a student thing and very innocent, despite the revolutionary rhetoric. They all came from middle-class backgrounds and there was no reason to think things would ever spiral out of control. That's precisely what did happen—everything spiraled out of control into a decade of violence." Spadano grimaced. "Cocco and his young wife were idealistic, practicing Christians in those days—sweet kids. Who'd've thought Cocco'd get life for murder? Who'd've ever thought his wife would be gunned down in daylight?"

"What's all this got to do with me, Spadano?"

Spadano was now smiling pensively. "I went to Sicily. I was there at the funeral in 1988, I was there when all his old Lotta Continua companions came down to Trapani for the funeral. And I saw Lakshmi's face. Not yet an adolescent and her sweet, sweet face swollen with tears. The pallbearers took the coffin from the cathedral and Gracchi was buried at Erice, in a piece of land that overlooks the sea, that overlooks the olive groves at BRAMAN, in a place where the Scirocco brings the warm sands from Africa. I was there, and all I could remember was that night in Trento and how he had come out of the beer cellar and how he had tapped at the window of the car."

"And?"

"He'd bought me a wurst and a beer. A bit embarrassed and said he realized I couldn't hobnob with the enemy, but that was no reason for my dying of pneumonia." Spadano smiled fondly. "That was Tino Gracchi—when you least expected it, he was capable of great kindness. He didn't have the killer instinct and that's why he could never be a politician—he liked people too much. Not the abstract idea of people, but people he could talk to, joke with. People he could love." Spadano nodded. "We became friends after that. I was supposed to be keeping an eye on this dangerous, revolutionary element, and instead we became friends. Like father and son."

"Well done."

"Twenty years later, when he was being lowered into the earth, when the dirt was being shoveled onto the flowers, it was then I swore I'd bring Tino's killer to justice. Not because Gracchi fought the Mafia or because he had set up a commune for addicts. It was something very personal, something I had to do to thank him for what he'd given me—me, the Carabiniere, me the enemy—over all the years. The friendship and the wurst."

93: West Bank

PEERING OVER THE wall, Trotti glanced down at the street below. The machine guns of the Carabinieri appeared no more sinister than the glinting cars or the occasional passerby in via del Tempio.

"The days Israel's on the front page of the papers, that's when they send in a couple of extra policemen."

"You know them?"

"The Carabinieri?" Lia Guerra raised her shoulder. "I recognize some of them. They smile their toothy smiles and ogle my legs."

"You knew the men who arrested me?"

Potted plants—cacti and bougainvillea and dates—stood along the low wall and incongruously, there was a line of sheets drying in the breeze.

The red tiles of the terrace tried to absorb the morning heat. Summer had already arrived in Rome, while five hundred kilometers to the north, the cherry trees were still struggling into blossom along via Milano.

Trotti returned to where Lia Guerra was sitting under the striped awning. Several wicker chairs and a low table. Beside the table was a wheeled refrigerator, and on a chaise longue, the morning's newspaper lay face down.

There was a glass of acqua brillante in her hand, "I didn't get to see their faces, commissario. I was too scared," Lia

Guerra said gently, more to herself than to Trotti. "Not every day armed men come bursting into your house and drag off a guest at gunpoint." She added, "Afterwards, they were very apologetic."

"That's reassuring. I was bundled into the car with a bag over my head."

"So I saw."

"Then I was beaten up."

Surprise in her voice. "By the Carabinieri?"

Trotti found himself scrutinizing the woman in front of him. "By one of Spadano's friends."

"Why?"

"I'd murdered a black girl."

"It was in the paper." A nod towards the newspaper. "I tried to contact you—I phoned the general. He didn't seem to know where you were."

"It was Spadano who made sure I was on the front page of every newspaper from Bolzano to Lipari. A retired commissario who's killed a black girl—it makes good copy. Your friend Spadano knew perfectly well where I was. It was his idea I'd killed her."

"Spadano lied to me?"

"Spadano lies to everybody."

"I like him. Why lie?"

"Because Spadano thought I'd help him find Enzo Beltoni."

"Why throw you in jail? Why put you in all the papers?"

Trotti made a gesture of resignation. "Enzo Beltoni held me responsible for his brother's death. With Chiara Gracchi's imminent arrest, Spadano knew Beltoni'd come back to Italy and finish me off."

"Finish you off," the woman repeated. She gave a little shudder.

"I was Spadano's bait."

"He wanted Enzo Beltoni?"

Trotti nodded. "Spadano believes Enzo Beltoni murdered your boyfriend, Valerio Gracchi. And thanks to me, Beltoni's now under arrest."

"All a bit dangerous, wasn't it?"

"Very dangerous."

"I've never been as scared as when those men entered this place, but I was sure nothing would happen to you—not at your age."

"Not sure that's a compliment. I was nearly killed by Beltoni. I ended up lying on the wet ground of the Po riverbank, tied up like a stuck pig. By the time Spadano finally got his hands on Enzo Beltoni, the man'd managed to beat the daylights out of an old man. And scare me to death."

"You seem alive."

"I do my best, signora."

"And your friend—the young man who was with you? Where's Signor Pisanelli?"

"On his honeymoon in Malindi. In Kenya."

Lia Guerra nodded with pleasure. "I saw him being accompanied downstairs by two women officers. The Carabinieri didn't rough him up or anything."

"Might've done him some good."

"The two had to carry him—the aluminum crutch was snapped. I was a lot more worried for him than for you."

"Pisanelli'll be delighted to hear that."

Her voice hardened. "You've beaten up enough people in your time, commissario."

(*The arm was scarred and hard where needles had pierced the skin.*

Lia Guerra pulled her arm free, fell backwards and crumpled onto the floor. "You bastard," she muttered as she scratched at her arm.)

"You still remember Porta Ticinese, Commissario Trotti?"

"A long time ago."

"A long time ago for you—but not for me."

"I'm sure you've forgotten."

"Perhaps I've forgiven you."

"You see."

"I haven't forgotten. You tricked me and you used me." She moved on her seat, and after all these years, Trotti was surprised how sensuous she was.

Trotti had always known Lia Guerra was pretty. In 1978, that long, hot May afternoon in the Questura, he had found her pretty, yes; several years later, when he had visited her in the Porta Ticinese shop, Lia Guerra was still an attractive young woman. Attractive despite the heroin.

It had never occurred to Trotti that Lia Guerra could be physically exciting.

Perhaps sensing Trotti's thoughts, the woman set down the acqua brillante, got up and went towards the balustrade. She lightly placed her weight on her toes. Her eyes never left him. She beckoned, and Trotti obediently rose and joined her.

The view of Rome from the rooftop was breathtaking.

"That's why you've come to see me?" Lia Guerra spoke with her Turin accent, deliberately softening the fricatives.

Trotti smiled and the smile felt awkward as it creased his cheeks, "The last time I was here, I didn't get to say goodbye."

"You can say goodbye, commissario, and then you can leave—without a bag over your head."

"You wanted to know who murdered Gracchi." Trotti raised his pitch in imitation of a woman's voice, "I need to know the truth, commissario. I need to know who killed him—it's the only thing that matters."

"You just told me."

"I didn't tell you anything."

"Enzo Beltoni murdered my Tino."

On the other side of the road, set back in the synagogue garden, Trotti caught sight of the bearded man with his broad-brimmed hat and dark coat. He had the bowed, thoughtful look of a priest reading his breviary.

"Spadano believes Enzo Beltoni murdered your boyfriend. I believe no such thing."

94: G7

"GENERAL SPADANO'S WRONG?"

"Spadano believes it's his duty to arrest Gracchi's murderer. Something he owes the little girl."

"Lakshmi?"

Trotti nodded.

Lia Guerra looked at him thoughtfully. "You think Enzo Beltoni didn't kill Tino."

"What I think doesn't really matter."

"It clearly matters to the general. It matters to me."

"What matters to Spadano isn't going to change things." Trotti gave the woman a weary smile, "Beltoni's not going to go to jail."

"Beltoni beat you up."

"Enzo Beltoni tried to kill me." Trotti rubbed at his neck where the rope had bitten into his skin. "More importantly, Enzo Beltoni murdered Gracchi—at least, according to Spadano. But Signora, I'm not important and Gracchi's not important. Nor is Beltoni."

Lia Guerra had returned to the chaise longue and Trotti sat down opposite her.

"Enzo Beltoni's a means to an end and Spadano knows it. He knows what the Americans want."

"What?"

"The Americans are going to do a deal, Lakshmi or no Lakshmi. The Americans want Craxi."

Her laughter was unexpected.

Lia Guerra put her head back and the Adam's apple jumped in her long, thin throat. She laughed happily. It was some time before she regained her composure and her glance returned to Trotti, amusement wrinkling her eyes. "The Americans want Bettino Craxi? What's Enzo Beltoni got to do with our Socialist ex-prime minister?"

"The Third Level—the level where Mafia and politicians meet. Andreotti being kissed by the Mafia bosses. Collusion between the state and organized crime. People've been talking about these things ever since the Americans brought back the Mafia in 1943, along with their tanks and jeeps and chewing gum. But until Craxi, the Third Level was within the Christian Democrats."

"And Craxi's a Socialist?"

"The Christian Democrats used the criminals, but Craxi is a criminal."

"He's in Tunisia now and out of the way. He's ill, probably dying."

"In Tunisia, but not necessarily out of the way for the Americans."

"I imagine the Americans have extradition treaties with Tunisia."

"Possibly."

"Then why the fuss?"

Trotti was silent.

"Why's Craxi so important? An exile and politically dead—just as the Socialist party is dead. Why bother the poor man? Let him live out his last years in peace."

"American bombers are based here in this country. For forty years, the Americans stifled Italian democracy because they were frightened of the Italian communists. Now the communists are no longer a threat, and the Americans no longer tell us what to do as if this were a banana republic. Italy's become the sixth wealthiest nation in the world."

"What's that got to do with Craxi?"

"A democracy washes its dirty linen in public." Trotti held up his hand. "After forty years of Cold War, the Americans've decided they need to speak to their allies on an equal footing. It's called the new international morality."

"That's just politics—empty words."

"Craxi's a criminal, and the Americans want him brought to justice."

"Criminal in what way?"

"You know perfectly well."

Lia Guerra put her hand to her throat, half smiling. "You're accusing me of being an associate of Craxi?"

"You were at BRAMAN in the mid-eighties. Here in Rome, you dealt with the politicians. You saw how BRAMAN changed from the idealistic commune your boyfriend Tino wanted. You saw how it was turned into a machine for making money—for whitewashing dirty money. Dirty money for Giovanni Verga and his Socialist friends. Friends in Milan, friends in Rome."

"That's got nothing to do with me."

"I hope not."

95: Buffoon

"PEDOPHILE?" A FROZEN smile on her face, her features suddenly weary. "You're joking, commissario."

"I'm afraid not."

"Giovanni likes women—he was married to an Austrian princess."

Trotti shook his head sadly. "Not women he's interested in now."

"Giovanni was desperately in love with Sissi. For her sake he went out to India—Giovanni did everything he possibly could to help the wretched girl. That's how he got into religion in the first place."

"Verga's a pedophile."

"It's just not possible."

"And Enzo Beltoni was blackmailing him."

Lia Guerra shook her head. "Giovanni once made a pass at me. I was shocked, but also a bit flattered that he should find me desirable. Giovanni Verga likes women—that's plain to see."

"I can make a pass at you, signora, but that tells you nothing about my sexual appetites."

"You don't find me desirable." Lia Guerra looked at Trotti with an appraising glance. "I doubt if you find any woman desirable. There are other things more important for you. I imagine you collect stamps or bonsai trees."

The empty glass stood on the terracotta floor of the terrace, and the black cat moved among the shadows on the roof. There was a light wind, but it was hot and brought little relief.

"Enzo Beltoni had photos—compromising photos. And he knew some of the boys."

"Tino would never have let Giovanni get near his daughter—near Lakshmi." Lia Guerra said, "Not if he was like that."

"Giovanni Verga's like that—and not particularly attracted by little girls. Nor by stamp collecting or bonsai trees."

She folded her arms against her chest. She looked healthier and happier than when he had last seen her.

"That's how you're going to get him out of Guatemala?"

"That's how Spadano hopes to get Verga out of Guatemala. If he does a deal with Enzo Beltoni and if it can be proved Verga's a danger to children in Guatemala, Giovanni Verga won't last very long—extradition treaty or no extradition treaty."

"Does it matter?"

"Personally, I couldn't give a damn about Giovanni Verga."

"You couldn't give a damn about anybody."

Trotti allowed himself a smile. "For all I care, Beltoni can rot in prison. For all I care Giovanni Verga can stay in Guatemala—and Bettino Craxi can stay in Tunisia." Trotti took a deep breath. "If Spadano hadn't told me his cock-and-bull story about Gracchi, I'd never have come to see you in the first place."

"You always hated Tino."

"I met Valerio Gracchi just once, signora."

"You hated him."

"Not sure he merited the effort." Trotti paused. "I'm finding it harder and harder to hate people as I get older—goodness knows why."

"Senility."

"Gracchi was a terrorist."

"Of course he wasn't. Tino abhorred violence."

"I believed he'd kidnapped my goddaughter and your

boyfriend spent a couple of nights in prison. I was wrong, but over the years I've not lost much sleep about that. Other, better people have spent time in prison and that hasn't worried me unduly."

"No one's better than Tino." Guerra shook her head. "That's what you don't understand, commissario. Tino was good, morally good."

"For some reason, Gracchi seemed to respect me. I wish I could return the compliment."

"Tino was a good man and could recognize goodness in others."

"What was it the Sicilian magazine said?" Trotti quoted, like a child reading aloud, "*A fascinating man. A thoroughly modern man, the bittersweet product of Postwar Italy, with all the conflicting contradictions, weaknesses and strengths of our nation. A flawed hero, an Italian hero, a poet, a crusader, at times even a buffoon.*" Trotti lowered his head. "I personally thought your boyfriend was a misguided crusader, naive and rather dangerous."

"Tino was never dangerous."

"I was wrong."

"Wrong, commissario?" There was a thin line of beaded sweat along her upper lip. "Beginning to think you don't know everything? You really are turning senile."

"I was wrong and I admit it."

"Perhaps you can admit Tino was a good man? That he had his values? That he wasn't afraid to fight for those values—in Trapani as in Trento?"

"That's what everybody says."

"Not you?"

"I don't give Gracchi much thought, signora—I have other things to worry about." Trotti nodded in concession. "But General Spadano considered him the son he'd never had. You apparently worshipped Gracchi, even if you never wanted to give him children. And his daughter Lakshmi's always idolized him, while not being blind to her father's shortcomings."

"And you, commissario?"

"Gracchi's been dead for eight years. What a slow-witted peasant from the Po valley thinks of a hero in the battle against the Mafia and the forces of evil—what a retired flatfoot thinks of Gracchi isn't important. What I think isn't important because I'm not important."

"Even your self-pity's insincere."

Trotti made a gesture of admission.

"Your opinion of Tino's never changed since 1978?"

"Gracchi was a fool."

She laughed in disbelief. "That's how you talk of the dead?"

"A buffoon who couldn't see who his real enemy was."

"His only enemies were people like you—people who didn't know him, who didn't trust him."

"You knew him—knew him as no one else did." Trotti paused before adding carefully, "You shared your bed with him and then, after years spent in Switzerland, you returned to that bed, although he was now happily married. You knew him, and you knew he was weak and a fool. If you loved him as you say you loved him, you really should never have murdered the poor fool. What a strange way to love a man, Lia."

96: Ispettore

SHE WAS WAITING for him, reading the newspaper on the terrace of the bar beneath a parasol. She sat in an aluminum chair, her bag at her feet and a pair of sunglasses pushed back into the thick hair. A blue ribbon ran through the curls and was tied into a knot above her neck.

She was wearing shorts with a white singlet, and for a brief moment Trotti thought it was Eva, but as the girl turned to face him, Piero Trotti saw that she was much younger than the prostitute from Uruguay.

"You never smile, signor ispettore. Not pleased to see me?"

"You've been waiting long?"

"Not more than a couple of weeks."

Trotti nodded to the portable telephone on the tablecloth. "You could've called Spadano."

"Spadano told me in no uncertain terms to leave you alone."

"I'd have appreciated a phone call while I was trussed up in the trunk of Enzo Beltoni's car."

It was indeed a beautiful day, with the afternoon sun shining on the open square and the central fountain. The car trunk, Enzo Beltoni and the chill of the sandy, wet banks of the Po seemed a world away.

Peace of the senses?

He sat down beside her and the girl placed a hand on Trotti's shoulder and she kissed him, a soft, gentle kiss on the forehead while with the other hand, she caressed what remained of his hair. "The general used me as much as he ever used you, signor ispettore."

In the Piazza Santa Maria in Trastevere, gypsy children were playing football, occasionally breaking off to beg from the passersby. A few foreign tourists entered the church or emerged from it.

Déjà vu?

Trotti had the impression of playing hooky, of being on a stolen holiday. It was as if a weight had been taken from his shoulders. "What've you been doing these last two weeks, Wilma?"

"Waiting for you."

"You still want me to find your father?"

"You find that funny?"

Trotti smiled crookedly. "You don't find it funny you lied to a gullible old man?"

"I phoned you, commissario—or perhaps you've forgotten. We were supposed to meet."

He shook his head. "I haven't forgotten." Trotti was still smiling.

"I needed to tell you the truth. You were good to me in Florence and Empoli and Siena. When I arrived in Rome, I felt very bad about all the lies."

"Not as bad as I felt when the Carabinieri started beating me. Or when I saw your dead body."

The same narrow-waisted waiter surged forward and brought the list of drinks to their table. Trotti smiled in surprise and pleasure as he ordered two spremutas. The waiter gave a brief glance at the American girl then nimbly returned to the interior of the café.

Trotti's eyes wandered to the church on the far side of the piazza, beyond the noisy children. He said, almost absent-mindedly, "Of course, I never did believe in coincidences."

"What coincidences?"

The eyes appraised him from behind the rim of the paper cup. Widely set brown eyes, and Trotti realized why she reminded him of Eva.

97: Pavé

WHENEVER TROTTI LOOKED at him, he had an ingratiating smile and his cheeks were creased in deep wrinkles. All the tables were served, and during the lull in customers, the waiter leaned against the doorway and carefully observed his patrons at their bright tables. The tight waistcoat was neatly buttoned.

Trotti turned back to the girl. "Spadano considered your father as his own son."

"My father's a bricklayer from Mestre," the girl said evenly, "and he's never met Spadano."

"For some reason, Spadano liked Valerio Gracchi—ever since they first met in Trento, when Spadano was supposed to be keeping an eye on the young revolutionary. Nearly everybody liked Gracchi. Even now, eight years after his death, everyone speaks well of him—an Italian hero."

"Except you?"

"With all his posturing, the man got on my nerves."

"You are going to arrest her?"

Trotti laughed. "A retired flatfoot—why do you want me to arrest the poor woman?"

"If she murdered him . . ."

"Nothing to do with me."

"You said the general wanted Gracchi's killer."

"I don't owe Spadano any favors."

"Spadano told me you were friends."

"That's what he told me, too—for twenty-five years, I believed him."

"You're not going to tell the general who killed Gracchi?"

"Spadano wouldn't believe me."

"If the general won't believe you, who's going to believe you?"

"Nobody—because nobody's going to know."

"Yet you're convinced Lia Guerra killed Gracchi?"

"That's what she said," Trotti replied softly and took another sip of the spremuta. He winced and stirred the long spoon. Granules of sugar danced against the side of the glass.

A gentle wind blew across the square. The smell of cooking came from the nearby houses—it was four o'clock in the afternoon.

Opposite Trotti, Wilma was both amused and puzzled. She was now sitting back in her chair. Beneath the parasol, the Roman light glinted off her skin.

"She admitted to killing her boyfriend?"

"She didn't deny it."

"Wasn't she in love? They'd lived together—and she'd returned to be with him in Sicily. Wasn't it Guerra who'd been trying to get the enquiry going again?"

"She wasn't interested in stirring muddy waters—all an act. She simply felt she had to imitate whatever Chiara Gracchi was doing."

"They'd been lovers—and they were still friends."

"Precisely why she killed him."

Wilma shook her head, "That doesn't make sense."

"Gracchi'd always been in love with Lia Guerra. Ever since she was a teenager, ever since the day in Milan they met during a fight with the Celere."

"Who?"

"One of those street battles between the armed police and radical students—they happened all the time in the early seventies. It was love at first sight—or at first hurled cobble. She was still a child, trying to break free of her home and her parents. He was a leading light in Lotta Continua. The night they met she was in his bed." Trotti added, "Like Laura and Petrarca."

She grinned with satisfaction. "You see, you are a romantic."

"Not Lia Guerra. She wasn't interested in sex. Not in those days. Dictatorship of the proletariat was more her line. More interested in the coming revolution than having the sweaty hands of a man all over her body."

"There's more to romance than just sex."

Trotti frowned.

"There's love."

"Lia Guerra'd grown up in a private school and the nuns'd put her off men. Which would explain why Gracchi left her in the end. After five years, they weren't going anywhere. He realized she'd never share herself with him. Gracchi'd always loved her—loved her a lot more than he ever loved his first wife in Turin. Unfortunately, Lia Guerra didn't love him in the way that every man wants to be loved."

"In the way every man wants?"

Trotti looked at the young woman. "You haven't found out?"

"Men can be very frightening, you know."

"I'm frightening, signorina?"

"An irritable mouse with a potbelly and a friendly smile."

"I'm supposed to be flattered?"

"Tell me about Lia Guerra."

Trotti put another sachet of sugar into the spremuta and stirred the milky, cool water. The ices cubes clicked noisily.

"Gracchi went off and married Chiara—while Guerra spent a couple of years with the unlamented journalist Maltese. Didn't take her long to see she couldn't live with Gracchi, but she couldn't live very well without him, either. She took up drugs, and from then on her life went into a downward spiral. Perhaps it was fortunate Maltese got himself killed."

"Fortunate her boyfriend was murdered?"

"Lia Guerra knew I wanted to arrest her—it was Pisanelli,

the man you saw at the Termini, who stopped me. Lia Guerra fled to Switzerland. Nearly thirty years old, the woman was on drugs and single. In Switzerland, she started to panic. She could do something about the drugs, but she couldn't do much about getting old. The two men of her life had disappeared, and Lia Guerra, the Marxist pasionaria, began to see she was no different from all other women. The sweaty hands of a man have their uses. Lia Guerra wanted a family of her own."

"But Gracchi was married?"

"Happily married and living in Sicily with a wonderful, loving wife and a beautiful child—even if perhaps he was still in love with his pasionaria from the Po valley." Another sip. "I can't say I ever found Guerra attractive."

"Surprised you find the time to think about that sort of thing."

"What sort of thing do you want me to think about, signorina?"

98: Genome

"EIGHT YEARS AND everybody's been looking for the killer—and it's the provincial flatfoot who's found her without even looking."

Trotti turned back to the girl. "Didn't really have to look."

"You wouldn't be arrogant, would you?"

"Why arrogant? Arrogant people want everyone to believe they're sure of themselves."

"You're sure of yourself?"

Trotti allowed himself a brief smile. "I don't much care what others think of me." He looked at the girl, at her high cheekbones. "You were working as a whore in Milan?"

"Don't be silly," Wilma retorted hotly, but the skin turned darker.

"That's what the paper said."

"Give up reading papers, signor ispettore, if you're going to believe everything they say. Or stick to the funnies."

"How else could Spadano blackmail you?"

"What blackmail are you talking about?"

"I'm too old to believe in coincidences. Your waiting for the same train at Santa Maria Novella wasn't a coincidence. Telling me you were looking for your father wasn't a coincidence."

"I just told you my father works in Mestre. He's a mason."

"On the train, you asked me to look for your father. You said your father was Valerio Gracchi."

A glint of teeth as her lips parted in a pretty smile. "I was lying."

"And that's funny?"

"It's funny seeing Commissario Trotti getting hot under the collar. You've never been lied to before by a pretty young woman?"

"Pretty young woman? You wouldn't be arrogant, would you?"

"Arrogant people want everyone to believe they're sure of themselves."

"You're sure of your youth and your beauty?" Trotti was no longer smiling. He leaned forward in his seat and tapped the tablecloth in poorly concealed irritation. "You were alone in Florence and you looked unhappy and lost. I tried to be helpful. Why'd you lie to me?"

"I was very cold."

"The long and convoluted story about your mother . . ."

"Is true." Wilma nodded briskly as the smile slowly died on her lips. "The wonderful black nurse who happens to be my real mother lives in Los Angeles, and she's just what I told you—a selfish bitch. An aging princess with beautiful black skin and thick, sensuous lips, with lustrous hair and a wonderful, doting husband. The black princess farmed me out—she farmed her own daughter out for adoption in Memphis, and I should hate her. I should hate the bitch—a complete stranger took me in and gave me more love than my own mother ever knew how to give. My adoptive parents in Evanston never skimped in their affection—and when I turned up at Los Angeles airport, all my real mother could spare me was a half-hour of her precious time. And a picture of her Nissan car."

Wilma was no longer relaxed, and she was no longer bantering or teasing. The dark pupils were immobile, while her hand on her thigh worried nervously at the fabric of the white shorts.

"The bitch's my mother and there's nothing I can do to change that, damn it. As tough as nails and she's a selfish, unfeeling monster. But the monster's my mother and her genes are my genes." Wilma shook her head vehemently, unhappily, as if trying to chase a bad memory. "I needed her to love me because I'd always loved her. Still do. And instead of telling me she was sorry she'd abandoned me or that she was pleased to see me, she talked to me about her car." There were fresh tears in her eyes as she asked, "Can't you see why I had to come to Italy?"

"To see your father in Mestre?"

She wiped a tear with the back of her hand.

"You met him?"

Wilma nodded glumly. "I found him in the telephone directory and he agreed to see me. We met up in a bar and all he could do was look at my chest."

"You wanted him to look at your shoes?"

"We met in a bar in the Piazza San Marco in Venice—like something out of a novel. It was romantic—it could've been the key scene in a romantic film. A bad romantic film."

"Why?"

"Where had he been these last twenty years? I wanted my real father to tell me he'd thought about me. I wanted him to tell me he was proud of his daughter, that I'd done well, that I'd gone to college. I wanted him to see his American daughter'd grown up into a serious, sensible, affectionate young woman. To see I'd learned Italian because my father was Italian. And all the stupid bastard could do was drool over me—his own flesh and blood."

"That's when you started prostituting yourself in Milan?"

Wilma banged the table, and heads turned in surprise. "You can't believe that crap."

"Spadano set you up as a decoy. He wanted to get his hands on Enzo Beltoni and he used me to do it. Spadano knew I wouldn't stick my neck out for his sake—so he used you. He knows all about my past, about Eva."

"Who's she?"

"A Uruguayan I once got involved with—I twice got involved with."

"A prostitute?"

"A black, Uruguayan whore who carries her prison around on her back, just like a snail."

"Where is she now?"

"How would I know?"

Wilma relaxed. She sat back in her seat and her hand smoothed the legs of her shorts. "You know, in your own way, you're rather sweet, ispettore. Anybody ever tell you there's something about you—something almost feminine?"

"Is that a compliment?"

"I can understand how a woman could fall in love with you—despite those terrible pink ears of yours that stick out like an irritable mouse's."

99: Two

"FEMININE?"

"You listen to people. Please don't take offense—it's just that men tend to be more interested in Juventus or Totocalcio than the workings of the human heart."

"I spent my last years in the Polizia di Stato shuttling between the Questura and the hospital, talking to abused girls. Or abused girls who'd grown up into abused women. I had no choice but to listen to what they were saying."

"What did they say?"

"You can't teach an old dog new tricks. I'm not a nurse, not a social worker—just a bad-tempered old policeman."

An exaggerated sigh. "What did these girls say to you?"

"They started pouring out their confessions. I became an ear for them."

"A big, pink ear."

"They saw me as a father."

"Me listening to you now—do I see you as a father?"

"You see me as a big, pink ear."

"Answer my question—you're a father figure to me?"

"How should I know?"

"Why do I listen to everything you say?"

"Your dream's always been to speak with the nasal accent of a peasant from the hills beyond the Po."

"I consider you as a surrogate father?"

"You grew up in Chicago, Wilma, where you were never wanting for love. No, I don't think you see me as your father. You've got a father back in America—not a blood father, but a real father all the same."

"If I have a father, why did I feel I had to find him? What brings me to Italy? Why look for the man who made me?"

"You're afraid."

"Afraid of what?"

Trotti had the feeling that they were alone, just him and the girl. The piazza— the other customers sitting under the bright Punt e Mes parasols, the waiter, the gypsy children— had nothing to do with either of them. He allowed himself a broad smile and with his open hand, he gestured towards the flat belly visible between her waist and the bottom of the short top. "There's a child in there."

Wilma retorted, "I hope not."

"Perhaps two children. At the moment, they're biding their time, waiting for their mother to decide on the road she wants to go down. In time they're going to start kicking and start wanting to come out."

"Not sure about that."

"A handsome stranger just a few years older than you is going to help you bring them into this world."

Wilma had raised an eyebrow.

"Those children, the children that you and this man are going to create—you're going to love them. Love them with all your heart. You know that, Wilma, better than I do, but sometimes, when you're thinking about Wilma's children—the little boy and the little girl—just sometimes you become afraid. Afraid Wilma Barclay'll turn out to be a mother like your Los Angeles princess."

The pretty face darkened.

"Being a mother's something you learn—it's not genetic. You know that—but still you're frightened. By looking for your mother and your father, you were looking for an answer."

"What answer?"

"And now you have it."

"What answer? What question?"

"You're Wilma Barclay, a young woman who grew up in a happy, close family, and within a few years you're going to have a happy, close family of your own."

A smile hovered at the corner of her lips.

"The only thing that matters is love—complete and unconditional love. The love you had in your adopted family—not what you hoped to find in Venice or Los Angeles."

She put her head to one side, paused, smiled brightly and said, "I was right when I said you liked children."

"You'll never be a Los Angeles princess."

"You see me as a child, signor ispettore?"

"I scarcely know you, Wilma."

"Just for once, answer the question I ask you—d'you see me as a child?"

"When I thought they'd killed you, you haunted my days and my nights and I wanted to die. Nobody deserves to die so young and so beautiful."

"You want to die now? Now that I'm sitting here in front of you?"

"They told me you were a whore."

"You believed them?"

"Never."

"But you thought I was dead?"

"Wilma, damn it. I saw your body and I saw the bloodstains and I saw your leg sticking out from under the sheet. I stood looking at your lifeless body and I wanted to die."

"I hated doing that."

"Then why did you do it?"

"I didn't have a choice."

"You always have a choice—it just takes a lot of courage to make the right one."

"They'd have thrown me out of Italy. They said I might even have to face charges of lewd conduct back home."

"What lewd conduct?"

"I'd gotten involved with a man and I thought he was my friend." Wilma bit her lip. "Not a good-looking man or anything, but he's American, and when I met him I was feeling lonely and he was kind to me. The family I was au pairing for wasn't very nice." She gave a small shudder. "I needed friendship—the little American girl all alone and lost in the big, strange city of Milan."

"Doesn't sound very lewd."

Wilma raised her shoulders in a resigned shrug. "He was sweet. A lot older than me of course—but then, as you say, I was probably missing Daddy—good, sweet, dyed-in-the-wool Daddy."

"What happened?"

"Harry got arrested."

"Why?"

"One day we were stopped in the street. Stopped by the cops in the viale Argentina. We were on the way to the cinema and he got arrested. Immoral earnings."

"You were hanging out with a pimp?"

"I swear I didn't know. To me he was lovely—ispettore, with me Harry was really charming."

"I've never met a charming pimp."

"How was I to know he was a pimp?"

"Where on earth did you meet him?"

"At the US consulate—and he made me laugh. An American, but the family came from Naples."

"Harry?" Trotti looked at the girl, frowned and held up his hand.

The gypsy children had returned to the plaza. They now had a different football; it was red and it seemed properly inflated. It bounced noisily off the walls of the church.

"A Neapolitan? About forty years old?"

"Thirty-seven."

"Tall, very pale and blond hair that's combed flat across the top of his head?"

"You know him?"

"Smokes a lot—one cigarette after another? And eats garlic?"

"You know Harry?"

Trotti laughed. "I hope you two made love."

"Why?" The face clouded with offense. "You have strange ideas about girls from Illinois."

"Not sure your Harry's going to get another chance to share his body with any innocent and naïve girl from Illinois. My goddaughter Anna was rather heavy-handed with him—or rather, with Harry's testicles."

"Your goddaughter's a surgeon?"

"I suppose she is."

100: Avignon

THEY SHOWED LITTLE generosity towards the shoeless young beggars; the Japanese tourists clutched their cameras nervously.

An American woman carrying a shoulder bag—Italy Tours Desmoines—smiled at a little boy. She was in her late sixties, her hair was tinted blue, and she wore bright pastel clothes, tan slacks and sensible shoes. She came out of the church hand in hand with her husband and gave a handful of coins to the boy.

The child's immediate smile was a brilliant grin that split the narrow face. Suddenly there was a crowd of children thronging the couple; the woman and her husband were importuned by the clamoring children until they had crossed the piazza and disappeared from Trotti's sight.

"She admitted she killed him?"

Wilma had been silent, and her question awoke Trotti from his daydreaming.

"Lia Guerra admits she's responsible."

"That doesn't mean she killed him."

"It's possible she flew down from Rome. She may have stolen the car in Messina—but I imagine she has an alibi. She may even have shot Gracchi in the head. More likely she got an accomplice from BRAMAN to do the job. One of the inmates."

"Enzo Beltoni?"

Trotti shook his head. "No reason for Enzo Beltoni to kill Gracchi. The Carabinieri always knew that, and I don't imagine for a moment he was a gun for hire. He was blackmailing Giovanni Verga—consequently any threat from Gracchi could be dealt with."

"Why did she kill her boyfriend?"

"Jealousy."

"All women are jealous." Wilma laughed. "That merited the life sentence?"

Trotti replied, "Guerra's existence was a life sentence."

Wilma sighed heavily. "You seem to think all women are abused."

"Unhappy children grow up to be unhappy adults—and Lia Guerra's unhappy. Says so herself. Always wanted to be loved, but she never learned how to love. Unfortunately, the man of her life—Gracchi, the flawed Italian hero—couldn't help her. He couldn't give her what she wanted."

"What did she want?"

"How do I know? How can anybody know when Lia Guerra doesn't know herself. Not sex—at least not sex with a man."

"She's a lesbian?"

"I imagine over the last twenty-five years she's been solicited by enough men—and by many women, too. She lives alone with a cat in rooftop flat near the Tiber—living in a golden past that never existed."

"If she's not interested in sex, why kill her boyfriend?"

"I never said she wasn't interested in sex. She clearly wasn't interested in the sex she had with Gracchi or with Maltese. After them, she graduated on to drugs."

"Drugs are better than sex?"

"Drugs give you the high of sex without the bother of sperm running down your legs. Or so I'm told."

Wilma flinched.

"She dried out in Switzerland, and there she was forced to face the future—her future. Her parents had paid for the rehabilitation, but she was thirty years old and needed to be free of them. Gracchi was still a good friend and, better yet, he was still in love with her, even though he was now married. Going down to Trapani and BRAMAN wasn't a decision Lia Guerra made. It was imposed on her. There was nowhere else to go."

"Going to Trapani'd mean returning to Gracchi's bed."

Trotti's eyes wandered to the church on the far side of the piazza. "Her options were limited. She was frightened of men—but she was also frightened of being alone."

"She slept with Gracchi?"

"You must ask her."

"Why kill him?"

"I imagine Gracchi's like most men."

"I know very few men." A grin. "Not counting the pimps."

"Once he could get what he'd pined after for so long, Gracchi was no longer terribly interested."

"You're forgetting Petrarch." Wilma shook her head vehemently. "Petrarch spent his life loving Laura. Loved her to his grave."

"Only because Laura was married and unavailable."

"You really don't believe in true love?"

"You're different, Wilma. You and your husband are going to live in perfect harmony—live happily ever after. After a long, hard day at the office, your husband's going to write sonnets to your beauty and purity." Trotti shrugged. "The rest of us—we're not like that. We forget about purity and beauty if the evening meal's not on the table, and we start to notice the orange peel on your thighs, the stretch marks."

"Perhaps Laura had stretch marks—but Petrarch loved her."

"Petrarch never had to share his bed with Laura."

The girl fell silent while the gentle breeze flapped at the fringes of the Punt e Mes parasol.

Trotti said, "Lia Guerra was frightened by the specter of years of loneliness opening up before her. She had to choose between her fear of loneliness and her fear of intimacy. When she returned to Gracchi, she rediscovered all his warmth, all his qualities. I don't know what happened—yet from the way she talks, you'd think everything was all very platonic."

"Why leave him?"

"She never left him—she was told to leave BRAMAN. Gracchi was married, and his wife saw what was happening. Chiara had Lia kicked out—Chiara got Verga to send the other woman to Rome."

"That's why she killed Gracchi?"

"Gracchi did nothing to keep her—but that wasn't why she killed him."

"Why kill the man of her life?"

Trotti paused, "Lia Guerra learned Chiara was pregnant."

"That was his death sentence?"

"Guerra'd always believed the love between her and Gracchi was special. When Chiara got pregnant, Lia Guerra had to admit to herself she wasn't his only true love, his only Laura. While Gracchi'd been sleeping with her, he'd also been sleeping with Chiara. He'd cheapened their love."

"He'd ceased to love her?"

"These things happen." Trotti shrugged, "Lia was no longer the young, passionate and beautiful woman he'd known on the streets of Milan. She'd turned into a middle-aged woman—and just like his first wife, Bettina, or just like Chiara Gracchi, Lia had started making demands on him. Expecting him to help her, to look after her—when he couldn't even look after himself."

"Look!"

The waiter who had been hovering by the open door of the café surged forward as the returning gypsy children descended upon the customers of the bar, winding between the tables, grubby hands held out as they begged and whined.

A larger, older waiter stood at the door of the café and watched the children with ill-concealed loathing.

The children laughed—one made an obscene gesture—then scurried away to their game of street football.

"Lia Guerra's completely insane."

Wilma asked, "Why?"

"She lives in a world of make-believe. She still thinks their love was something special, something pure and enduring. Lia Guerra lives in the past."

"It's all she has."

"Not the past at BRAMAN, but her years as a pasionaria. Her years with Lotta Continua. In the photograph taken by the Nucleo Politico, Lia Guerra had an intense, proud beauty as she hurled a missile at the Celere—she was young and beautiful and her Tino loved her to distraction."

"When she was Laura."

"When Gracchi was her Petrarch—and he never got to touch her."

Wilma Barclay frowned. "Petrarch could never love a woman who wants to touch him?"

It was indeed a beautiful day, with a warm sun shining on the open square and the central fountain. The damp of the Po valley seemed a world away.

The American girl placed her hand on Trotti's and for a while sat in silence, staring at the two hands. His old, pale and wrinkled; hers soft and dark.